Lie of the Needle

Cate Price

BERKLEY PRIME CRIME, NEW YORK

THE BERKLEY PUBLISHING GROUP
Published by the Penguin Group
Penguin Group (USA) LLC
375 Hudson Street, New York, New York 10014

USA • Canada • UK • Ireland • Australia • New Zealand • India • South Africa • China

penguin.com

A Penguin Random House Company

LIE OF THE NEEDLE

A Berkley Prime Crime Book / published by arrangement with the author

Berkley Prime Crime Books are published by The Berkley Publishing Group.
BERKLEY® PRIME CRIME and the PRIME CRIME logo are trademarks of
Penguin Group (USA) LLC.

For information, address: The Berkley Publishing Group,
a division of Penguin Group (USA) LLC,
375 Hudson Street, New York, New York 10014.

ISBN: 978-0-425-25881-1

PUBLISHING HISTORY
Berkley Prime Crime mass-market edition / January 2015

PRINTED IN THE UNITED STATES OF AMERICA

10 9 8 7 6 5 4 3 2 1

Cover illustration by Ben Perinil.
Cover art: *Logo pin* © Roman Sotola; *Floral pattern* © LDesign.
Cover design by Diana Kolsky.
Interior text design by Laura K. Corless.

Praise for the Deadly Notions Mysteries

A Dollhouse to Die For

"Nicely written . . . The book pays off with intriguing characters with plenty of small-town charm."   —*RT Book Reviews*

Going Through the Notions

"A quaint little village, quirky characters, and a crafty killer—I loved it!"

>—Laura Childs, *New York Times* bestselling author of *Gossamer Ghost*

"Cate Price's *Going Through the Notions* has everything I read cozy mysteries for—a terrific setting, a smart plot, and well-rounded, clever characters. Lucky us—it's the first in an all-new series (Deadly Notions)—and I can't wait for the next one!"

>—Mariah Stewart, *New York Times* bestselling author of *On Sunset Beach*

"A fun fast-paced debut filled with eccentric characters, quirky humor, and small-town drama."

>—Ali Brandon, national bestselling author of *Literally Murder*

"This is a promising start for a fun new series. Cate Price writes with a natural tone, describing the characters and the settings with just enough detail to make this reader feel as though I was already visiting old friends and places. The story is unique and funny, with enough small-town antics and drama to make it a true cozy. The town of Millbury, Pennsylvania, will welcome you, too."   —Myshelf.com

"Cozy fans, there's a new author in print and you are going to love her stories. Small-town charm, quirky characters, a dose of humor, a bit of romance, and murder. Just the way we love them!"   —*Escape with Dollycas into a Good Book*

Berkley Prime Crime titles by Cate Price

GOING THROUGH THE NOTIONS
A DOLLHOUSE TO DIE FOR
LIE OF THE NEEDLE

For my mum

Acknowledgments

For help with zoning information, I am grateful to Lee Milligan, building code official of Upper Providence Township, Pennsylvania. Also, many thanks to Leslie Lighton-Humphries, fellow author and local reporter who was so generous with her input and time to critique relevant pages. If there are any mistakes, please blame me, not them.

I appreciate Nannygoat Antiques, my favorite store in the world, for hosting me at their very first author showcase. Also, thanks to Kathleen Rogers at Set to a Tea for assembling such a fun group for our talk, and who remained calm and collected even when the power went out on that dark and stormy night!

For friendship, writing support and nourishment of my soul, I am beholden to Eileen Emerson, Maria Entenman, Jackie Himmel, Stephanie Julian, and Jeannine Standen.

To Lynn Wilson, whose heartfelt and wonderful notes of encouragement always seem to come at exactly the right time—thank you, with deep appreciation.

Thanks to everyone at Berkley Prime Crime for all you do for me, in particular Amanda Ng, Kayleigh Clark, and Danielle Dill. Thank you to vice president Natalee Rosenstein, not only for the opportunity to write this series, but for knowing how to throw the best parties evah.

As usual, gratitude to my wonderful editor, Jackie Cantor, and my terrific agent, Jessica Alvarez. I'm so lucky.

And finally, to all the teachers in the world, underpaid and underappreciated, doing one of the most important jobs I can think of, keep doing what you do. You never know how your words can inspire a young mind, and how they will be remembered for years to come. I still treasure an inscription my English teacher Beryl Shorthouse wrote in a book I won at school when I was eleven. She urged me to reach for the stars. It gave me chills at the time, and it still does.

Chapter One

It's not every day you have the opportunity to see the best-looking men of your acquaintance naked. Almost never, in fact. And after tonight, I doubted I ever would again.

The shoot for the Men of Millbury calendar had been going on all week in the carriage house of a local estate. It was a fund-raiser for the Millbury Historical Society and we were desperately trying to save an old farmstead once inhabited by one of the founders of our nineteenth-century village. However we were up against a builder who was intent on knocking the house down and putting up a slew of cookie-cutter condos on the accompanying thirty acres unless we could stop him.

We'd done the bake sale route. Now we needed some serious cash.

"Having fun, Daisy?" Mr. February, who also happened to be my very handsome husband, Joe Daly, came over and wrapped his arm around me.

I grinned and leaned into his embrace.

Not only did we want to save the character of our quaint neighborhood situated in bucolic Bucks County, Pennsylvania, but if we prevailed, the rambling farmhouse would be turned into a community center, providing badly needed recreation space for the local children.

Somehow my best friend, Martha, secretary of the society and a fiery redhead, had convinced these twelve brave souls to take it all off for the sake of historical preservation. Perhaps the fact that it would benefit the children had been the motivating factor, and not so much Martha's salesmanship or, should I say, relentless arm-twisting.

"It's crazy out there tonight," Joe said to me. "Think you might need a couple of bouncers for the next guy."

There was high excitement in the air. Tonight we would see the crème de la crème.

Dark and dangerous Detective Serrano, in the flesh.

Literally.

Although these guys weren't completely baring it all. Depending on the way they made a living, the photographer had used a discreetly placed object to cover the family jewels, like a fire helmet, a barbershop chair, or a farming implement.

We were working in the garage of the carriage house, a beautiful space with heavy wooden timbers overhead and whitewashed walls. It was even heated, which was a definite plus on a wintry night. It would certainly have been easier to produce this calendar in the summer, when we could have used outdoor locations, but seeing as it was early November, the clock was ticking to get it printed and into stores in time for Christmas.

By the way, I'm Daisy Buchanan, the fiftysomething-year-old proprietress of Millbury's antiques and sewing notions store called Sometimes a Great Notion. Actually I'm fifty-eight, but fifty-something sounds better. I'd kept my maiden name of Buchanan when we married. Joe was secure enough in his masculinity that he didn't have a problem with that, or with sitting bare-bottomed on his lovingly restored vintage bicycle.

All in all, this project had been a lot of fun. Our models had been pretty good-natured about the whole thing. Privately, I think they'd quite enjoyed the fuss.

Tonight Joe had helped us by hauling in bales of hay and stacks of gourds into the garage, because first up under the lights was Mr. October, a former mailman whose hobby was growing giant pumpkins. He was in his early sixties now, but still in good shape thanks to years of extreme gardening. The plan called for him to hold a pumpkin in front of the essential bits, and there'd been lots of cheerful ribbing going on.

"Hey, that's a mini pumpkin!" he'd yelled, still fully clothed, when Martha handed him his prop. "I'm gonna need a bigger one than that!" Martha had finally given Mr. October a large enough pumpkin to satisfy his manly ego, and she swept over to us, carrying a clipboard and trailing Cyril Mackey in her wake. I wasn't sure what the clipboard was for, seeing as we only had two models to keep track of, but I didn't dare ask.

She was wearing a gold wrap shirt, harem-style pants in a black-and-gold Japanese design, and high heels. The shirt gapped dangerously over her impressive curves, and I hoped the little snap fastener at her cleavage was up to the challenge, ready to give its all for God and country. Her bright red hair was twisted up into a thick knot, showing long shimmering earrings.

If need be, the photographer could always use her as another light reflector.

Eleanor Reid, president of the society and my other best friend in the world next to Martha, also sidled up to us, her gray eyes sparkling with anticipation. She wore her usual all-black attire—a long-sleeved baseball shirt and yoga pants—which actually seemed to fit tonight with her role as photographer's assistant. Her white hair was cropped mannishly short.

"There's a huge crowd outside those garage doors," she said in her husky voice. "All kinds of women from the village, not just from the Historical Society. Like a rock concert or something. Far out, man. I feel like I'm back at Woodstock."

"How did you ever talk these guys into this, anyway?" Joe asked Martha. "I mean, I know *I* was a pushover, but it can't have been that easy with everyone."

"Well, some were easier than others," she said with an arch look at Cyril, the cantankerous owner of the local salvage business.

He glared at her. "I still don't know how I feel about taking my kit off in front of a bunch o' gawping women."

Cyril was originally from Yorkshire, England, and until recently, a bit of an outcast whose wardrobe left a lot to be desired. The village was still intrigued as to how he and Martha, a wealthy widow, had embarked on their strange and precarious new romance.

I grinned at them. As a former cheerleader, prom queen, and trophy wife, Martha had spent a lifetime perfecting her stage presence. Even in her early sixties, she was still a knockout. Cyril, despite his tough demeanor, had swiftly gone down for the count.

"Come on, man, be a sport," Joe said. "We've all sacrificed our pride for a good cause."

Cyril took his tweed cap off and ran a hand through his thick gray hair before jamming the cap back on his head. "I know, and that old bugger what owns the place has already scarpered to the bloody Outer Banks. So I hope a lot of people buy this damn calendar, and right quick."

He was correct that the current owner of the historic

property had no real emotional attachment to Millbury anymore. The only thing he cared about was getting a nice fat check to fund his retirement. He'd simply sell to the highest bidder.

I gave Martha a hug. "You did such an amazing job putting this together. And Cyril, don't worry. We'll keep our eyes closed, I promise."

No women were allowed to stay for the actual shooting, well, except for the designated photographer's assistants— Martha, Eleanor, and me.

"There have to be *some* perks of sitting through the insufferably dull Historical Society meetings," Martha had declared when she'd made the arrangements.

Far from my words providing comfort, Cyril's expression turned even more dour, if that was possible. But I knew there was no question he would come through. Cyril was nothing if not dependable.

At the rear of the garage, there was a wooden screen behind which the model could change. To protect his modesty as much as possible, we kept our backs turned until he was posed with his strategically placed item, and only came forward when requested to reposition something on the set or to hand Roos a new roll of film. The photographer was going old-school instead of using digital because he said he preferred the result.

Joe clapped him on the shoulder. "Well, Cyril, after tonight, you'll be the last one, and then the ladies can get this calendar into production." He cleared his throat. "So, Daisy, where's Serrano?"

"Mr. July should be here any minute," I said, not even bothering to check my watch. Serrano always showed up on time for his rendezvous.

"Excuse me while I kiss the sky." Eleanor inhaled as if already catching a hint of his intoxicating aftershave in the air. "Ah. The hot detective. Every woman's fantasy."

Martha shook her head. "No. Trust me, dear. At our age, it's a fantasy to have someone *cook* for you every night. Like Joe does for Daisy."

My husband had blossomed into quite the gourmet cook, seeing as Millbury didn't have a restaurant, only a diner that closed at 3 p.m. He'd convinced me to take early retirement two years ago from teaching high school, and we'd moved into our former vacation home, a Greek Revival on Main Street. Joe had settled comfortably into country life, but it had been harder for me, and when I bid on a steamer trunk full of sewing notions at the local auction, it had been the inspiration to open my store. And my salvation.

So not only was I a resident, but as a store owner, I was doubly interested in what happened to our little village.

At that moment, the photographer, Alex Roos, strolled past our group, performing the habitual stretching moves that signified he was finished shooting in his crouching pose. "People, people, how's it going?" He flashed a wicked grin at Eleanor, showing capped teeth that were startlingly bright against his tanned skin. She blew him back a kiss. Martha just shook her head.

Roos wore black jeans, pointed emerald-green snakeskin boots, and a black leather vest that showed off his wiry surfer's body covered in myriad tattoos. His hair was cut in a Mohawk style, about an inch long, like the bristles on a silver-backed antique brush, and so blond it was almost white, the way some fair-skinned children get after a summer spent playing outside.

And like a soft brush, it seemed to invite the touch of your fingers.

"Today's cock, tomorrow's feather duster," Cyril muttered. He would have probably spit on the ground if he was back in his junkyard and not in this garage that was nicer than a lot of people's living rooms.

The lanky photographer had caused quite a stir himself

around these parts during the week he'd been shooting. Even without knowing he was from California, it was clear to see he was an exotic bird among a flock of country fowl. It was rumored he'd had almost as many liaisons as there were months in the calendar, including a dalliance with one of the married women. There was more than one jealous significant other who would be glad to see the back of him when he left town.

I narrowed my gaze at him. Was he really wearing eyeliner? In spite of his affectations, I had to acknowledge that he did have some strange sort of charm. But give me Joe's wholesome good looks or Serrano's dark and debonair sex appeal any day.

Roos clapped his hands together. "Okay, peeps. Time to rock 'n' roll. Next set, please." While I swept the garage, and the others removed the pumpkins, Joe loaded the bales of hay back into Cyril's truck.

"I'm going to catch a ride back to Millbury with Cyril, so I can let the puppy out," he said as he kissed me goodbye and handed me the keys to our old Subaru station wagon. "See you later, babe."

As I watched Joe and Cyril pull away in the truck, I blew out a breath against the guilty flutter in my chest for the imminent arrival of our next model.

Eleanor had borrowed a fake brick wall from the local theater, and the plan was to back the detective's Dodge Challenger on an angle into the garage and create the illusion of a grimy alleyway with a couple of garbage cans and some moody lighting. Serrano would stand partway behind the open driver's door, pointing his gun at an imaginary assailant.

"Now, aren't you glad we talked you into joining the society?" Eleanor said as we maneuvered the wall into place.

"Yes," I answered dutifully, grunting as I pushed.

"Well, it was about time you joined, seeing as you were

a history teacher, after all," Martha said, peering at us over her clipboard.

Okay, Tom Sawyer.

While Eleanor and I worked, and Martha supervised, I could feel the tension building, like the pressure in the air before a summer thunderstorm. The mailman was nice enough to look at, but he was nothing compared to the main attraction.

At the sound of a powerful muscle car rumbling up the driveway, we scrambled to open the garage doors. We stepped out of the way as Serrano executed a swift three-point turn and slid the gleaming black vehicle into position. He got out and, with a respectful nod in our direction, headed over to talk to Roos, exuding authority with every movement. I could see there would be none of the usual banter that we enjoyed when he stopped by my store in the mornings for coffee and baked goodies.

Tonight was a necessary evil he obviously wanted to get over and done with as efficiently as possible.

He was wearing a dark gray suit that complemented his closely cropped salt-and-pepper hair. Serrano had the perfect physique—muscular, yet lean—to wear a suit, and wear it well.

Eleanor narrowed her gaze in his direction. "God, I can't wait to see that man with his shirt off."

Neither, apparently, could the crowd of women waiting outside, who had rushed into the garage now and were leaning against the car, trailing their fingers over the warm hood and giggling in feverish anticipation.

Detective Serrano was a transplanted New Yorker, like Joe and me. He was the hottest, most exciting import into Millbury in years, and he spent as much time fending off the local females as he did catching criminals.

Somehow I'd become a bit of an amateur sleuth, thanks

to my, um, inquisitive disposition, and I'd helped him solve a couple of cases, whether accidentally or on purpose.

His ice-blue eyes surveyed the scene, taking in everything, missing nothing.

"It's a good thing it's cold enough to wear gloves tonight, or he'd have a heart attack at the fingerprints on that paintwork," I murmured.

To say that Serrano was slightly anal was like saying Philly sports fans were somewhat enthusiastic about their favorite teams.

Suddenly there was a loud beeping outside, like someone leaning on a truck horn with both hands.

"What on earth is that terrible racket?" Martha exclaimed.

"Oh, probably Sally McIntire's husband, here to pick up his wife," Eleanor murmured, cocking her head toward a lithe, well-endowed blonde hanging on to the photographer. "She's been flirting with Roos all week, and I hear her old man is mad with jealousy."

We shooed everyone out again, including the reluctant Sally, and I closed the doors to a chorus of groans. While Serrano took his jacket off and laid it on the backseat of the car, Alex Roos adjusted the lighting. Martha dusted the car with a sheepskin cloth, and Eleanor and I pulled the garbage cans into place.

We stood back to admire our tableau.

Suddenly I spotted faces popping up outside the row of windows at the top of the garage doors. The groupies must be giving one another piggybacks to try to steal a peek.

I got up on a stepladder, and Martha handed me pieces of seamless black background paper that I taped carefully over the square panes so that not a crack of light shone through.

The stage was finally set.

"Okay, ladies." Roos clapped his hands. "I think I can handle it from here. Good night. Thanks a million for your help."

Eleanor sucked in a breath, but she couldn't really object, not with Serrano standing right behind him. The photographer had obviously been given strict instructions to clear the scene.

One by one we trailed into the house.

"*Damn* that Roos. Now *we* can't see anything either," Eleanor grumbled as I pulled the door to the kitchen closed behind us. "What a spoilsport. And why the hell did you have to be so efficient and cover up all the windows, Daisy?"

The tastefully remodeled carriage house had the same heavy ceiling beams as the garage, but the whitewashed walls and exposed stonework were softened with paintings of rustic subjects like a folk art pig, and there were top-quality Persian area rugs covering most of the stone floors. It was a simple layout. A huge sleeping loft and a sitting room above, and a good-size living room, dining room, and kitchen with walk-in fireplace downstairs.

Ruth Bornstein, the owner of this estate, was standing at the maple wood kitchen counter making a fresh pot of coffee. She had more connections than a crocheted shawl and had talked the photographer into doing the shoot for a cut-rate price. The gorgeous fieldstone building served both as his studio and temporary living quarters.

She grinned at our downcast expressions. "Don't despair, my friends. All is not lost."

Ruth made a beckoning motion, and we followed her to an alcove off the kitchen that was set up as an office. It also housed a closed-circuit TV system. She poked the power button on the computer monitor and it flickered into life, showing a quadrant of pictures of the front of the house, the back door, the main gate, and the interior of the garage.

There was quite a bit of pushing and shoving so everyone could get into a good viewing position before the show started.

We didn't have long to wait.

Serrano didn't bother going back to the changing area to

don a robe or a towel like the other guys. He simply pulled off his tie right where he stood and stripped off his shirt while we held our collective breath.

Even in a grainy black-and-white image, the hard-muscled body was awe-inspiring.

"Good *God*," Martha said.

The nighttime gray hues accented the rippled stomach and strong biceps that flexed as he moved, like a prowling mountain cat that wastes no energy, but is a focused, tightly coiled killing machine.

I swallowed, but there was no moisture left in my throat.

As Serrano slowly reached for his belt buckle, he glanced in the direction of the security camera, and it seemed as though his eyes met mine. Roos triggered the strobes to test the light meter near Serrano's face, and the resultant flash made my heart bounce.

With shaking fingers I turned the monitor off, suddenly ashamed of myself.

Serrano was my friend, above all else, and not only was I betraying our friendship, but his hard-won trust in me with such giddy, schoolgirl behavior. "We shouldn't be spying on the man like this. We're just a bunch of sick old women getting our jollies."

"And *you're* jolly annoying." Eleanor pouted and slumped back in a chair, crossing her arms over her narrow chest.

"Daisy, why don't you come up to the house with me and visit with Stanley while the shoot is going on?" Ruth urged.

"Okay." My heart was still racing.

"We'll clean up here when it's all over, dear," Martha said to Ruth. "Don't you worry about a thing."

As we left the room, I thought I could hear the whir of the monitor starting up again.

I grabbed my coat from the kitchen, and Ruth and I walked the short distance up the curving driveway toward the magnificent main house.

The original section was from the eighteenth century, with random width floors and fireplaces in most of the rooms. It had been added on to over the years, and the newer wings had the same sage-green siding as the carriage house. The carefully tended rose gardens, tennis court, and pool were situated behind with breathtaking views of the countryside, and verdant acres rolled away in every direction.

The wind whipped across the land, and even though we were only open to the elements for a minute, I felt my body temperature plummet. I huddled down inside my jacket and walked faster.

Ruth's husband had been diagnosed with Alzheimer's a few years ago. Before his illness, Joe and I used to join the Bornsteins occasionally for dinner during the summers when we vacationed in Millbury. Stanley Bornstein had been a successful chemist for one of the large pharmaceutical corporations based in Montgomery County. He'd made a fortune for the company, and for himself, and had retired in his early fifties.

I'd always thought of him as a highly intelligent, fascinating man. Brilliant, in fact.

And now he barely knew his own name.

Ruth hung our coats in the foyer closet and then took a deep breath. "Daisy, you haven't seen Stanley in a while. I don't want you to be upset, but he . . . Well, he's gotten much worse lately. He probably won't recognize you."

"That's okay." I smiled up at her in reassurance. I'd never seen the tall, elegant Ruth not perfectly coiffed, and tonight was no exception. She wore a long ecru flowing sweater over a silk top and dress pants, together with a necklace of intertwined gold rings. Her bobbed hair was dyed a rich chocolate brown, and her dark eyes were enhanced with eyeliner of the same shade.

She'd always looked years younger than her husband, even before he got sick, but in the light cast by the chandelier there were fine lines of exhaustion drawn around her eyes and mouth that even the most expensive night creams couldn't erase.

I followed her upstairs. We passed a guest bedroom on our way, and I caught a glimpse of some of Ruth's things. When we walked into the master bedroom, I could see why. The imposing cherry four-poster bed was gone. It must have been dismantled and stored somewhere else and replaced by a metal hospital bed.

I'd steeled myself for this, but I had to press my lips together to hide my shock at Stanley's wasted appearance. He'd always been a slim guy, but now he was incredibly thin, his cheeks sunken and gray hair standing up in wisps on top of his head.

His hands looked like bird claws resting on the starched white sheets.

"Stanley, Daisy's here to see you," Ruth said.

He didn't turn his head.

It must have been six months since I'd last seen him. At that time he seemed to know who I was, although he couldn't quite follow the thread of the conversation. He kept asking Ruth about someone named Mickey. Turns out that Mickey was the cocker spaniel he'd had as a kid.

There were sheets covering the mirrors on the dressing table and also draped over the closet doors. Ruth followed my gaze. "Sometimes we see imposters in the room," she said softly.

I bit my lip and nodded.

An array of medicines stood on the bedside table, and a nurse sat in an armchair next to the bed, knitting a pink-and-orange scarf. She got to her feet with a grunt.

"He wouldn't let me change him, Miz Bornstein," she said, pursing her full lips together.

"I'll do it, Jo Ellen. You were right not to push matters. Evenings are always the worst time."

Stanley coughed, a painful dry wheeze.

"His sinus infection is getting real bad again, too." The nurse shook her head. "Doctor was here earlier to do his blood work and said he's probably gonna need another course of antibiotics."

"I'll pick up the prescription tomorrow." Ruth walked over to the table and trailed a graceful hand over the bottles. "Did you give him his meds?"

"Yes, Miz Bornstein."

"And did you sign off on the chart?"

"Yes, ma'am."

The nurse glanced at me. She stopped short of rolling her eyes, but she may as well have. I gathered they'd been through this routine many times before.

Ruth touched a hand to my shoulder. "Daisy, I'll be right back. I'm just going to see Jo Ellen out."

They walked out of the room, and I sat in the chair next to the bed. Even though I didn't know much about how to deal with a person afflicted with Alzheimer's, I knew I should talk to Stanley as normally as I could. If there was a part of him that could still comprehend, I wanted to respect his dignity.

I tried to ignore the faint odor hanging in the air that reminded me of the early days of teaching, when some of the little kids didn't always make it to the bathroom in time. I wondered how long he'd been lying here like that. Surely Ruth paid the nurse well enough that she could have handled the task, difficult and unappealing as it admittedly was.

I struggled to think of something to say.

Throughout the house there were hundreds of books. He'd been such a vibrant, educated man. There were even two bookshelves on the back wall of this huge master bedroom.

I'd always relished our conversations about novels we'd enjoyed, the current state of world affairs, and even news of his chemical research. He had a way of explaining things that made it easy to understand.

We also shared a passion for quirky historical facts.

"Hey, Stanley, did you know that Charles Dickens always faced to the north when sleeping?" I said to him, hoping to see some sort of familiar answering spark in his eyes. "That the first novel ever written on a typewriter was *The Adventures of Tom Sawyer*? Or that ketchup was sold in the 1830s as a *medicine*?" He used to tease me about my penchant for putting the tomato condiment on anything and everything.

He stared unblinking at the ceiling.

Never mind not recognizing me; it was as if he couldn't hear me at all.

I sighed, remembering one time when the four of us had gone out to dinner, right before he retired. Stanley insisted on taking the bill when it came to the table because Joe and I had treated the time before. But then he took so long figuring out the tip that Ruth pulled out her own credit card. Stanley was furious at his wife, and it was an uncomfortable scene, to say the least. She'd excused the episode afterward by saying he'd been under a lot of stress at work.

Now I wondered if Stanley had retired because he'd had a premonition that something might be going wrong.

His thin fingers plucked restlessly at the sheet, and he turned to look at me.

"I know you." His face crumpled and he started crying. "It's your birthday, isn't it? That's why you're here. And I forgot your birthday."

"No, no, it's not my birthday. It's okay. Really."

"Card. I should have bought you a card."

I tried again to tell him it wasn't my birthday, but he wouldn't be consoled. In fact, the more I protested, the more agitated he became. Desperate, I looked around. There was a small writing desk near the window with a stack of expensive cream-colored writing paper.

A memory flashed into my head of making Mother's Day cards with the elementary school children, cutting hearts out of paper doilies and decorating borders with snippets of lace, sequins, and buttons.

"Okay, you know what, Stanley? You're right. It *is* my birthday. So let's make a card. What should I put on it?"

But he lapsed into silence once more.

I hurried over to the desk, folded a piece of letterhead adorned with an embossed *B* in half, and selected a fountain pen from the marble cup. I knew he liked dogs, so I drew a stick figure of a dog that looked a bit like my golden retriever mix puppy. I added a bunch of flowers and wrote *Happy Birthday* inside.

I went back to the bed and sat next to him. "Look. Here it is. Do you want to give it to me now?"

I held it out, but he suddenly gripped my wrist so tightly that the paper fell from my fingers onto the stiff sheets.

"Help me, Daisy," he said in a hoarse whisper, his eyes focused and very bright. "She's trying to kill me!"

Chapter Two

"*What?*" I sucked in a breath.

Soft footsteps sounded in the hallway, and Stanley slumped back against the pillows.

"Everything all right?" Ruth came back into the bedroom, worry etched across her beautiful face.

"Yes, fine," I said, forcing a smile. "Stanley was just giving me my birthday card."

For a second she frowned, and then she nodded in understanding.

I cleared my throat and gestured to the bedside table. "Um, I was wondering, Ruth. All those drugs. What do they do?"

She explained that some were to try to delay the progression of the disease as long as possible, some were for anxiety and depression, and some were sleep aids or antipsychotics.

I glanced over at Stanley for any kind of signal, but

after his startling pronouncement, he was staring blankly at the ceiling again.

"Seems like an awful lot." The sea of brown plastic bottles all looked exactly the same to me. "Must be hard to keep them straight."

"That's why I have a checklist." Ruth sighed. "Jo Ellen's a wonderful nurse, but she and I butt heads sometimes. She has her own way of doing things, and it's not always the way I've instructed. Like signing off on giving him this medicine."

A little while later, I got up to leave. If Stanley needed changing, I wanted to give them some privacy.

We walked downstairs, and when we got to the foyer, Ruth hovered in front of the door as I slipped on my coat. "Thank you for your kindness, Daisy. About the birthday card, I mean. It's easier to go along with him than argue. It just gets him more upset." She ran a hand across her forehead. "I'm sorry. I shouldn't have asked you to come over here. I guess that selfishly I wanted you to see . . ."

I swallowed against a lump in my throat. "What you have to deal with every day? Oh, Ruth, it's okay. And I'm so sorry." I hugged her and she hugged me tightly in return, like she never wanted to let me go. I rubbed her back a little to comfort her, feeling the bones of her spine through the silk. "You can share anything you want with me. This must be such a huge burden."

She nodded, but didn't speak again.

When I left the main house and walked back down the driveway, snow was falling. Huge, feathery flakes that tickled my nose and brushed against my eyes. The carriage house was dark now, and my car was the only vehicle parked outside. Our photogenic detective must have made for a quick shoot, or maybe Roos wanted to hurry things along and get down to the Sheepville Pub for one last fling.

I turned and looked up at the main house and toward the master bedroom, where light still blazed from its windows.

What the heck was *that* all about? Should I take the wild statement of a delusional man seriously? Was someone really trying to kill him?

I couldn't believe it.

I swiped the feathery dusting of snow off my windshield and tried to shrug off my unease as I slid into the cold driver's seat.

The next morning, as I opened up Sometimes a Great Notion, I was still troubled.

My store was situated in a former Victorian residence a short distance down on Main Street from our house. Joe and our good friend Angus Backstead, the auctioneer, had made several improvements to the interior, including installing two display windows that jutted out onto the black-painted front porch. The former living room and parlor had been opened up into one space, but I'd kept the dining room intact for consultations with customers. There was a small kitchen and a powder room in the back.

I went through my usual routine of starting the coffee brewing and turning the stereo on, but instead of 1940s jazz, I slipped in a CD of Sinatra's Christmas songs.

It was time to decorate the store for the holidays, too. I'd stockpiled some suitable merchandise and I clambered onto one of the wide windowsills. My work outfit consisted of a plain T-shirt and comfortable jeans, as I often had to lug boxes around or go up and down the stairs more times than I wanted to count. I'd twisted my hair up into a knot to hide the insidious gray roots that were creeping through the brown, applied some lip balm, and that was about as good as it got.

An antique wooden children's sleigh would fit well in one corner, and I filled it with boxes that I'd wrapped with scraps of pretty vintage fabrics and decorated with old millinery trimmings, like rosettes and silk flowers. I put a tiny blue spruce tree potted in a red Transferware footed serving bowl in the middle of the window and a stack of hatboxes, each tied with some gold ribbon and a piece of white netting, in the opposite corner.

Refreshing the displays was usually one of my favorite things to do, but today my mind was still replaying the scene in Stanley Bornstein's bedroom. He'd suddenly seemed so lucid, so intent on trying to get his message across. But what the heck should I do about it, if anything?

And which "she" had he been talking about?

I hated to entertain even a moment of doubt about Ruth. Not only had we been friends for years, but she was a pillar of Millbury society, always ready to help a needy cause.

Although if it was the nurse who had frightened him, why hadn't Stanley confided in his wife?

I sighed and went over to the other window, where I created a mini dining tableau using a gorgeous Irish linen tablecloth and napkins, some mercury glass candlesticks, bundles of silver flatware tied with holly-patterned ribbon, and a set of six ruby wineglasses.

My store was mainly geared toward sewing notions and fabrics, but I allowed myself the leeway to pick up other interesting items at auction. Everything sold in the end.

A collection of vintage evening bags filled with tiny baubles, spools of thread, and mother-of-pearl buttons completed the festive design.

I'd just lit a couple of clove-scented candles and placed them on top of the Welsh dresser that held my antique linens when the doorbell jangled.

"Good God, it's cold out there," Martha said as she hurried in, with Eleanor close on her heels.

I nodded. "I think it's going to be a hard winter."

It was snowing out on the street, and a few flakes sparkled on Martha's shoulder-length hair. She was wearing a voluminous crimson-colored wool jacket that made her look like an older, more imposing version of Little Red Riding Hood, and she was carrying a foil-covered plate. I wondered what deliciousness lay underneath.

Martha was a fabulous baker. She said it was her way of relaxing—to spend hours in her kitchen whipping up artistic treats—and she was a fearsome competitor at the local Bake-Offs. But because she didn't need those tempting creations sitting around at home, she brought them in every day for my customers.

"That maniac Tony Z popped out with a sprig of mistletoe when we walked by," Eleanor said. "He kissed me before I could stop him. On the *mouth*. Do you believe that?"

The Millbury barber had had a crush on Eleanor for years, but she'd never taken his pursuit seriously. Tony Zappata, or Tony Z as we called him, was certainly an ardent suitor. He'd gone so far as to get himself arrested by singing arias outside her bedroom window at night.

I smiled and poured coffee into three mugs. I added cream and three heaping spoonfuls of brown sugar to the first one and handed it to Martha.

"He's persistent, I'll give him that." Martha nodded her thanks as she shivered and sipped her warm beverage.

"So is poison ivy, but that doesn't mean you want it to stick around," Eleanor snapped. She hadn't bothered to wear a coat on her short trip across the street, and she swiped at the snowflakes dotting the sleeves of what looked suspiciously like an extra small men's tailored black shirt.

Eleanor owned a store across from mine on Main Street called A Stitch Back in Time, where she restored and restyled vintage wedding gowns. She only worked when she felt like it, which wasn't very often, but in some mysterious manner she always seemed to maintain an exceedingly comfortable lifestyle.

Enough to put gas in her red Vespa and chilled Beefeater in her martini glass, anyway.

"You two are rather late this morning," I said. They were usually here on the dot of ten, when I unlocked the door to Sometimes a Great Notion.

"We were trying on *the dress* again." Eleanor made quote marks in the air with her fingers.

Martha and Cyril were planning to attend the Give a Buck Charity Ball in December, which raised money for wildlife rescue in Bucks County and the surrounding areas. I'd been hearing about this ball gown for months. Eleanor had agreed to alter it, and as far as I could calculate, this must be the sixth fitting.

"Those seams are at their absolute limit, and I'm not going to take them out one more time," Eleanor declared. "It's getting ridiculous."

There was a moment of uncomfortable silence.

I slid a mug of black, unsweetened coffee down the counter toward Eleanor, and she sucked down half of the contents in one gulp.

"I can't help it," Martha finally said with a sigh. "You know how I eat when I'm under inordinate stress. I *wish* I was one of those people who waste away because of their troubles, but anxiety has the opposite effect on me. It just makes me feel like consuming everything in sight."

As loyal a friend as I wanted to be, even I had to secretly admit that Martha's normally voluptuous figure had ballooned a bit over the past months.

I quickly took the plate of treats out of her hands. "Well, what the heck are you so stressed about?"

She blew out another sigh that was so full of exasperation, angst, and high tension that she could have taught a master drama class at the Sheepville Players. "It's *Cyril*. My dear Cyril. I keep hoping the man will propose, but he never does."

"Marriage is a fine institution, but who wants to live in an institution?" Eleanor said. "Sorry. Old joke."

Martha ignored her and spoke directly to me. "Each time I think the perfect opportunity arises, I hold my breath, but nothing ever happens. I'm beginning to think he never will."

"Sure he will," I said, mentally crossing my fingers. "He's just taking his time working up to it. He's not the kind of guy who can be rushed."

Cyril Mackey was a difficult character, but he really did care for Martha. A couple of months ago he'd shown me the weather vane he was planning on giving her for Christmas. He'd spent hours and hours on careful restoration, and the result was spectacular. You didn't do all that work for someone you didn't love. Plus it proved he was capable of long-term planning for the relationship.

But I didn't think Cyril was the type of man who would want to be asked for his hand in marriage, so I prayed he popped the question before Martha's impatience got the better of her.

"You realize if you married him that it would make you *Martha Mackey*, don't you?" Eleanor snickered as she peeled back the foil and snatched a handful from the mountain of spice cookies.

"Those are supposed to be for Daisy's customers." Martha glared at her. "And don't be absurd. I'll still be Martha Bristol."

I could sympathize. I'd kept my maiden name for that very reason, not relishing the prospect of going through life as Daisy Daly.

"Let's hope to God that he musters up the courage before Christmas," Eleanor whispered in my ear.

Martha had wandered over to the children's section of the store. She selected a vintage lunch box and brought it to the counter. She placed a linen napkin on the bottom of the box, piled the rest of the cookies on top and was about to pop one in her mouth when she turned to see Eleanor and me watching her.

She blew out a long breath. "Okay, okay, you're right. That's it. I'm going to put myself on a *strict* diet between now and December fourth. No more treats for me."

She handed the cookie to me. I handed it to Eleanor.

"Or there'll be hell to pay." Eleanor took a big bite and chewed with relish. She ate like a teenage boy after football practice, drank like a dehydrated rugby player, and never gained an ounce on her slim frame.

I decided to change the subject. Quickly. "So. Did you guys enjoy the rest of the show?"

"We didn't watch any more." Eleanor's expression turned glum. "You made us feel too guilty. Ruined the whole thing."

I smiled and set some fresh bay leaves and eucalyptus on the counter. I gathered together bunches of the aromatic greens to make a wreath.

"You know, it's been quite a week so far," Martha said. "Starting with the cute little barber. Even though he was the first to take his clothes off, you didn't have to ask him twice."

"The man's an exhibitionist." Eleanor sniffed.

"I must say, I'd never realized how well-built he was," Martha continued. "I mean, he's short and everything, but very nice-looking. Especially with his clothes off."

"I suppose." Suddenly Eleanor brightened. "Hey, remember when Angus mooned us?"

"Ew, yes!" I said. Our irrepressible auctioneer had loved every second of his fifteen minutes of fame.

The door banged open, and Alex Roos strode in. He wore a long black trench coat, black leather pants, and a bright aqua-colored V-neck shirt, together with a lemon-and-blue scarf tossed around his neck.

"My mains!" he said to us, flinging his arms wide. "How's tricks?"

Martha looked at me and shrugged one plump shoulder. She'd told me once she couldn't understand half of Roos's West Coast expressions. To Martha, it was like he was speaking another language.

"Did you get what you needed last night?" Eleanor asked, and then she smirked. "With Serrano, I mean."

"Oh yeah, awesome. He's a cool dude."

"And do you need any help with the shoot today?" She didn't sound as enthusiastic as she had for the night before.

Roos winked at her. He was such a raging flirt, it seemed that he couldn't help himself, no matter what the age of the female. "Nah, we're not shooting at the studio. We're going to an undisclosed location, but if I told you where, I'd have to kill you. My man Cyril is all about his privacy."

Martha planted her hands on her ample hips. "Oh for God's sake, he's making such a fuss about one dinky little photo."

Roos chuckled and glanced around the store. "Daisy, this place is *epic*, man."

"Thanks. Come take a look at this." I showed him the box in the back that Joe kept filled with an interesting mix of odds and ends for any male customers that happened to visit. I'd taken an old MAIL sign, crossed it out, and written MALE. Everything was priced at five dollars.

He sorted through eagerly and held up one of the vintage cameras.

"Oh, man, an Argus C3! These old cameras were *great*. And this was the best-selling one in the world. Peeps in the biz called it 'the Brick.'"

I looked at the boxy Bakelite-and-steel treasure he'd found and could see why it had earned its nickname.

He perched on the edge of a hope chest to inspect his find, long legs encased in skintight leather stretched out

before him, exposing the familiar bright green snakeskin
boots. "It had such a dynamic range, man. Awesome for
picking up highlights and shadows."

His yellow-and-blue scarf fell forward, and he tossed it
back over his shoulder.

"We lost something when we moved from film to digital. Back in the day, you had to *think*—about light, compo-
sition, exposure, and depth of field. You had to plan your
shot instead of banging off a hundred in digital and hoping
you got one good one."

The over-the-top showboating was suddenly gone as he
bent his bleached head over the old camera in intense con-
centration. I'd seen his portfolio, the depth of emotion he'd
coaxed from his subjects, and knew how good he was,
although you'd never know it from the flamboyant way he
carried on.

"And then it was like Christmas morning to see what
you'd captured on film," he continued in a low voice, warming to his subject. "No instant gratification and models
peeking over your shoulder, telling you how to do your job."

He fished around in his pocket, obviously searching for
his wallet. But in those pants, I doubted there was room for
much.

"That's why I'm using old-school film for the calendar,"
he said, turning his attention now to the pockets of his
coat. "Really makes a difference in the quality, you know.
Richer, somehow. Plus I like to do my own prints and pro-
cessing. It's like meditation, man."

I might have to revise my opinion of him as a flaky vag-
abond. Anyone who had respect for the past was okay in
my book.

"Take the camera. It's on the house," I said. "A little
memento of Millbury for you."

"Word! Thanks, Daisy. Hey, maybe I'll use it for the

shoot with Cyril this afternoon." He stuffed the Argus into the deep pocket of his trench coat. "Yeah, especially for a mature dude, the black-and-white will really rock it."

Cyril did look like an aging rock musician, with his long gray hair, temperamental green eyes, and deep lines worn into his face by a rough life.

When they first started dating, Martha had done her best to clean up his act, but you know what they say about old dogs and new tricks. He'd cut his hair a few inches and she'd smartened up his wardrobe, but lately he seemed to be regressing. Almost like a kid rebelling against too many rules. Now he looked more like Mick Jagger's evil twin after a killer weekend.

Still, he had a relatively fit body and should prove to be an interesting moody contrast to the sunny-faced mailman or the young firefighters.

"There should be something for everyone in this calendar," I said.

"Fersure." Roos smiled at me. "I can't wait to get that film developed. Hey, Daisy, man, is it okay if I use the facilities?"

"Help yourself."

The doorbell clanged as Dottie Brown, the owner of the yarn store and wife to Mr. October, the pumpkin man, came bustling in. She was a solid, capable woman with white hair cropped in a no-nonsense cut, a stocky build, and an attitude toward life that allowed her to trundle over any of its little inconveniences.

"Did you hear the news?" she asked us. "Stanley Bornstein died."

"*What?*" I gripped the counter. "But I just saw him last night!"

She shrugged. "Didn't know if you knew."

"My God. No, we did *not*," Martha said, frowning. The neighboring town of Sheepville had the *Sheepville Times*, but our village didn't have a local newspaper. However, we had Martha, and she hated to be scooped on a headline event. "When did this happen?" she demanded.

I sank onto a stool behind the register, my heart pounding in my chest, as I stared at Dottie.

"It must have been early this morning." Her eyes were somber. "My daughter, Kathleen, was called in first thing to clean the place from top to bottom. A special cleaning for the shivah. The funeral is at four o'clock."

Kathleen Brown was cut from the same sensible cloth as her mother, with the same sturdy build. They even had the same hairstyle, except Kathleen's brown locks were streaked with chunky highlights. She owned a successful cleaning service, and the Bornsteins were one of her clients.

"This afternoon? So soon?" I could barely get the words out past the tightness in my throat.

"In the Jewish religion funerals happen very quickly, Daisy," Eleanor murmured. "It's considered a humiliation of the dead not to bury them right away."

"Was there any sign of foul play?" I managed. "Was it the Alzheimer's that finally killed him?"

"No one actually *dies* from Alzheimer's, you know," Martha said with a note of authority in her voice. "It's usually from some secondary cause. In my support group after Teddy died, there were several women who'd lost their husbands to that dreadful disease. But it was pneumonia or another infection that took them in the end."

Dottie pursed her lips. "Well, supposedly he'd been very sick with a bad cold. Ruth is such a good person. I feel so sorry for her."

"Poor Stanley," Eleanor murmured. "And poor Ruth."

"Yes, it's terrible," Martha said. "Still, perhaps it's for the best."

There was a pause while we each absorbed the news and the toilet flushed faintly in the back.

"How's your calendar coming along?" Dottie asked. "Sounds like a fun project."

"Good. We're almost done," Martha said.

Eleanor drained her mug of coffee and smacked her lips. "I must say *I'm* seeing things I haven't seen in a long time."

Martha waved a hand in the air. "Meh. Seen one, seen 'em all."

Dottie smiled, and Eleanor burst out laughing.

I couldn't join in the frivolity, though. I was sure that to everyone else Stanley's death must seem like a blessing, and if I hadn't had the odd experience in his bedroom last night, I might have been able to adjust as quickly, too.

But as things were, I went through the motions of pouring more coffee while my pulse raced and my mind struggled to make sense of it all.

A few moments later, Roos sauntered out of the bathroom, adjusting his leather pants. "Hey, that's sad news, man. About ol' Stanley, I mean."

Suddenly it hit me. "Alex, why on earth didn't you say something to us before?"

"Had no clue the dude was toast until I heard you guys talking. Excuse me. I mean, *ladies*. I . . . ah . . . crashed someplace else last night," he said with a hint of a boyish grin.

Martha rolled her eyes at me.

"Well. I must be going. See you all later?" Dottie asked. "At the funeral?"

"Yes, we'll be there," I said firmly.

She hurried out with her usual purposeful stride, as if she was on some kind of important mission.

"Yeah, I gotta cruise, too," Alex said. "Thanks again for the camera, Daisy. I'm stoked."

Martha frowned as she watched him trail out onto the street after Dottie. "I still think that photographer is quite strange."

Eleanor slipped a couple more cookies out of the lunch box.

"Oh, Martha, he's okay," I said. "He's just a free spirit, and he shoots from the hip—pardon the pun."

"Very punny. Did you see those leather pants he was wearing?" Eleanor mumbled, her mouth full. "They didn't leave much to the imagination, that's for sure." She wrestled a few cookie crumbs back up into her mouth. "And believe me, I have a *very* vivid imagination."

I twisted some wire around a bunch of bay leaves, and then another twist to hold it on to the circular metal frame.

Martha sniffed. "I'm positive he wasn't wearing any underwear."

"Even though he's so overblown that he's almost comical, there's something oddly sexy about him," I said as I pulled out a few more stems from the bunch, trying to match their length. "I just can't put my finger on it."

Eleanor arched an eyebrow at me.

I pointed a eucalyptus stem in her direction. "Don't say it, Eleanor."

Martha shrugged on her coat. "Well, I'd better get on home and pick out a black outfit for the funeral. And maybe I'll stop and see Ruth on the way."

Eleanor hopped down from her stool. "I'll go with you."

For the funeral.

I tried to gather some more fresh bay leaves into a bundle, but my hands shook so badly that the cut end of the wire pricked my finger. I gasped and dropped the leaves onto the counter.

"What's the matter with *you*?" Martha asked.

I sucked down some coffee for strength. "Jeez. I don't even know if I should say anything about this to anyone. It was just so bizarre . . ."

I'd said the magic words as far as Martha was concerned. If sweets fueled her body, gossip fueled her soul. I knew she wouldn't leave now until I'd spilled the beans. So I explained about visiting with Stanley and his dramatic announcement when we were alone in his bedroom. "I know it sounds hard to believe, but he seemed so perfectly lucid. I don't know what to do. Should I say something to Detective Serrano?"

Martha and Eleanor exchanged glances.

"What?"

"Let's face it: Stanley was a few sandwiches short of a picnic," Eleanor said.

I winced. "Don't talk like that, please."

"Sorry."

In my mind's eye I saw the vast array of bottles on the bedside table. "He was taking a ton of medication. You don't think that Ruth could have, you know, been tempted to . . . ?"

Martha shook her head firmly as she buttoned up her coat. "Ruth spent an absolute *fortune* caring for that man. I've never seen anyone more devoted. She acted like she wanted to keep him alive at all costs. Round-the-clock medical care, a physical therapist every day, you name it. I don't see how you could possibly take it seriously."

Martha edged toward the door. I could see she was on fire to get over to Ruth's and dive into the middle of the action. She wasn't about to waste any more time with me.

I frowned. "But what if it was a deathbed statement? What if he was murdered? What if he was being slowly poisoned?"

"I don't think you should worry about it any more, Daisy," Martha called over her shoulder as she hurried out, with Eleanor close behind. "See you later?"

I nodded and sucked my finger, where blood oozed out of the cut from the wire.

Chapter Three

That afternoon, I was sitting on a wooden pew in the chapel of the local synagogue next to Joe, still shaken by the speed of events.

I'd closed Sometimes a Great Notion early and put an apologetic sign on the door. I hated to disappoint any customers, but in the winter it was really only the weekends when our little village came alive. I had tried to call Ruth, but Kathleen Brown said she was indisposed. According to Martha, who'd made a futile visit to the house and been turned away, the doctor had given her a sedative and she was lying down to rest.

On the ride over, I'd told Joe about Stanley's dying declaration. Joe hadn't been as adamant as Martha that I was barking up the wrong tree, but it was evident that he thought I was reading way too much into one rambling comment by a highly medicated man suffering from the final stages of dementia.

As we waited for the service to begin, I tried to imagine what Ruth's life must have been like for these past few years in the grueling role of caregiver. How hard was it to change the diaper of a man who had once been your lover?

And Ruth was lucky, if you could call her that, in that she was wealthy enough to afford nurses to give her some respite. What about the people who couldn't?

I swallowed against a wave of sadness, remembering my last sight of Stanley. The husk of the person I'd known had been lying in that bed, but the kernel was gone.

I slipped my hand into Joe's and he squeezed back. I mentally said a prayer of thanks. Even though I wasn't in my own church, I was sure it would be heard somewhere up above.

My husband was very much alive, healthy, and gorgeous. To me, anyway. I held his hand tighter. We could still ride our bikes, make love, savor romantic dinners, and enjoy each other's company. There was a lot to be thankful for.

I blinked against a sting of tears.

Eleanor slid along the pew to sit on my other side. "You okay, Daisy?" she whispered. She wore a designer black cashmere sweater with smart dress pants and black boots.

I swallowed and stared into her gray eyes. "It's just that this is all happening so quickly," I murmured, softly enough that Joe wouldn't be able to hear me. "I'm wondering if I should have done more. Asked Serrano for an autopsy, a toxicology report, *something*."

She shook her head. "Autopsies aren't allowed according to the Jewish religion. Unless it's a criminal case, of course."

I sighed and leaned against the hard seat, looking around the modern chapel. The backs of the pews were a brilliant blue, and the white beams radiating like a sunburst from the raised platform in front of us soared up into the ceiling. There were no flowers, only the simple wooden coffin draped in black.

Eleanor pointed to the raised platform in front of us. "That's the Ark, where the holy Torah scrolls were kept."

I stared at the highly decorated cabinet in front of us that was flanked by two columns. The pulpit stood off to one side.

"How come you know so much about the Jewish way of life?" I asked.

She shrugged. "Lots of friends in the film business, I suppose. As a matter of fact, some of the best parties I've ever been to in my life were for thirteen-year-old boys."

I smiled at her. Eleanor had worked as a costume designer for years before she moved to Millbury. She had even been on some of the same film sets as our daughter, Sarah, who lived in New York and worked as a script supervisor.

I tried to save a spot for Cyril and Martha, but the church was filling up and we had to keep sliding down the pew. Where the heck were they? Martha was usually the first to arrive at any kind of event, not wanting to miss a moment.

The place was packed. Obviously there were many people who remembered Stanley as fondly as I did. Amazing that so many were here, especially on such short notice.

Ruth was sitting in the front row now. I spotted most of my fellow store owners, other members of the Historical Society, and the local newspaper reporter, PJ Avery, who was slinking around the edge of the room. The Bornsteins didn't have any children, but they were both involved in so many philanthropic endeavors that they had a wide circle of friends and acquaintances. The cream of Philadelphia society and the upper echelon of city government were also in attendance.

"There's that creep Beau Cassell," Eleanor muttered, nodding toward the builder who planned to destroy our village if we didn't stop him. He was a well-built man in his forties, sandy-haired and strangely tanned for this time of year, wearing a tweed jacket with a black turtleneck underneath and dark pants. With his vigorous good looks, he could have been a politician himself.

A well-dressed couple walked down the center aisle, the man extending a hand in front of the woman as if parting the waves for her. She swept the folds of her ermine coat close to her body as she slid onto the pew.

"And there's Nancy Fowler, and her milquetoast husband, Frank," Eleanor said.

Nancy was currently a commissioner for Bucks County, but it was rumored she had ambitions of becoming Pennsylvania's governor some day. Frank was our township solicitor.

I glanced over in surprise at the fervent disdain in Eleanor's voice. "What's the matter with them?"

"How many defenseless animals do you suppose died for that woman's coat?"

I nodded. "Ah, I see."

Eleanor had been quite the radical back in her day. I'd seen photos of her at various political events and sit-ins, usually wearing a psychedelic scarf around her head and chained to a railing, protesting the use of performing animals in circuses or the clubbing of baby seals or some such cause.

A couple of minutes later, there were so many mourners crammed in next to me that in spite of the fact it was early November, my heart started pounding and a thin film of sweat covered my forehead.

Oh, no, not now.

There were too many people, too close. Too late I wished that I'd sat at the end of the aisle.

I concentrated on my breathing, fighting the panic. In. Out. In. Out.

Many years ago, I'd tried to protect one of my students in a violent altercation and had barely survived. Sometimes when I felt cornered, the old fears and the panicked urge to flee came raging back.

Eleanor glanced over at me and fanned me with her funeral program. I smiled faintly, turning my face toward the welcome brief gusts of air.

Martha hurried down the aisle and forced her way into the end of the pew in front of us. Her freckled cheeks were pink, and she looked even more flustered than me, if that was possible. She rolled her eyes at us, obviously irritated, as she settled herself and took off her coat.

"Where's Cyril?" Eleanor muttered in my ear. "I can't believe he wouldn't come."

I nodded in agreement, my pulse settling down with something else to focus on. This wasn't like him. Admittedly he didn't know Ruth that well, but he certainly knew what was expected by his commander in chief.

"Where's Cyril?" I mouthed when Martha turned around.

She shook her head and made the motion of dialing a telephone. "I've been calling and calling, but he never answered. Finally I said, *Screw him*, and came on my own," she hissed.

A couple of people glanced at us with forbidding expressions, and we subsided into silence.

The rabbi stepped up to the pulpit, and I checked my watch. Four o'clock. Unlike many other ceremonies I'd attended, this one started exactly on time.

As he started the reading of Psalm 23, my thoughts drifted to Stanley and then quickly sank back into the quagmire of doubt. Had the nurse with the attitude wanted to get rid of him? Or the doctor who'd visited earlier? Perhaps the physical therapist?

But it didn't make sense. It was in those people's best interests to keep the goose that laid the golden eggs alive as long as possible. Now that he was gone, they were all out of a job.

At the very least, had he been overmedicated? It could have been a simple mistake for the nurse to confuse those different medicines on the bedside table. Come to think of it, the only person I hadn't spotted in the congregation was Jo Ellen.

Oh, Daisy. Stop being so melodramatic. The poor man was just delusional. You're reading way too much into it. I tried to concentrate on the eulogy and on my own memories of Stanley. His warmth, intelligence, and gentle humor.

Suddenly I sucked in a ragged breath.

Ruth had made a Very Big Deal about stating that Jo Ellen was the one to give him his meds. Is *that* why she brought me up to the house? So good old Daisy could be a witness? And later she could slip him something extra and, if there were any inconvenient questions, blame it on the nurse?

Wild thoughts rampaged through my brain. Funerals should give the public the opportunity to speak, like at a wedding, when the person officiating asks if anyone has anything to say before the proceeding continues. I pictured the rabbi intoning, "Does anyone have any objection to this funeral, or any reason why this man should not be buried?" At which point I could jump up and say, "Yes, because I think he's been murdered!"

My stomach clutched into an aching knot. Did I owe it to Stanley to make sure justice was done? But what should I do?

Maybe Ruth didn't *mean* to kill him. Even if she'd been tempted to give him a hefty dose of sleeping pills so she could get a good night's rest for once, could anyone really blame her?

Just when I was toying with the idea of making a complete fool of myself, the cantor chanted the memorial prayer in a plaintive voice, and mercifully, the ceremony was over.

This had to be the quickest funeral I'd ever attended.

As soon as the casket was carried out and the family left

the church, I jumped to my feet. Even though the worst of my panic attack was behind me, I still wanted to get the heck out of Dodge. Ignoring the frowns of those who rightfully thought I should wait my turn until each pew emptied in order, I hurried toward the exit, alternating between apologies and pushing past bodies. Just the act of standing up and moving was something to be thankful for.

The synagogue was an attractive building, with a preschool and religious school attached. Outside were tree-lined walkways and places to sit, and the bracing cold was a welcome respite from the stuffy interior. I sank onto a concrete bench to wait for Joe, wiping my clammy forehead and sucking in large gulps of frigid air.

He found me a few minutes later, and we joined the line of cars heading for the cemetery.

At the gravesite, I stayed at the back of the crowd. I wasn't about to make the mistake of being trapped in that mass of humanity again. There were several chairs placed before the grave, but the majority of people were standing.

Serrano materialized at my side, wearing a black suit and gray overcoat.

"Everything okay, Daisy?" he said quietly.

Same comment as Eleanor. My face must mirror every thought in my brain.

Men were normally not detail-oriented, but Serrano had eyes like telephoto lenses, and right now he was zooming in for a close-up.

"Fine," I answered, wishing I could blurt out all my anxieties and suspicions. But what if I was wrong? Did I really need to heap more suffering on this day?

"I almost didn't recognize you with your clothes on, Detective," I said, hoping to distract him with a joke.

A hint of a smile played around his firm mouth, but we fell silent as there was another reading, another psalm, and a recitation of an ancient prayer in Hebrew.

Too soon, I watched as the coffin holding the body of
Stanley Bornstein was lowered into the ground. My eyes
stung as Ruth tossed a shovelful of dirt on top of the coffin
and placed the spade back in the earth.

The announcement had been made earlier that shivah
would be held back at the Bornsteins'. When we arrived,
the front door was standing open and there was a table
with a pitcher of water and towels for mourners to wash
their hands before entering the house.

Martha and Eleanor caught up to us, and we all walked
in together. Martha had brought a cheesecake, I carried a
dried fruit and nut platter, and Eleanor had a box of dark
chocolates under her arm.

Inside, every mirror was covered now, and tall candles
burned on every tabletop. There were so many people
crowded around Ruth in the living room, I suggested we
head for the kitchen first with our food offerings.

Dottie's daughter, Kathleen, seemed to be in charge in
the kitchen, bossing everyone around and organizing the
care and feeding of the guests. She commandeered Joe to
fetch more cases of water from her van, and Martha, Eleanor, and I made ourselves useful by bringing platters to the
dining room and unwrapping them.

"It's really a blessing he's gone, you know," one woman
near me whispered to another as they helped themselves to
large quantities of smoked salmon.

"Oh, yes, can I tell you? Poor Ruth was at the very end
of her rope," murmured her friend. "I don't know how
much longer she could have coped."

I frowned as I stared at the array of bagels, hard-boiled
eggs, tuna salad, cookies, and cakes galore. How desperate
was Ruth to be free of her demanding and frustrating patient?

"So much food," Martha murmured.

Eleanor and I dragged her away from the buffet and
back to the living room.

The mass of people seemed to have swelled even more. Frank and Nancy Fowler were doing their civic duty and greeting Ruth as we joined the end of the line. I watched her carefully through the gaps in the crowd, cursing myself as I did so.

"She seems to be in shock, poor thing," Martha said as we waited for our turn to approach. "The doctor must have given her something to get her through this."

When we finally made it through a gap in the crowd, I could see what Martha meant. We each hugged Ruth in turn, but her eyes were glassy and it was as though she could hardly stand up under her own power. The frailty of her thin frame seemed even more pronounced in black attire, and she wore a torn black ribbon over her heart.

"I'm so sorry, Ruth," I said. She didn't speak, just nodded. "I'll call you tomorrow," I promised, not knowing what else to say.

"She'll need us more later on," Martha declared once we were all outside the house again. "Days from now, when this crowd has gone home and the shivah is over, she'll be feeling lonely, and that's when we'll show up with a casserole and a bottle of wine."

Beau Cassell stepped out of a metallic brown Mercedes and came striding up the driveway. I caught a whiff of fresh cigar smoke as he gave a curt nod in our direction and walked inside without washing his hands.

At the bottom of the hill, the carriage house was dark.

"So where the heck *are* Cyril and Alex?" Eleanor said. "I can't believe they'd be shooting this late. The light's gone."

I stared at Eleanor in admiration. She was braver than me. I wasn't about to bring up the elephant in the room. I suspected that Martha was embarrassed at having to justify Cyril's absence, which only added to her fury.

Her eyes blazed and her freckled hands fisted into

knots. "When I get hold of that man, he's going to feel the sharp edge of my tongue, let me tell you."

I winced and glanced at Joe, who closed his eyes briefly in dismay.

Cyril was probably enjoying a whiskey at the pub right now with Roos, but he was playing with fire in his quest to break loose. I didn't envy him the reception he'd receive when he finally did decide to show up.

Martha was going to *kill* him.

Chapter Four

As I hurried down Main Street the next morning, frost mottled the car windshields and a covering of white blanketed the sidewalks. A bitter wind tossed the light snow into swirling flurries and made me run the last few yards from our house to Sometimes a Great Notion.

Winter was early this year. I hated these dark mornings and brief afternoons before the dark descended again. My favorite season, fall, had been late to arrive and quick to leave, like a boorish dinner guest.

On the porch in front of the shop, a merry arrangement of holly branches sat in an oversize tin watering can. Red berries on the vine wreath I'd hung on the door peeked through the recent powdering. Once inside, I cranked up the heat, set a pot of coffee on to brew, and plugged in the string of white lights that were arranged like a three-strand necklace on Alice, the mannequin. I dressed her according to the season, and today she was sporting a 1960s holiday dress with a velvet top and a plaid taffeta skirt. I would have loved to put a fur muff on her hands, but didn't want to catch any flak from Eleanor.

The store was full of extra-special merchandise now that would be appropriate for holiday gifts, like linen dish towels bundled with red rickrack trim and Belgian linen pillows stitched with crewel wool in a holly pattern. There were lots of affordable stocking stuffers, too, like wax seals, potpourri sachets, holiday postcards, or sweet antique Christmas ornaments in the shapes of a pine cone, trolley car, or owl.

I walked back to the ten-drawer seed counter with glass-fronted loading bins that housed all kinds of magical sewing notions. On top was an ornate National cash register, and next to it was a bowl full of handmade bookmarks for sale at a dollar each. My clever assistant, Laura Grayling, who usually watched the store on Fridays so I could attend some auctions, had taken strips of wide satin ribbons, studded them with a row of vintage buttons, and added a knotted fringe at one end. A simple design, really, but so appealing.

The bookmarks made me think of Stanley, and I leaned against the counter, allowing my mind to flood with memories. The way I wanted to remember him.

He was a fast and voracious reader and had introduced me to so many of my favorite authors. He bought the latest hardcovers the instant they came out because he couldn't wait for the paperback editions, and I'd been the lucky recipient of many of his top literary picks. He loved nothing better than to discuss the book with me after I'd read it, while Joe and Ruth chatted about gardening or the weather.

The last of the coffee dripped into the pot, and the front door opened. Eleanor had impeccable timing, always seeming to appear just as it finished brewing.

I poured coffee into two mugs. We wrapped our cold fingers around the hot pottery and shivered.

"Wonder what Martha's bringing today?" Eleanor said. "I could really go for some of her shortbread lemon bars. Ooh, or maybe the orange-scented mocha truffles? It *is* the season, after all."

But when our redheaded friend arrived a few moments later, her arms were empty. Eleanor and I glanced at each other in dismay.

"No cakes today. I could barely drag myself out of bed as it is." Martha heaved a sigh so deep, it seemed to suck all the breath from her body. "Let me tell you, I am completely *exhausted*. I couldn't sleep a wink last night, wondering what on *earth* that man is playing at." She slammed a hand down on the counter. "Where the hell is he? Is he trying to drive me insane, or *what*?"

Before we could come up with an appropriately comforting response, the shop door banged open, flung wide by the wind. Detective Serrano strode into the store, grabbed the wayward door, and shut it firmly behind him.

"Detective, Officer, sir. I need to speak to you!"

Serrano came up to us and laid a hand briefly on her shoulder. "Hold on, Martha. Listen, ladies, I'm afraid I've got some bad news. The photographer's missing, and his studio in the carriage house was trashed."

"Do you think something's happened to him?" I whispered.

Eleanor arched an eyebrow as if that went without saying. "I thought it was weird that he never showed for the shivah. I mean, Roos was a flake, but not *that* much. And he definitely knew about Stanley's death."

Serrano adjusted the bowl of bookmarks one millimeter to the left, so the design on the bowl was facing directly forward. "Mrs. Bornstein wasn't up to answering too many questions. I wondered if you ladies could help me."

"Of course." I poured another mug of coffee.

"Kathleen Brown discovered the mess when she went

in to clean this morning. All the equipment's gone, too. Cameras, lights, film, the whole shebang."

"Oh, no." I stared at him. "The calendar!"

"This is a disaster," Eleanor said glumly. "We'll need to reshoot the whole thing, assuming we can convince the guys to go through the process again. The printer was already freaking out as it was about the tight deadline to get it into the stores before Christmas."

"Oh, good God, Cyril!" Martha pressed a hand to her mouth as she sank into a nearby boudoir chair.

Serrano looked at me for an explanation.

"Alex Roos and Cyril were doing the modeling shoot together yesterday."

"Don't panic, Martha," Eleanor said. "Maybe they took a trip to Atlantic City together or something. Or maybe Roos ended up at some woman's house like he did the night before. There's lots of possible explanations."

I poured a glass of water for Martha. "When did the break-in happen, Serrano?"

"Tough to say—last night, maybe. Coulda even been during the shivah. People were coming and going, making enough commotion to cover up the noise. It looks like a professional job. Nothing else in the house was taken. All the artwork and antiques are still there. Trust me, Roos was targeted, and more specifically, his stuff."

"Was there any blood in the studio?" Eleanor asked.

I elbowed her as Martha picked up an antique postcard and started fanning herself.

"Not that I could see, but our guys are going over everything now." Serrano scanned the empty counter where there were no plates piled high with the usual baked goodies. He sighed. "So. How did Ruth find this photographer?"

"I think she has contacts in California. Somebody in the fashion industry?" Eleanor wrinkled her nose.

"I called Cyril this morning," Martha said, still fixated on the subject of her missing love. "He didn't answer, but then he often doesn't, so I didn't think much of it. Honestly, I can call that man *ten times* and he won't pick up."

Was I the only one who detected the whisper on the wind of Serrano's slightly indrawn breath?

"But what if something's really wrong? What if something's happened to him?" She tossed the postcard back into the basket and stood up. "That's it. I'm going over to that godforsaken junkyard right now to see what's going on."

As far as I knew, Martha had never set foot in Cyril's kingdom of rusty delights.

"Um, I still have a key to his place from when I fed his cat the last time you and he went on vacation." I turned to Eleanor. "Could you watch the store for me for half an hour? Please?"

Serrano helped Martha into her copious red coat. "I'll go, too."

Eleanor crossed her arms. "Sure, sure, leave me out of all the fun."

A few minutes later, we stepped out of Serrano's Dodge Challenger into a wintry wasteland. It was impossible to drive all the way up to the trailer that was Cyril Mackey's home because towering piles of junk barred our way.

The snowfall had softened the sharp edges of car doors, old radiators, and gasoline signs, which were now bumpy, indefinable piles of white. As Martha glanced dubiously around the salvage yard, I fancied that Mother Nature had wanted to make this as gentle an introduction for her first time here as possible.

We trudged across a smooth, untouched crust of snow, heads bowed against the cruel cold that seemed to sink its talons deep into our skulls.

Serrano rapped on the trailer door, but there was no answer. He stuck a hand in my direction. "Give me the key."

I placed the key obediently into his outstretched palm.

"Stand back, ladies. Do *not* enter until I give the all clear."

I did a mental eye roll as he disappeared inside the trailer. Serrano was in his bossy mode today.

About thirty seconds later, he came back to the top step and motioned for us to enter.

Martha gasped and grabbed my arm as she stepped into the bright kitchen. Ahead of us was a double doorway to the living room.

"Good God, he's been robbed! Call the police!"

"Martha, it's okay," I said. "Serrano's already here, and besides, it always looks like this. You know, sort of, um, minimalist. Cyril doesn't have very much furniture."

Cyril and I had formed an odd acquaintance before he and Martha ever embarked on their romantic journey. He was surly, cantankerous, and rude, even, but somehow I'd seen beyond the bite of the junkyard dog to the sweet soul beneath.

True, steady, loyal, and ready to lay down his life for those he loved.

The spare décor was clean and neat, in complete contrast to the exterior yard. In the kitchen, near the window, there was a white Formica round table covered with a lace tablecloth, and a vibrant Boston fern hung in the corner. There wasn't much in the living room except a recliner covered in an afghan, a china cabinet, and a grandfather clock.

"Well at least the inside is somewhat respectable." Martha sniffed and ran a finger over the spotless kitchen counter.

While Serrano inspected the latches on the windows, I picked up the cat's food and water bowls and refilled both.

"So where's this cat?" Serrano asked.

I took a quick look around for the black feline who had a habit of hiding on top of cabinets and ninja-diving past unsuspecting humans. I wasn't sure Martha's nerves would survive the shock in her present condition.

"I'm not sure, but I don't think he'll show himself with this many people around."

Serrano was busy opening the kitchen cabinets. I glimpsed some Liquorice Allsorts, a box of English tea-bags, and a jar of Marmite.

I shifted uneasily. If Cyril came home now, he would be royally pissed at this invasion of his privacy, and especially peeved at the person who had helpfully offered the key to gain access. He'd have my guts for garters, as he would say.

"Look, Serrano, it's obvious he's not here and no one has ransacked the place," I said. "We should get going."

He gave no sign of listening to me and strode off to Cyril's bedroom. Martha and I scurried after him. He opened the sliding doors of the closet, which hardly had any clothes hanging inside, but probably usually didn't anyway.

He shook his head. "Can't tell if he packed for a trip or not."

Next came the bathroom, and Martha and I crowded in behind him as he opened the medicine cabinet. No medicine inside, just an old-fashioned shaving brush and mug and a plastic bottle of store-brand mouthwash.

Serrano shut the cabinet, and we headed into the living room. There were a few framed photographs scattered around, including one of a much younger Cyril with a rugby team.

Martha picked it up and ran her fingers over the edge of the frame. "Detective Serrano, sir, I wish to file a missing persons report," she murmured.

"Don't you think you're jumping the gun a bit?" he said.

Martha shuddered, and I gave Serrano the most chiding look I could muster.

"Okay, okay. Well, we're gonna need some more recent photos than this. Do you have any?"

"Oh, I have a million. From the Walnut Street Theatre,

the Horticultural Society luncheon, the Pennsylvania Ballet, the fashion show fund-raiser. And that's just from last week."

"Cyril Mackey went to *all* of those events?" Serrano asked faintly.

Again, I gave him the hairy eyeball.

He cleared his throat. "Are you sure he's not just lying low for a bit, Martha? Didn't you say it's customary for him not to answer calls?"

She bit her lip.

I'd been in this trailer before when Cyril let the phone ring, not even bothering to see who was calling. Cyril was his own man, and as much as Martha bossed around her friends and anyone else she came in contact with, she'd never really been able to do the same with him.

"When I find that man, I am going to commit grievous bodily harm to his person for worrying me like this." Her words were harsh, but I could hear the catch of tears in her throat.

"You know, sometimes guys just need to get away," Serrano said. "It's nothing personal. They don't think about the consequences or who's at home worrying about them."

I had to agree. Even though I had been married for thirty-four years, men were still a mystery to me. I appreciated the fact that Serrano was downplaying things for Martha's sake. Sometimes there was a real kindness that glimmered through the tightly controlled persona. He was even convincing me until I glanced toward the kitchen and the cat's bowl.

As much as Cyril might be feeling suffocated by his high society schedule, he wouldn't have left without asking me to take care of His Nibs.

"I'm sure there's a very good explanation," I said firmly.

Serrano followed my gaze, never missing a thing. "Will the cat be all right here by himself, Daisy?"

"It's warm enough inside this trailer, and he can come and go as he pleases through the cat flap." The little feline was an independent spirit, just like his owner. "I'll come by every day and make sure he has food and fresh water."

The detective walked through to the kitchen and I followed, leaving Martha still gazing at the rugby photo. I moved closer and grabbed his sleeve. "What the hell's going on, Serrano?" I hissed. Up close, I could finally read the concern in his eyes.

"I don't know, Daisy," he murmured, "but I've got a bad feeling about this whole situation."

That night, there was a Board of Supervisors' meeting where one of the topics on the agenda would be the proposed zoning change that Beau Cassell would require to develop the land for his townhomes.

Before the meeting, and what promised to be a contentious public hearing, Martha, Eleanor, and I went over to see Ruth. I picked them up in my old Subaru, because for one thing, Eleanor didn't own a car, only a red Vespa, and for another, Martha was the worst driver in the world, and I was an even worse passenger.

But when we got there, Kathleen Brown said that Ruth was not up to seeing anyone. We reluctantly handed over our chicken enchilada casserole, green salad, and bottle of wine.

"Isn't that rather strange?" Martha whispered to me as we got back in the car. "Shivah is supposed to be where you have people come over all the time, right?"

I shrugged. "Yes, I thought so. Traditionally it lasts a week. Ruth must really not be feeling well."

"We'll come back tomorrow." She settled herself in the front seat. "Now, let's put the pedal to the metal, Daisy."

I ignored her and drove carefully. The roads were still

slick, and I didn't want to drive too fast, even in a Subaru. Every once in a while, I could feel the tires lose traction on a slippery patch, and by the time we reached Sheepville, I breathed a sigh of relief.

The meeting was scheduled for 7:30 p.m. at the Sheepville Town Hall, so we had plenty of time to kill. We'd planned to share the meal with Ruth, and I could feel my stomach rumbling. Maybe we could grab a bite in town.

But when I pulled into the parking lot, Martha hopped out of the car almost before it had stopped moving.

"You two go on ahead to the meeting without me," she said. "I'm going to file a missing persons report at the police station. Time to take action." She bustled off down Main Street toward the intersection with Sheepville Pike.

Eleanor and I looked at each other for a moment.

"What do you think about this whole state of affairs, E? Do you really think Cyril just took off with Roos and they're hanging out in some cheap Atlantic City motel?"

Her gray eyes were somber. "Not unless he's savagely hungover and can't face the music yet, no. Nothing against Cyril, but I don't think he's *this* brave."

I had to drive all the way around the nearly full lot before I finally squeezed into a spot. "This place is packed. I guess we should skip dinner and go find a seat inside."

Eleanor sighed as we got out of the car. I guessed she was as hungry as me.

We walked into the town hall situated at the corner of Porter and Main, across from the glorious Sheepville Library. It was built in the same grand style as the library, with a brick façade and tall Palladian windows.

The town of Sheepville oversaw the zoning and building codes for several smaller towns and villages, including Millbury. In the meeting room that held about a hundred seats, most of them were occupied tonight, with the first few rows filled with township experts like the engineer, fire marshal, and code enforcement officer. The supervisors were ordinary citizens, mostly small business people and volunteers, and they relied on the advice of the paid experts. I was pleased to see a good showing by Millbury residents. The Historical Society had worked hard to get the word out about this meeting.

The court stenographer was setting up before the curved podium that was flanked by the Stars and Stripes on one side and the Commonwealth's flag on the other. The appearance of the board, probably waiting in the wings with their laptops, would be a well-orchestrated production.

"Eleanor, you go ahead and sit down. I'll just hang out here in the back." My rush of claustrophobia and near panic attack at the funeral was still fresh in my mind.

"I'll stand with you, you crazy old woman."

I bumped shoulders with her. "Hey, not so much of the *old*."

Warren Zeigler, a local lawyer, came up to us, wearing his customary bow tie and round horn-rimmed glasses. He was representing the Historical Society for free, thankfully, because he also had a vested interest. It wasn't just the society that was against the builder. Many other residents of the village didn't want the landscape spoiled by a condo development either.

I smiled at him. "So what do you think of our chances tonight, Warren?"

"Yeah, do you think that if Cassell's bid falls through, the farmer will be willing to make a deal with us?" Eleanor asked.

"One step at a time, ladies. Let's first state our case at this meeting." He pushed his glasses up a fraction. "I think that once we educate people to what construction will mean, they'll see the danger. Not just the negative aesthetic impact on our village, but increased traffic, higher school taxes, and a greater drain on the township resources."

The Historical Society had been blindsided when the old farmer who owned the land had suddenly signed a conditional agreement of sale with Cassell Builders. Glory Farm had lingered on the market for over two years, partly because of the downturn in the real estate market, and partly because it was priced far too high. We'd been lulled into a false sense of security.

Cassell had preempted us, but undeterred, we'd resolved to drum up enough support within the community to block him. Builders often optioned a piece of land before buying it outright, but if he couldn't get the zoning approved, he wouldn't be obligated to go through with the purchase. Our hope was that we could raise enough money with the proceeds from the calendar, combined with funds accumulated over the years, to step up and make our own offer when that happened. It would take everything we had, but it would be worth it.

Now the calendar had hit a road bump, but we still needed to do whatever we could to make sure he didn't get the necessary approvals.

"Now here's a sight for sore eyes. Brat One and Brat Two!" Angus Backstead, the auctioneer, came up and threw his huge arms around me and Eleanor. We found ourselves crushed against his mountain man frame. "What's goin' on, girls? Good turnout tonight for the NIMBY meeting, eh?"

"The what?" Eleanor had almost disappeared under the folds of his ski jacket, but I could still hear her muffled voice.

"NIMBY. Not in my backyard." Warren took off his glasses and polished them carefully.

Angus chuckled. "Yup. Always produces a good showing. We like the concept of affordable housing, but just not here. Right, missy?"

I almost expected Angus to rub his knuckles across the top of my head. He was like the big brother I never had, and we'd spent many an enjoyable day hunting for dusty treasures at flea markets and yard sales.

"I'm warning you, things could get ugly," Angus said. "If we're going to win the war, we gotta be ready to fight. Cassell knows he'll make a boatload of dough in the end and he's used to dealing with these types of legal battles for his builder's remedy. Right, Warren?"

Warren nodded. "I'm going to look for an opportunity to accuse the board of spot zoning. They'll hate that." He straightened his tie one last time and headed for the front of the room.

"What's that?" I whispered to Angus.

"Spot zoning is when a certain party is being favored for no good reason. Or at least not one that's made public." He nodded toward the podium. "It's *showtime*, folks."

With the appropriate amount of fanfare, the supervisors, township manager, solicitor, and police chief entered the room, took their seats, and the meeting was called to order.

After the pledge of allegiance, roll call, and the approval of minutes from the last meeting, the chairwoman announced the first item on the agenda. One resident was seeking a variance to the ordinance that required a three-acre lot to keep livestock. She owned two potbellied pigs and argued that they weren't really livestock, but pets. She went on at length how the pair, called Eggs and Benedict, were docile, intelligent, and well-trained, and brought up a seemingly endless parade of people to testify on their behalf.

"Dang, but she's makin' me hungry," Angus murmured.

Eleanor sighed. "Yeah, Daisy, we could have skipped all this nonsense. We would have had time for dinner after all."

The variance passed, probably because the supervisors were so glassy-eyed they could hardly see their notes.

After we suffered through various other mind-numbing

matters on the agenda, the chairwoman finally announced that Beau Cassell was filing a request to have Glory Farm rezoned. The builder had already presented his preliminary plans before the zoning hearing board.

"Now we are going to open up the meeting for citizen comments. Please state your name and your association with the property address at the microphone."

Althea Gunn spoke first. She was our church secretary and a forbidding woman who cowed much of the congregation into submission. "I, for one, would like to see that old farm sold as soon as possible. The place is a nuisance and an eyesore. Neighborhood kids have broken in, *partying* and doing who knows what else. It's only a matter of time before something bad happens. I hope that Mr. Cassell's request is approved without delay."

Odd. As a longtime resident of the village, one would think she'd want to protect open space as much as we did. Although it wasn't just Althea. As other members of the public got up and spoke in support of the development, it seemed there was a small faction that really liked the idea.

"Just like Glory Farm, my land is my 401(k)!" one man shouted. "It's all I have to take care of my retirement. It's builders like Cassell here who are going to pay me what it's worth. We need to work *with* them instead of the municipality stonewalling and taking money out of my pocket!"

"That old retirement nest egg line has been heard enough times around here," Angus muttered to me and Eleanor. "It's a personal dig that works well. Plays on the board's sympathy."

We looked at each other in dismay. This meeting wasn't going according to plan. Not at all.

Next it was Warren's turn, and I crossed my fingers.

"The farmland is the buffer between our historic village and the new construction that's happening all over Bucks County," he began in his measured tone. "Many villages have already been lost to growth and development. How many other farms like this one have disappeared? Gone for good. Do you realize that we've lost almost seventy percent of our open land since 1950?"

I could see heads nodding in the audience. Warren had a quiet intelligence that made people calm down and listen.

"Wider roads have spelled the death of villages that sit at a crossroads like ours. Where a blacksmith's shop or a tavern used to be, it's now a strip mall or gas station. And let's not forget skyrocketing school taxes. A new development adds about five thousand dollars per child to the tax burden on a township."

The audience was spellbound, the court stenographer rapidly taking down every word, and I grinned at Eleanor. This was more like it.

Now it was the builder's turn at bat. Beau Cassell was an attractive man and a smooth speaker, but a faint flush on his cheeks hinted at high blood pressure and a volatile temperament.

"New development *can* offer affordable housing to your township without changing its character. As you've seen, my plans have been carefully designed to provide for a limited number of units, as well as keeping back five of the thirty acres for open space. The plan also included renderings of the exteriors, and much care was put into façades to blend with the environment."

Right. As if his vinyl boxes could compare to a village of historic homes. Especially the two-hundred-year-old farmhouse he would raze with his development.

I watched one of the younger women chewing on her lip thoughtfully, as if an affordable condo would fit the bill for her. I knew that a lot of young people preferred new construction. This generation didn't want to deal with redoing kitchens or stripping off wallpaper. They wanted any place they bought to be move-in ready.

"You're welcome to visit any of my completed developments and see how well we have assimilated our designs into the landscape."

"Your houses are crap!" came a shout from the back of the room. "Shoddy construction that could kill someone. You oughta be ashamed of yourself!"

Frank Fowler, the township's solicitor, patted his balding forehead with his handkerchief. He looked a little under the weather, his pale skin more colorless than usual.

More voices chimed in. It became obvious that a contingent of homeowners who lived in Cassell-constructed homes had shown up with serious axes to grind. I recognized Jim McIntire, the husband who had been mad with jealousy over his wife's infatuation with the photographer, and who had been beeping frantically outside the garage on the night of the calendar shoot. "Cassell never finished half the stuff on our punch list after we moved in!" he yelled.

"Slaps them up, takes the money, and doesn't care that they fall apart a year later," another one shouted.

I saw a muscle clench in Beau Cassell's cheek, the flush noticeable even through the tan.

Everyone was shouting now, whether they were a resident or not.

"Goddamn it, Fowler, *do* something." Even though I wasn't a lip reader, it wasn't hard to decipher the words Cassell growled at our hapless attorney.

Althea Gunn stuck both her pinkie fingers in her mouth and sounded a piercing whistle.

The room fell silent.

The chairwoman took a deep breath and took advantage of the sudden quiet. "Now, please settle down, everyone. The issue here is the zoning change, not the quality of the builder's construction."

Cassell glared at her.

"Not that I'm—er—commenting on that, however." She cleared her throat in confusion.

One of the supervisors leaned forward. "Has a traffic study been done yet, Mr. Cassell?"

Cassell shook his head, his mouth compressed as if he was holding on to his temper with an effort.

"Well, I think we need to learn more about that issue. Also about the additional load on the sewer system. You're talking two hundred EDUs on land that was only zoned for thirty. I propose we defer a decision for this evening and meet privately with Mr. Fowler and the rest of our consultants to review more of the facts." He nodded at the chairwoman.

"Ahem. Due to—er—time constraints, we are going to table the discussion on the Glory Farm property. Meeting is adjourned." She banged her gavel, and a few minutes later, amid some residual grumbling and the shuffling of chairs, the crowd began to disperse.

Angus, Warren, Eleanor, and I gathered again in the back of the room.

Angus ran a hand through his thick snow-white hair. "Whew! Hell of a shindig, eh? Me and the gals didn't even get a chance to speak. And after the reaction tonight, I can't imagine the supervisors approving this unless some serious money exchanges hands. *If* you know what I mean."

Warren delicately cleared his throat. "I couldn't possibly comment. But if the rezoning request is denied, Cassell can file a substantive validity challenge."

"But the longer this whole thing drags out, the better for us, right?" Eleanor said. "Gives us more time to raise the money."

"Possibly. However, if you fight too hard, the courts will make the decision, and it may not be the one you want," Warren said. "Sometimes it's better to compromise a little. More open land preserved to create a larger buffer between the development and the village of Millbury, for instance."

"He's going for two hundred units, so they can shoot him down to one-eighty, and he'll still be happy," Angus said. "He knows how to play this game."

Warren nodded. "I'm sure he has a contingency plan up his sleeve."

"The board will probably reintroduce it when the weather is bad and there's poor attendance, and it'll get pushed through," Angus muttered darkly. "I've seen this tactic before, and especially when it comes to a Cassell build. Just need to figure out who the rat is in the woodpile."

The lack of dinner and the overabundance of hot tempers in the room combined to make my head swim. "I need some air," I said. "I'll meet you guys outside."

I stepped out of the town hall into the parking lot and caught a whiff of cigarette smoke. In deep shadow cast by the eaves of the grand building, Frank Fowler seemed to be in an intense discussion with a stranger, an imposing, rough-hewn man wearing a long, black leather coat.

The stranger towered over the slim lawyer, almost threatening, or at least invading, his personal space.

One of the genetic gifts I had honed during my decades as a high school teacher was my excellent sense of hearing as I caught the whisper of test answers or the rustle of notes being passed in class. I half closed my eyes now to concentrate.

They were arguing about something, and I caught a word here and there, but I needed to get closer.

I walked across the lot as if heading to my car and, once I got as near as I dared, stopped and bent my knees slightly, shrinking into the shadow of a big Chevy Suburban.

"What the hell do you want?" Frank Fowler sucked on his cigarette as he glared at the stranger.

"You owe me, Fowler. Big-time."

"You're mistaken. I don't owe you a damn thing."

The stranger's voice lowered. "You and me, we have a

lot of history between us. A lot of secrets to keep. I'm sure you wouldn't want certain information made public, now would you, Frankie?"

Fowler glanced in my direction, and I pretended to fumble inside my pocketbook as if searching for my keys. I looked up to see him staring directly at me. I straightened up and decided to take the bull by the horns and see if I could get a better look at this intimidating companion.

I walked over to the two men. "Hey, Frank. Interesting meeting, eh?" I turned to the tall stranger. "Hello. I'm Daisy Buchanan."

The man didn't speak, just stared at me without any change in his expression.

"This is—er—Randy," Frank said. "He's—er—Beau Cassell's new foreman."

The stranger flicked a disparaging look at Frank, but stuck his hand out. I shook it and got a quick impression of a large, smooth palm before he yanked it away. He stayed sullen and silent, and the moment became uncomfortable until the door opened and Angus and Eleanor came out into the lot in a burst of laughter.

"Well, nice to meet you, Randy," I said. "Good night, Frank."

I scurried over to my friends, thinking that the newcomer's gruff persona would be a good match for the builder. One was just as obnoxious as the other.

Chapter Five

When I got home, starving and chilled, Joe had already pulled the heavy curtains in the living room against the cold. I followed an enticing aroma toward the kitchen, where I found him stirring a huge pot of turkey chili.

"Wow. You have no idea how good it is to see you." I breathed in the steam from the stove. "And your chili."

"Hungry, Daisy?"

"I could eat my arm off, that's how starving I am."

Joe laughed, and while he opened a bottle of cabernet, I ladled the spicy bean mixture into two soup crocks. I set them on the table next to a basket of crusty French bread and farm fresh butter. As we ate, I told him about the meeting and the encounter with Fowler and the other man.

It was one of those nights when all I really wanted to do was snuggle on the couch with my husband and sip some more red wine, but once I'd finished eating, our retriever puppy, Jasper, fixed me with an unblinking stare, as if willing me to put my coat on.

I tried to squash the rising guilt as I rinsed the dishes and put the rest of the chili into plastic containers, some for the fridge and some to go in the freezer.

Like a lot of married couples, we'd made pacts about how to divvy up the household chores. Joe did the cooking and I cleaned up. He did the laundry and I walked the dog.

Most days I felt like I was getting the better end of the deal as, truth be told, I enjoyed the walks as much as Jasper, but on nights like tonight, I had to dig deep into my suitcase of courage.

Joe came up behind me, wrapped his arms around me, and I turned and kissed him. Things were progressing nicely until I heard the tiny whine in the back of Jasper's throat. A bark I might have been able to disregard, but this plaintive plea was impossible to ignore.

With a sigh, I gently disengaged myself from my husband's embrace and bundled up to brave the elements.

Outside, I gasped at the unforgiving chill and tucked my face inside the collar of my jacket like a turtle. Gray strips of clouds lay across the moon, like someone shining a torch through a mummy's shroud. Ice-crusted snow on the grass verges crunched underfoot as we hurried down Main Street. Or at least I hurried, trying to keep the dog moving.

When we got to the end of Main Street, I took a right on Grist Mill Road. I'd already walked farther than I wanted to in this weather, but now I was so close to the farm, I had an urge to see it one more time.

What would happen if this land was turned into yet another cookie-cutter development? The wild turkeys, foxes, deer, and other wildlife would all disappear.

"Suppose I should thank you for keeping me fit, Jasper," I huffed out against the wind. "There's no way I'd have taken this walk tonight if not for you."

The names of some of the developments in the surrounding townships gave a hint as to what had come before, like Meadow Farms or Hilltop Forest or Pleasant Woods, except there wasn't a farm there anymore, and most of the trees were gone. The McMansion had ridden the wave of the real estate boom of the eighties and nineties, and there seemed to be no way to stop the powerful force of development raging through the remaining available land like a voracious combine harvester. It seemed as though the builders always won, and I sucked in a breath of frigid air at the thought of this peaceful expanse of countryside becoming yet another victim.

My face was freezing, and my gloves weren't doing much to protect my icy fingers. I alternated keeping one hand in my pocket and one holding the leash. Jasper snuffled in the undergrowth by the side of the road, probably catching the scent of a rabbit.

Why had Sheepville Township done nothing to stem the flow of this destruction? Was there someone on the board, or close to them, who was doing a backstreet deal with the developers and had helped push deals through for Cassell before? Was Fowler accepting bribes to finance his wife's political campaign?

Was Frank Fowler the rat in the woodpile?

On Friday, the bitter cold eased up a little, with a forecast of forty degrees later in the day. Early that morning, I walked up to the salvage yard. As I got closer, I caught a glimpse of Cyril's cat disappearing through the flap into the trailer.

I knocked on the door before I went in, just to be on the safe side, but there was no sign that his owner had returned. I swallowed against a rush of disappointment. I'd have put up with any amount of tongue-lashing to know that Cyril was still around.

The little cat peeked at me from behind the grandfather clock as I filled his food and water bowls. "It's okay, buddy. Don't worry. I'll take care of you."

He blinked his topaz-colored eyes, but didn't venture any nearer.

The other end of the trailer served as Cyril's office, and I hung a CLOSED sign on the door. In some silly way it made me feel better, as if he would be coming back at any minute.

I trudged back up the long potholed driveway to the intersection with Main Street. Seeing as it was Friday, Laura would be managing the shop, but there were no auctions on my schedule because Angus and I were going house hunting with Patsy Elliot and her daughter, Claire. As a first-time home buyer, Patsy had asked us to come along and give the benefit of our experience.

When I arrived in Sheepville, I stopped at the hardware store to pick up some more pet-safe ice melt and a few other necessary items that I couldn't get in Millbury. Apart from the specialty stores like mine, there was only the post office with a tiny convenience shop attached and the diner. That was it, apart from farm stands in the summer. Residents had to make this five-mile trip for any major shopping. As I walked out, the sun was shining, and the snow was melting in earnest on the salt-encrusted sidewalks.

Suddenly I gasped as I saw Ruth Bornstein walking along the other side of the street with an attractive man in his forties.

I skidded on a patch of slush, dropped the bag of ice melt, and grabbed hold of a lamppost for balance. Ruth was laughing up at the man, who had his arm around her. I peeked around the pole, wondering if they'd seen me, but they were too engrossed in each other.

According to Jewish custom, Ruth should be sitting shivah

at home, at least for a week, shouldn't she? Should I say anything to Detective Serrano about this merry widow?

I pulled out my cell phone and stood there for a few moments, wracked with indecision.

Come on, Daisy. Why don't you mind your own business for once?

Time was ticking away and I didn't want to be late, so I stuffed the phone in my pocket, threw the ice melt in the trunk of the station wagon, and headed up Sheepville Pike toward Backstead's Auction House.

The auction building sat on three acres, with parking for a hundred cars, plus room for more on the surrounding fields. I pulled up in front of the low-slung corrugated metal structure and parked next to Angus's Ford F-150 pickup truck.

"Hullo, Brat," he greeted me as he strolled out of the double front doors, wearing his usual uniform of plaid shirt, jeans, and mountain boots. He handed me a coffee to go from the snack bar.

"Ah, a savior has come! Thank you, Angus." I took a grateful slurp of the caffeine. "This is so exciting, isn't it? It's been a long time since I went house hunting."

Angus grunted. "Yup. We just need to make sure that crazy gal doesn't buy some ol' money pit today." He crossed his massive arms across his chest. "You know, Daisy, I still miss my Betty, but teaching Patsy the ropes around here is helping take my mind off things."

A month or so ago, Angus's wife had left him after twenty-five years of marriage, saying she wanted to "find" herself. Poor Angus didn't really know what that meant and was utterly devastated, until Patsy, who had been a part-time auctioneer, quit waitressing and came to work for him full-time. With her no-nonsense practicality, she was pushing Angus to revamp his ancient business practices and distracting him from pining so much for his lost love.

At that moment, a gold-colored sedan that had seen better years zoomed along Sheepville Pike, clanged into the parking lot, and came to a stop in a cloud of smoke.

Claire, Patsy's ten-year-old daughter, rushed out of the car and into my arms, reminding me of a galloping colt with her long limbs and shining dark hair. "This is so fun, isn't it, Daisy?" she exclaimed, echoing my enthusiasm for the outing.

"You're getting too tall and grown-up. You need to stop that right now." I grinned at her as I hugged her back. I'd insisted she call me Daisy, instead of Mrs. Daly or Mrs. Buchanan or whatever else I could be.

Patsy got out of the car, too, but the unfortunate vehicle still sounded like it was running along the road until she thumped the hood a couple of times and it shuddered into silence. She had the same slim build as her daughter, and she wore jeans that encased her long legs, plus a red T-shirt under a leather jacket. "Yo, guys, wazzup?"

Angus glared at the beat-up contraption. "You need to get rid of that crappy car, missy."

Patsy frowned. "What for? It runs fine."

"Gimme a break. I can tell you're coming a country mile away by the black clouds."

"House first, and *then* maybe I'll think about getting a new ride. My sister's been awesome, but I think she's really ready for us to get our own place."

Patsy and Claire had been living with her sister in the same condo development as Serrano, and while they had the whole huge finished basement to themselves, there was nothing like owning your own home. At a recent auction, the antique doll collection on sale had blown the doors out with the sky-high price it fetched. In fact, it was the biggest auction that Backstead's had ever seen, and Patsy's share of the healthy commission was enough for a down payment on a house, and then some.

Thinking how Cyril and I had restored a Victorian

dollhouse for Claire's birthday this past Halloween brought a rush of renewed anxiety for his safety, but I tamped it down and pasted a smile on my face.

Claire kept an arm around my waist as she looked up at her mother. "Do you think we can be in the new house by Christmas, Mommy?"

"Not sure about that, sweets. Heck, Christmas will be here before we know it. Look at all the stuff in the stores already, and it's not even Thanksgiving. Drives me *crazy*."

I winced as I thought of my festive and decidedly Yule-like store.

"I don't understand why you guys don't just move in with me," Angus said. "I got lots of room. Hell, I'm rattling around that old place by myself." He nodded toward the pristine white stucco three-story farmhouse across from the auction building. Angus had sort of adopted these two, like the child and grandchild he never had.

Patsy stifled a sigh, as if they'd had this conversation many times before. She looked at me with a plea in her eyes.

I cleared my throat. "Well, that's certainly very generous of you, Angus, and I'm sure Patsy appreciates the offer. But with you two working together, it might be best for all concerned if she had her own home. As a woman, I can tell you that sometimes we just need our space."

Angus grunted, but he was a smart enough man to know that three females were too much to take on at once.

We'd arranged to meet the real estate agent at the first listing, so we piled into Angus's truck and headed toward the south end of Sheepville.

"The first one we're going to see is a resale in a development that Beau Cassell built a couple of years ago." Patsy consulted her sheaf of property listings. "Fairview Farm Estates. He's still building over in the newer section, but this one's well within my budget." She directed Angus through the development until we found the right road.

The agent was waiting for us in a common parking area near a row of beige single homes, built close together with tiny yards in front.

"Are we the only crazy people looking for a house at this time of year?" Patsy called to her as she got out of the truck. Claire bent and gathered some snow into a snowball.

The real estate agent shook her head and smiled. "It's the serious buyers who are looking now, and so sellers are generally willing to make a deal. But I have to point out up front that this one is a foreclosure."

"So? What's your point?" Patsy demanded.

"Foreclosures can be tricky because you're dealing with the banks. It could take longer than the average sale and may not go through at all. But if it works out, you can get a great value. Anyway, here's the house."

She led the way to one at the end of the row.

"This is it?" Claire murmured, dropping her snowball in dismay. "Ooh, Mommy, it's *ugly*!"

"Shh. Knock it off," Patsy hissed over her shoulder as she followed the agent into the foyer.

I had to admit it wasn't the most attractive place I'd ever seen. Just a plain shingled box with four windows and a door in the center of the bottom story.

Glancing back toward the newer section, I saw the same unappealing cubes going up in rapid succession. Even a gable or two or some decorative feature above the front door would have helped. Guess Beau Cassell hadn't spent much on architectural design. This one could have been sketched on the back of a napkin.

The previous owners hadn't done any additional landscaping either. The three stunted bushes that the builder had originally supplied were spaced far apart, far too few for the front of the house.

Inside, it was frigid and the living room carpet was badly stained and needed a good vacuuming. It looked as though someone had punched a huge hole in the drywall in a fit of rage.

Patsy flipped a light switch, but nothing happened.

"The electricity was shut off. By the electric company," said the agent apologetically. "The couple who owned the house are getting divorced and I guess they didn't pay the bill."

The tour didn't improve as we continued. In the kitchen, white countertops made of laminate to look like Corian were marred by cigarette burns and red wineglass stains that no one had bothered to try to remove.

I swallowed against the acrid odor of bleach overlaying mold. The owners must not have emptied the fridge when they left, and when the electricity was turned off, everything had rotted. Now the door was propped ajar from a recent cleanout. I wondered if the real estate agent had done it.

"Guess we'd need a new icebox." Patsy shrugged her shoulders as she inspected the upper kitchen cabinets.

Feeling my stomach lurch, I blew out a breath and hurried out of the kitchen with Claire right behind me.

"I don't like this place, Daisy," she whispered. "It feels bad." Claire was normally a sweet-natured child, but she was obviously violently opposed to the two-year-old building with holes in the walls. She'd once shown me a painting of her dream house for herself and her mom that won first prize at a country fair. This was definitely not it.

I had to agree with her. Houses had personalities just like people, and there was something very angry and bitter about this one.

By the time we made it down to the basement with its broken window and piles of black garbage bags holding who knows what, Claire had had enough.

"Mom! I don't want to live here. It's a *horrible* house."

"Yo, don't be a brat. Lose the addi-tood." Patsy ruffled her hair. "Just use your imagination. Picture this place

with some fresh paint and cleaned up a bit." She glanced
around. "Okay, maybe a lot."

I could tell that the ever-practical Patsy liked the low
price and the idea of getting a real bargain. Some might
call her tough, and she could be brash at times, but she was
also good-hearted and devoted to her daughter. Despite a
hard start in life, she was making her own way.

"I'm glad you could come, Daisy," she said to me. "You
know about all the things that could possibly go wrong in a
house."

I chuckled ruefully. "Sad, but true." Our Greek Revival
had been a never-ending repair story. Even now, some thirty
years later, we still weren't finished working on it. Speaking
of money pits, Joe and I knew we'd taken on a big challenge
when we bought it. But it didn't matter—we'd fallen madly
in love and had overlooked the leaking roof, ancient electri-
cal fuses, and drafty windows. Angus had been a big help
with fixing up the house as well as remodeling my store.

I thought it would behoove the bank to pay a few bucks to
get this place properly cleaned if they wanted to see it sold.
Most buyers were distracted by details like carpets that
needed vacuuming and wouldn't be able to see the potential.

The smell of mold was strong in the basement, too, which
was surprising for a young house built using modern drain-
age systems. I couldn't see any water on the floor, but it could
be a potential issue down the road.

We headed upstairs where the same sad feeling per-
vaded. The bathroom tiles were grungy, a broken venetian
blind hung down in one of the bedrooms, and the closet
doors were off the track. There was another hole smashed
in the drywall.

Angus was inspecting the master bedroom. He had
worked in construction for years before he opened his auction business. "Well, I don't need a split level to see that
the walls aren't true. Even when this place was brand-new,

it wasn't up to snuff. In my opinion you'd be better off with an older home with solid construction and good bones. Something with only some cosmetic touches needed. I can help you with that."

Patsy glared at him. I'd seen that same bullish expression on Angus's face a thousand times before. If a person didn't know otherwise, it would be easy to think that they were father and daughter. Of course, the fact that they were alike in lots of ways meant they butted heads all the time, but I knew Angus hoped Patsy could take over the business someday. He absolutely doted on Claire, too.

Patsy hitched her leather jacket back and stuck her hands in the pockets of her jeans. "I can't deal with pink-tiled bathrooms and psychedelic wallpaper, Angus. I don't want to do a lot of rehab. I want something newer."

"You'd have to do just as much work with this place. Look at all the damn holes in the walls!"

Claire held out her palm and Angus fished in his pockets, looking for a quarter as penance for his cuss word. Claire had done her best to clean up her mother's language and was now working on Angus, twenty-five cents at a time.

He grunted as he pulled down the steps to the attic and one of the hinges swung loose. "Sloppy. No excuse. Cassell is banging these dumps up as fast as he can go. There's no quality workmanship here." Angus, who took his job as surrogate parent to Patsy very seriously, climbed the attic steps to inspect the roof construction.

The real estate agent shifted nervously as we watched his large frame disappear into the rafters. Patsy sighed.

"Don't worry, dear," the agent murmured as she laid a hand on Patsy's sleeve. "You know, sometimes when parents are involved, they can be overly picky. It's how they justify why they've been brought along."

I gritted my teeth. I viewed Patsy and Claire as my family, too. I wasn't about to let them make a mistake either.

A few moments later, Angus clambered back down. "Some of those rafters have been spray-foamed and some not. I've never seen such an uneven and unprofessional job in my life." He let go of the attic steps, and they swung back into the roof with a clang.

"Nope, you gals are not buying this place. No way. It's a disaster waiting to happen. Come on, we're leaving."

The real estate agent pressed her lips together, probably wishing Patsy hadn't brought her "dad" along.

Outside, as we headed toward Angus's truck, Beau Cassell himself was getting out of a big pickup truck, a length of metal rebar in his hand. Patsy walked past him with her rangy stride that made men stop and take a second look when she walked by. Beau Cassell was no exception.

Angus took a step in front of her. "Hey, Cassell, congratulations, you did a real crap job on this place," he said with a nod of his head toward the house we had just vacated.

"What the hell are you talking about, Backstead?" Cassell's cheeks flushed.

"That spray foam in the attic? It's not even finished, and it's way too thick in some places, not enough in others. Your fricking building technique is for the birds."

Cassell gripped the rebar so tightly, I could see the white on his knuckles. "The owner must have done it himself, because spray foam wasn't an option when we built this section. I remember these homeowners. What a pair. They had a huge fight right in the model home." Suddenly his eyes narrowed. "That son of a bitch! He must have been stealing my construction materials."

"Or maybe some of your crew are doing work on the side and pocketing the cash?" Patsy suggested.

Cassell's face turned a purplish-red, and he hurried toward the house with Angus hard on his heels, obviously eager to personally point out the rest of the builder's failings to him.

"Oh, jeez," I said. "Patsy, you stay here with Claire. I don't want Angus getting into a fight."

I ran after the two men. To say Angus was a hothead was an understatement, and he'd already been in trouble with the law for brawling. It wouldn't take much of a cinder to ignite the simmering resentment between these two into a firestorm.

As I hurried up to the second floor, Beau was already at the top of the pull-down steps.

"This foam smells as though it's been recently applied," he said as he heaved himself into the attic.

"Angus, wait," I pleaded, but Angus was following Cassell, and with a sigh, I grabbed the side of the steps and gingerly climbed up until I could peek inside.

In the dingy light I could see puffed rows of cream-colored foam piled high between the wooden rafters. Even though I wasn't a construction expert, it looked like a holy mess to me.

"Son of a . . . It's way too thick. How deep did this idiot spray this stuff?" Cassell took his length of metal rebar and poked at the end of the thickest pile.

A jagged piece of foam broke off, exposing the tip of a brilliant emerald snakeskin boot.

Chapter Six

The missing photographer.

I gasped and clung to the wooden rail as my knees went soft, but Cassell was already heading for the steps. I had to scurry back down and out of the way before he trampled over my fingers with his big construction boots.

"Everyone out of here now!" he yelled. "It's a frigging fire hazard!" Without looking back he was gone. I grabbed Angus's hand as we ran for the front door.

Once we were all a safe distance away, Angus called the police and fire departments.

Who on earth could have wanted to kill Alex Roos?

I joined Patsy and Claire near the retention pond, my heart racing. It wasn't long before we heard the whine of sirens. Two police cars flew into the lot, and a fire engine rumbled up in front of the house.

"What's going on, Daisy?" Patsy asked.

"The builder thinks the house is dangerous and may catch on fire," I answered as carefully as I could.

Claire gasped. "I knew it! Didn't I tell you this wasn't a good place, Mommy?"

"So why are the *police* here?"

As Cyril would have said, Patsy wasn't as green as she was cabbage-looking. I shook my head slightly and glanced meaningfully at Claire. "Fill you in later, okay? Just keep Claire as far away from this scene as you can."

It didn't take long for Serrano to roar up in his Dodge Challenger and bark out orders to secure the area and keep the gaggle of interested homeowners at bay.

One old man behind us was pushing his way to the front. "What's going on here?"

"Unsafe situation," I said, but didn't elaborate.

"I'm not surprised. Cassell did a crap job on my house, too. Everything's falling apart on a house that's barely two years old. Criminal, it is. Good to see the police finally took some notice."

Serrano caught my eye and motioned me through the yellow tape. I passed the builder, who was explaining the dangers of oversprayed foam to an officer.

"You're going to have a helluva job here, Serrano," Angus was saying as I caught up to them. He nodded toward the roof. "You're gonna need a reciprocating saw or sabre saw, something like that, to cut that guy out."

"Oh, God, Angus, please." I shuddered and wrapped my arms around my chest. The charismatic photographer had been in my shop only a couple of days ago. If I let myself imagine the hideous reality of his last moments on this earth, I thought I might crumble into a million pieces.

"Sorry, Daisy, but seems like someone was royally pissed off at this guy, don't it?"

"Yes, but who on earth could it be?" I glanced over to

where Beau Cassell, still vermilion in the face, was gesturing wildly at the police officer. I was relieved to see that Patsy and Claire were well away in the grassy common area and Claire was bending to pet a neighbor's dog. "As much as I don't like Beau Cassell, it seems a bit far-fetched for him to have done it to block the production of the calendar and maybe win the bid for the farm."

For some reason the night of the calendar shoot popped into my head and I told them about Stanley's panicked deathbed statement. I didn't miss the look that passed between Serrano and Angus.

"Bornstein had dementia, right?" Serrano said. "Anyway, what's this to do with the situation at hand, Ms. Buchanan?"

I inhaled, prayed for patience, and tried again. "Maybe Alex caught something on film that night that someone else would not want to be common knowledge. Like someone murdering a defenseless old man, for instance."

Serrano sighed. "Facts, facts, Daisy. How many times must we repeat this? There's nothing concrete here, just speculation."

I bit my lip. Sometimes Serrano was just great to me, valuing my help and my opinions, and other times he was so high-handed and dismissive that I wished he was a student in one of my elementary classes of yore and I could make him sit in the corner for a long time-out.

"But that's not all. This morning I saw Ruth Bornstein walking through Sheepville with a very attractive younger man."

"There's no law that says she can't have a little romance in her life." Serrano winked at Angus, who smiled benevolently at me.

I wanted to smack them both.

Serrano consulted his notepad. "Now, Daisy, you say

that the last time you saw Roos was the day of the shoot for Cyril Mackey?"

An even more disturbing image popped into my head. Had Alex been attacked while they were taking pictures? Was Cyril hurt and bleeding somewhere, or perhaps tied up and held for ransom?

"Do you think Cyril could have been kidnapped?" I gasped.

Serrano shook his head. He glanced at Angus again, but there was no humor in their eyes this time.

After we had finished giving our statements, we walked back to Angus's truck, where the agent was saying something about vacant houses being targets.

Her mouth pressed into a thin line at the sight of Angus. She must have thought she could talk Patsy into this place, but now it was a crime scene and off the market for a little while at least. "Well, we've run out of time for today," she said, as if a dead body was just a blip in the schedule. "I have another appointment now, but I'll line up some more places for us to see soon."

After we dropped Patsy and Claire off at Quarry Ridge, the development where they lived with her sister, Angus drove back to the auction house. I was silent as we drove, my mind speeding a million miles faster than Angus's pickup.

"Now what, missy? What's going on in that head of yours?"

"I've been trying to think of places where Alex and Cyril may have done their modeling shoot. I have a hunch it might have been at the old farmhouse. I think I'll stop there on my way home."

"Oh no, you don't. Not by yourself, anyway. I'll go with you."

"Angus, that's ridiculous. It's five miles out of your way, and back. I'll be fine."

Angus drummed his meaty fingers on the steering wheel. I sighed. Me and my big mouth.

I hopped into my Subaru, and Angus followed me to the outskirts of Millbury. As I got closer, I felt a racing tingle in my skin, the way I usually did when I listened to my intuition. The rough, rustic setting would fit Cyril's character perfectly and be a nice tie-in to the purpose of the calendar.

When we pulled into the rutted driveway, where the entrance sign for Glory Farm hung askew on the pole, I was glad Angus had insisted on coming with me. The farmhouse was set a good distance back from the road. In the waning light of a winter afternoon, it suddenly seemed eerily remote.

The last time I'd seen the place up close was a few months ago when the Historical Society had toured here, trying to come up with ideas to save it. It was boarded up then, too, but not so condemned-looking.

"Don't look too glorious now, does it?" Angus said once we were out of our vehicles and picking our way over muddy puddles and patches of gravel in the melting snow. In late summer there had been perennials in the garden, albeit overgrown, and in the glow of the sun it had seemed a whole lot better.

"Careful, Daisy." Angus reached out a hand as I stepped onto the porch and almost lost my balance when one of the rotted boards sank beneath my feet. Some of the gutters were missing, and long treacherous icicles hung off the sides of the house. I spotted some shingles lying on the ground from the recent storms. If someone didn't do something soon, the roof would leak and the cost of restoration would zoom to astronomical.

I peered through a gap where one of the slats had been ripped away from the boarded-up kitchen window. The

room was a mess, with a table overturned, beer bottles on
the ground, trash everywhere. Kids must have been in here
at some point, just like Althea said. Or had there been a
struggle? It was tough to tell.

There was still quite a bit of furniture in the house from
what I could see. My heart raced as I spotted some earth-
enware jars in the corner.

"Wonder why the farmer left all this stuff here?" I
whispered to Angus, who was looking over my shoulder.

He shrugged. "Shame to see those jars broken by van-
dals or squatters. They're probably worth a couple of hundred bucks each."

"The sooner we sort this out, the better. I can't bear to
think of this place being bulldozed." If houses could speak,
this one was crying out for help. Even in the terrible shape
it was in, it still had way more character and beauty than
Cassell's boring boxes.

Above us the sky was streaked with deep purple and violent pink, almost Technicolor. A vivid contrast against the
white of the farmhouse and the snowy fields. It would make
a great watercolor painting, except it wouldn't look real.

The main house was closed up, but there also were
plenty of outbuildings where the shoot could have taken
place. As Angus and I were walking over to the barn, with
its bird coop built into the top, I suddenly spotted an
unopened pack of Benson & Hedges cigarettes on the
ground. Cyril, a former smoker, always carried one as a
security blanket. He used to say if he knew he had them, but
chose not to smoke, the urge went away. He'd had them for
so long that if he ever did succumb to the urge, his head
would probably explode.

My heart was racing as I traced my fingers over the battered gold foil box.

I wasn't a particularly mystical person, but I didn't get the
sense that Cyril was dead. If he was, I thought I should feel

an ache in my heart, but I couldn't, especially not in this run-down atmosphere where he would have felt so at home.

"Oh, Cyril," I whispered, "where the heck are you?"

That night I came home to find Martha in my kitchen with a large cosmopolitan in her hand and a distressed look on her face. Joe was chatting with her as he busied himself at the stove.

"I heard what happened on the house hunt, Daisy." He gave me a meaningful look. "I figured Martha would like to hear the story directly from you, so I invited her for dinner."

My kind, thoughtful husband knew that news about the murder would have reached her already and she'd be panic-stricken for Cyril's safety. The Millbury village grapevine was faster than any ultrahigh-speed fiber-optic network.

I smiled at him. "Thank you, Joe."

"Daisy!" Martha got up and flung herself into my arms, and I braced my legs so we both didn't topple over backward. "I hope you don't mind that I accepted your dear husband's invitation, but I am simply *beside* myself with worry."

"I'm so glad you're here." I kissed her soft cheek and urged her to sit down at the butcher block table. Jasper slid in between us and rested his head on her knee.

"You need to tell me exactly what went on today," she said. "*Everything.* Don't you dare leave anything out."

Joe poured me a glass of cabernet and I told them the story from beginning to end, including every tiny detail I could remember.

Martha seemed to relax a little as I spoke, as if the information gave her some sense of control. "Do the police think that Roos was attacked at the house? Or earlier in the day?"

I shook my head. "They don't really know anything yet."

"You know, if Cyril needs his space, as *everyone* keeps

telling me, why isn't he calling after all this happened? So I don't worry?"

She was twisting the long chains around her neck into a tangled mess. I took her hands gently away and set them in her lap before a million beads burst all over the kitchen floor.

I was worried about Cyril, too, but I tried to hide my anxiety for Martha's sake. I didn't tell her about finding the cigarettes on the farm. Perhaps it was kinder for her to think he was safely out of the picture, blowing off steam in some dive bar somewhere.

When I got to the part about the disgruntled homeowners complaining about the quality of their Cassell-built homes, she sniffed.

"Well, the only thing *well-built* about that man is himself. His houses are a rip-off. I can tell you about so many people who have had problems. Even with a brand-new place. Take Terri Jones, for instance. Mold throughout, and so bad that her poor child has terrible asthma now."

I sipped my wine thoughtfully. "You know, I could see if it was Beau Cassell who had been murdered instead of Alex. There must be a thousand people who bear him a grudge."

At that moment, Joe came to the table with a steaming casserole dish. I breathed in the aroma of pot roast as he ladled out three generous portions. Jasper took great, gulping sniffs of the air.

Conversation ceased as I dug in, savoring the succulent meat and trying not to moan at how spectacular it was. "Joe, this is *so* good." Pot roast was one of Joe's signature dishes anyway, but he'd really outdone himself tonight.

He smiled at me, but then a shadow crossed his face as he glanced at our other dinner partner. "Don't you like it, Martha?"

She sighed, a long breathy sound that could have given Marilyn Monroe a run for her money. "Oh, it's wonderful, you darling man. It's just that my stomach is *completely* and *utterly* in knots."

I looked up guiltily from where I had been shoveling in the delicious meat, potatoes, and carrots as fast as I could go. The aftermath of the adrenaline surge from the discovery of a dead body, plus the fact that I'd missed lunch, had left me famished.

But Martha's plate was barely touched. Her stress-o-meter must be through the roof, yet she wasn't eating a thing.

I set down my fork and glanced at Joe, reading the same concern in his eyes.

"How about another cosmo, Martha?" he said. "You look like you could use one." He got up and fixed her another drink without waiting for an answer. Joe was a very attentive host, sometimes overly so, but we all lived within walking distance of one another.

After Joe and I had finished eating and Jasper had inhaled his portion of pot roast, Joe said, "I'll do the dishes tonight. Why don't you girls go and relax?"

Martha and I took our drinks into the study and set them on the steamer trunk that served as a coffee table. The color was coming back to her pale cheeks. Joe had been right. She needed this tonight.

Flames leapt in the fireplace, and for a while there was no sound except for the crackling of the logs and the hiss of fresh wood succumbing to the heat. Martha sipped her cocktail and stared into the fire. There were stress lines around her mouth evidencing the toll that the past couple of sleepless nights had wreaked on her freckled skin.

I couldn't bear this sad Martha. She was always my warm comfort and stalwart refuge from the storms of life, ebullient and fearless, large and in charge, as she liked to say. My heart ached for my best friend, helpless to give her any guarantees that Cyril would ever come back.

"Hey, Martha," I whispered. "You remember when we

were at Cyril's trailer? Did you happen to notice that weather vane propped up against the living room wall?"

If Cyril *was* alive, he'd be mad that I spoiled the surprise, but I couldn't worry about that right now. If this disappearing act was just about the fact that he craved some personal space, then too bad. He shouldn't be putting her through this stress.

She nodded slowly. "It was beautiful."

"He's going to give it to you for Christmas. You should have seen it when he first bought it, all blackened and dented. He spent hours, I mean *hours*, on restoration. You don't spend that much time on a present for someone you don't care for. Deeply."

A tear trickled down her cheek. "I fancy that the weather vane is trying to point me in the right direction to find him, Daisy. That little guy has wangled his way into my heart like no one else. I mean, I loved Teddy very much, don't get me wrong, but it's as if Cyril *needs* me more."

I nodded, my throat tight. I handed her a tissue, and she patted at the dark shadows under her eyes.

I racked my brain for something to cheer her up. "Oh, Martha, here's a tidbit I forgot to tell you before. I saw Ruth Bornstein in town today." Here I paused for dramatic effect. "With a *very* good-looking man in his forties. He had his arm around her *waist*."

Martha gasped, and I saw a hint of a sparkle in her eyes from the injection of some life-giving gossip. "Good God! Isn't she supposed to be sitting shivah all week? What do you suppose is going on there?"

I sat back, gratified by this properly impressed reaction to the news that I hadn't received from Serrano or Angus.

"You know, according to my sources, Ruth had a prenup," she said. "Stanley made a fortune with his pharmaceutical research and those patents of his, and she had to be married a certain number of years before he died to collect.

I would expect that the time period is up by now, but if she divorced him, she got nothing."

"Did she kill him to get the money?" I mused. "He would have died soon anyway. Why not wait? Was she getting impatient?" My mind was racing now. "They didn't have any children. Do you know if Stanley had any other heirs?"

"I don't know." She stood up and swayed a little, whether from weariness with my questions or the cosmos, I wasn't sure. "Daisy, I'd better go. Suddenly I'm very tired."

"I'll walk you home."

"You don't have to do that. I'm fine."

I put an arm around her. "Jasper needs a walk, anyway. Come on."

Joe hugged Martha good-bye and handed her a bag with a Tupperware container. "Take some pot roast home with you. Maybe you'll be hungry later."

"Darling, Joe." She looked at me sadly. "Daisy, you have no idea how lucky you are."

Chapter Seven

On Saturday, it turned even colder, and the wind kicked up as I hopped out of the car at the salvage yard, hoping to see my irascible friend standing on the stoop of the trailer in his sweatpants, his long gray hair brushing the shoulders of his white T-shirt, ready to give me an earful.

But the trailer was empty, except for the tiny black cat curled up on the recliner. He jumped down and came into the kitchen at the sight of me. After I filled up his bowl, he even let me brush my hand briefly against his fur before he bent his head to eat.

Progress.

At some point I might try to pick him up and take him home with me, but I wasn't sure how that would work out with Jasper. Besides, he seemed fairly content here.

"But I'm sure you miss Cyril, too. Right, buddy?"

He surveyed me with dark yellow eyes before he bent down again and lapped at the water.

I sat on the floor next to him, closed my eyes, and fancied I could almost smell the familiar scent of slightly burnt toast in the air. I squeezed my eyes tightly, and it was as if Cyril was at the stove, making his usual cups of tea. He'd hand me a cup of the strong, sweet, delicious brew that he called "builder's grade" and say, "There, lass. That'll put hairs on yer chest."

Whenever something was bothering me, or I wanted an unvarnished opinion, or just a fresh view on the world, I came down to this rusty paradise, counting on Cyril to give it to me straight.

Well, now I had a real problem, but the problem was, the problem was *him.*

I got up with some effort. "Well, ah'd better get cracking," I said to the cat, in what I hoped was a reasonable imitation of Cyril's accent.

The cat didn't deign to favor me with a backward glance as he turned away and sprang back into his position in the recliner.

"Okay, okay. Give me a break. I'm trying."

Before I headed over to open Sometimes a Great Notion, I had another errand to run. During most of the year, the store was open from 10 a.m. to 5 p.m. during the week and Saturdays only by appointment. In the winter, with slower traffic, I modified the hours from noon to 5 p.m., but included Saturdays, when some brave souls ventured out for a drive in the country.

I'd heard that Dottie Brown held a needlework class in her yarn store on Thursday and Saturday mornings, and I wanted to ask her advice on some samplers I'd recently purchased at an estate sale. I had a rough idea of their value from my own experience and the research I'd done on the Internet, but it would be nice to have confirmation.

Dottie was ringing up a customer, and I waited until she was free, smiling as I saw the stack of my business cards on her counter. We attracted some of the same clientele, and we were each other's best cheerleaders.

"Hi, Dottie. I was wondering if I could pick your brain to price these antique samplers I bought last week." I held up the tote bag I carried.

"Oh, you should talk to Althea, over there, teaching the class." Dottie nodded her head toward the back of the store where I saw a group of women. "She's the real expert."

I sighed. It was common knowledge that the formidable and deeply religious Althea Gunn vehemently disapproved of the Men of Millbury calendar. She wasn't my favorite person, but hey, beggars couldn't be choosers.

"Go on. The class hasn't started yet. They're still waiting for a few more. Unless—wait, don't tell me . . . You're *scared* of our church secretary?"

I shook my head at her. "Very funny. Everybody's a comedian."

Dottie grinned as I sucked in a breath, straightened my shoulders, and walked to where Althea sat, ramrod straight, at a large frame, while several other women were unpacking their embroidery hoops. She was wearing a gray serge dress that was almost nunlike, secured with a wide leather belt around her narrow waist. Her snow-white hair was cropped short, but in an uneven fringe, as if she'd cut it herself.

Althea ran the operations of the church with an iron fist and had most of the flock cowed and completely in awe. She edited the weekly bulletin, maintained the calendar, answered the phones, and was the first point of contact for anyone inquiring about our community. She also kept the database of parishioners and probably knew more than most people where the bodies were buried. Literally and figuratively.

"Good morning, Althea." I gave her the brightest smile I could muster.

"Daisy Buchanan." Her voice was a low alto. She peered over the rims of her bifocals at me. "I heard that your fancy-pants photographer came to a very unfortunate end. Just as well. It's immoral that those men were taking their clothes off for money."

I gritted my teeth. *Just as well?* Where was her respect for the dead?

"The profits from the calendar would go to a good cause, Althea. To save Millbury!"

"I heard that someone ransacked the carriage house where he was staying." Grace Vreeland, the local tax collector, didn't look up from where she was sorting pearl cotton threads. "I bet he was involved in marijuana or something like that." She pronounced it *marry-jee-wahna.*

Althea made the sign of the cross over her chest. "It's the wrath of God."

I quickly took the first sampler out of the bag, hoping it was enticing enough to overcome her disapproval of the activities of the Historical Society.

"And that Cyril Mackey? I hear he's gone, too," Grace said as she paired a skein of ecru with a darker shade of beige. Her milky blue eyes went round with excitement. "Do you think he—you know—he was murdered, too?"

I could feel my blood pressure rise and I wondered if an antiques appraisal was really worth all this aggravation. "I sincerely hope not."

Althea nodded at me in agreement. "He must have figured it was a good excuse to disappear. You know what a loner he was. Martha Bristol and her big plans were enough to scare the devil out of any man. That woman paraded him around to every social event under the sun like a pet Chihuahua. He probably tired of the pressure."

In desperation, I shoved the sampler under her nose. "Althea, I was wondering if you have a moment to take a look at these items that I plan to sell in my shop. I have some idea of what they're worth, but I'd really value your input."

Althea's mouth was still set in a scowl, but her eyes brightened at the sight of the pretty antique needlework, and she took the frame out of my hands.

"Hmm. This one is likely early nineteenth century. See the pair of bird-in-branch designs, the floating swans, the floral sprigs? All classic Quaker motifs." She peered at it closely. "This could possibly have been worked at the Quaker Westtown School in Chester County. Somewhat plain, but distinctive. Some of the best school samplers in that time period were made in Pennsylvania."

Over her shoulder I admired again the peaceful scene of a humble house near a pasture with a sheep and a cow, surrounded by a decorative border.

Althea tapped on the glass. "Originally samplers served as a way for women to store their personal repertoire of stitches and patterns. But at the beginning of the eighteenth century, their purpose gradually changed to become a teaching tool for young girls. Not just for needlework, but also to learn their alphabet and numerals."

Even though Althea was quite thin, she must be heavy-boned, as my mother liked to say. Her hands were large enough to be a man's hands, and I wondered how she managed such fine work with those big, blunt fingers.

"Let's see. Silk on open mesh cotton. A wide range of stitches—the usual satin, cross, chain, and eyelet, but here's some upright Gobelin. And Queen stitch for these." Althea pointed to a crop of strawberries. "The linen has some slight overall discoloration, but that's consistent with its age, and the colors of the silks are good. Nice condition. I would think this should reach in the twenty-five hundred to three thousand dollar range."

Pleased that her estimate of value and mine were in sync, I handed her another. This one was signed by Eliza

Franks, who was nine years old in 1846. The top section of the sampler was decorated with an elaborate urn, stags, butterflies, and a honeysuckle border. The central section had this verse:

Hide me, O my Savior, hide till the storm of life is past
Safe into the haven guide, Oh receive my soul at last
Other refuge have I none, hangs my helpless soul
   on thee
Leave oh leave me not alone, still support and
   comfort me

"I can't believe this fine work was done by someone so young," I said, marveling at the tiny stitches.

"A young woman needed needle skills to be suitable for marriage. One of her primary responsibilities was to mark and mend the household linens," Althea said. "Again, very good condition. Same price range. Where on earth did you get these?"

"At a local estate sale." I was on a roll now, so I handed her a third, dated 1830. This time the needlewoman was only seven years old.

It looked almost like Claire Elliot's painting of her ideal home—a large house surrounded by fields and trees with birds flying overhead and a floral border, done in numerous colors, with a section of letters of the alphabet. A bird nearly the size of a dog sat in a tree, and flowers reached halfway up the side of the house.

Althea frowned. "The Y is stitched backward, and it lacks proportion."

I gritted my teeth. Again. "I was a teacher for most of my life, so I did notice that, yes. But personally, I think those little irregularities give it charm."

Althea peered over the top of her glasses at me. "You

were a teacher, were you? Well, teachers played a significant part in the rise of popularity of needlework. Speaking of which, it's time to start this class. Sit down, Daisy Buchanan. You might learn something. I shall inspect the rest of your samplers later."

"Thank you, Althea." Obediently, I sat.

A couple more ladies hurried in. I smiled at Liz Gallagher, a young farmer's wife. She had five children, taught spinning classes, was the president of the PTA, and had enough energy to run the Northeast power grid if they hooked her up to it.

Liz sat next to me and pulled out a Christmas sampler. It was a manger scene with the words *Come let us adore him, Christ the Lord* on cream linen, with a pretty combination of greens and terra cotta threads.

"That looks great, Liz," I said. "I don't think I could do this, even though I think samplers are beautiful and I love the finished product." One of the necessary qualities I'd unfortunately lacked as a teacher was a sufficient supply of patience. "My grandmother was a milliner, and I loved to watch her work on projects."

Liz laughed. "Oh, I stick to the simple, easy designs. Drives Althea crazy, but I let it roll right off. When you have as many kids as I do, you can't sweat the small stuff. Seems like I constantly have friends who are getting married or having babies. I have a huge family, too, so there's always something going on with birthdays or anniversaries. I can make a nice, personalized gift for them this way."

"Abigail Weller!"

We jumped as Althea's voice thundered across the table. "You're supposed to be doing *marking* cross-stitch. It should be reversible, so each stitch forms a cross on the front and a square of straight stitches on the back. All of you: Make sure the back of your work is as immaculate as the front."

Liz took a quick look at the back of her hoop, grimaced, and then grinned at me. "This is my weekly ordeal, but I don't dare quit," she whispered. "I'd kill for a cup of coffee right now, too, but Althea won't allow any food or drink in class. Our hands have to be spotless."

"Sounds like Eleanor." I said, with a chuckle. Eleanor made everyone take their shoes off at the door to her shop and don pristine white gloves before they came anywhere near the exquisite wedding gowns.

Althea cleared her throat, fixed me with an eagle eye, and Liz and I subsided into silence. She pointed at Grace. "Look at what Grace is doing, everyone."

Grace flushed.

"She is quite *right* to decide on a color *scheme* and select all the threads she will require at the *same* time for the most *harmonious* combination of colors." Althea emphasized every third word or so in her delivery in a voice that carried clear to the other end of the store. I wondered how many of her students zoned out after a while from this bombastic technique. Sort of like someone e-mailing in capital letters.

"Also remember to choose a nonshrink fabric and *do not wash it.* You can work more easily on fabric that still contains dressing. Remember, don't make a knot at the end of the thread when you start. Leave about two inches loose. You can darn in later."

A slight figure with spiky black hair slunk into the chair next to me. She wore a vintage motorcycle jacket, black jeans, and a T-shirt that looked like it had been dug out of the bottom of a laundry basket. I caught a whiff of the cigarette that must have been hastily stubbed out before she entered the shop.

"PJ! What the heck are you doing here?"

PJ Avery was a reporter for the *Sheepville Times*, and the last person in the world I would have ever thought to see.

She glared at me. "Is there some kind of law against reporters doing needlework?"

"No, of course not," I stammered, wondering how on earth the twitchy PJ would sit still long enough for this kind of work. If I didn't have the patience, how would she?

"Ms. Avery!" Althea's voice boomed. "Not only are you late, but now you compound your sin by disrupting the class."

"It's my fault, Althea. I apologize," I said before PJ could open her mouth.

The disheveled reporter reminded me of a bantam hen strutting around the barnyard in her abrupt no-nonsense way, but actually she was more fragile than any of us. She'd lost most of her family recently in various tragic ways, and I'd taken on a protective role in her life. It was a different dynamic than the walking-on-eggshells routine I did with my daughter, Sarah. PJ and I could give it to each other straight, but we were okay with it. And as much as she liked to act like she didn't need anyone, she seemed to relish the time with me, Joe, and my friends. She'd certainly never declined a dinner invitation.

"Now class, today we are going to learn Scottish Cretan stitch."

I saw a few worried glances pass back and forth between members of the group.

Althea showed us an example of a rich, ornamental stitch. "It is basically blocks of open Cretan stitches that are linked together without picking up the ground fabric. Tension the thread carefully before proceeding to the next block. If the thread is pulled too tightly, the stitches will become distorted."

Abigail Weller glanced up, simply shook her head of white curls, and continued doggedly with her basic cross-stitch.

I looked over at PJ's sampler. She was doing some kind of weird abstract design, but her stitches were very neat. It looked a bit like a sea serpent swimming through a montage

of flowers and buildings, reminding me of the back of a
Chinese silk robe. Different, but good.

Althea came over to inspect, and we both watched PJ's
tattooed fingers with skull rings deftly wield the needle as
she slipped it under the base of the stitches in the previous row.

"A closed wave stitch. That's a useful and economical
one because nearly all the thread remains on the surface of
the fabric. Good technique, Ms. Avery."

PJ was working each row in a different color. Like me,
she never took the easy road.

"This is a combination of vertical satin and looped
stitches." Althea directed me to pay attention, stubbing her
thick finger at PJ's work. "Satin stitch can be worked in any
direction, and encroaching satin is especially useful for
shading and blending naturalistic designs."

Althea patiently showed her pupil how to finish each
row. In spite of her off-putting demeanor, she was a good
teacher. Even the most annoying people had some redeem-
ing qualities, although sometimes they were only revealed
upon the closest inspection.

"However, I don't expect you to be late for my class
again. And that shirt could certainly use a good ironing."

I sucked in a breath, but PJ just shrugged, like Jasper
shaking raindrops off his coat in a wet swirl.

Althea walked around the table, taking one look at Abigail Weller, who was methodically continuing with her
wobbly cross-stitch. She simply shuddered and moved on.

I got up to check out everyone's projects, too. There
were a few stitches I recognized. Of course, the basic cross-
stitch, which was a great favorite for marking household
linen. I'd seen plenty of examples on 1920s table runners in
my store.

Not everyone was creating a sampler. One quiet, indus-
trious woman was working on a pillow, adding a sweet

nosegay of pink roses with a curling ribbon bow underneath. She gave a soft cough every minute or two.

I was entranced with another woman's stunning white-on-white embroidered purse. "Is that for a wedding gift?" I asked, watching her long elegant fingers sew a tiny seed bead in the center of each flower.

She smiled gently at me. "Yes. This is Kingston linen with satin and buttonhole stitch. I'm using Japanese ribbon stitch for the buds and petals."

"It's exquisite."

Althea's sampler was by far the largest piece in the class. Everyone else was using a hand-held embroidery hoop, which was two circular sections that fit one inside the other, but hers was on a freestanding floor frame. The sides of the fabric were bound with tape, and the top and bottom edges were sewn to webbing that was attached to rollers and tensioned with wooden screws.

The sampler was absolutely magnificent, but the verse it contained was appropriately grim:

Little white house where the road doth bend
Let the wickedness of the wicked end
Hell and destruction are never full
Oh, what will become of my poor soul

When I am dead, laid in my grave
And all my bones gone rotten
When this you see, remember me
That I be not forgotten

True to her word, Althea appraised the rest of the samplers for me after the class. When I thanked her effusively, I even received an invitation to attend the next class if I liked.

I left Dottie's shop with my head buzzing full of images of Maltese crosses, Sprat's Heads, and French knots.

Chapter Eight

Everyone who came into my store that Saturday seemed to have the same topic on their minds: Cyril and Martha. Like the women in the needlework class, most people thought that Cyril had left because he was tired of the pressure. Not only from having to participate in the calendar shoot, but from the ardent attentions of his new girlfriend.

When there was a break in the action, I took the samplers out of the bag and hung a couple on the wall. I hoped they'd sell quickly, before I got too attached to them, especially the one that had been stitched by Claire's counterpart in another lifetime. Our modern lives were so different today, with our instant communication, global travel, and career aspirations.

Or maybe not that much. Maybe we all still longed for the same things deep down. A safe, happy home. A loving family.

I was standing there lost in thought when Eleanor slipped into the shop.

"What's going on, Daisy?"

I sighed. "Oh, it's just that if I hear one more denigrating comment about Cyril today, I'm going to scream."

"Well, I wouldn't blame him if he *had* decided to get out of here and fly south for the winter. God, I hate the cold. And it's snowing early for this time of year."

"How do you know something didn't happen to him? I'm not convinced Cyril would leave Martha without a backward glance. I don't think he'd be that unkind."

I picked up a rare Red Wing beehive salt-glazed jug, similar to those I'd glimpsed through the window of the farmhouse, and set it next to a display of vintage dish towels. I'd paid $75 for it at auction, but I thought I could get at least $185. I wrote up a price tag and tied it to the handle.

"Hmm." Eleanor frowned at the empty surface of the seed counter. "What, no treats *again*?"

"Martha didn't feel like baking. She's too upset."

"Daisy, you have to do something! This is serious. She needs to get a grip. Winter is depressing enough—getting up in the dark, coming home in the dark. I feel like a mushroom. I can see why all those people in Norway drink vodka and kill themselves. A deficiency of chocolate gâteaux and honey madeleines is going to make me want to do the same."

"Have some coffee in the meantime." I poured us each a mug. "Then there's this bad business with Stanley. I wonder if a toxicology report would have shown a slow poisoning."

Eleanor heaved a sigh. "Oh, you can't be serious. Come on, you know that Ruth's not a murderer."

"I can't forget Stanley grabbing my hand and saying, 'She's trying to kill me!'"

"Are you sure he said 'she'?"

I stared at her. "You know, now that you mention it, I'm not sure whether it was 'he' or 'she.' His voice was quite faint. I was just so shocked that he was talking normally.

Or seemed to be." I sipped my coffee. "I wonder if it's too late to exhume the body."

"What would that do to Ruth if you stirred things up now?" Eleanor caressed the sides of the mug with her elegant fingers.

"Do you think I'm crazy?"

There was a short silence.

"Well, sometimes you can take things a bit too far."

While I was staring at Eleanor, openmouthed, Serrano strode into the store. I snatched another mug from the shelf, splashed coffee into it, and thrust it at him.

"How're you doing, ladies?" he said, looking carefully at each of us.

"Daisy wants to dig up a body," Eleanor said.

"This again?" He accepted the mug, nodding his thanks as he wiped the drips from the rim. "Daisy, the death certificate states Stanley Bornstein died of pneumonia. Anyway, the testing would have had to be done within forty-eight hours. It's too late now. Let it go . . ." His voice trailed off. "So. No treats today?"

"Mais non," Eleanor muttered. *"Tant pis."*

I didn't think Eleanor was actually fluent in French. She tossed in a few phrases here and there to impress her bridal clients, but the little she did know was fairly pithy.

"Come again?"

"She said, 'It's too bad,' but don't worry about that right now," I said. "Look, did you know that Ruth Bornstein had a prenuptial agreement? If she divorced Stanley, she got nothing. But if he died, it was a different story. Remember how I told you about that guy I saw her with in town?"

I must have had a stubborn look on my face, because Serrano apparently felt compelled to give me a brief lecture.

"Do you know how they catch monkeys in Borneo, Daisy? They make a small hole in a coconut, hollow it out, put a green banana inside, and chain the coconut to a tree. The monkey puts his hand in to get the banana. While he's clutching the fruit, he can't pull his hand back through the hole, so he's stuck. All he has to do to free himself is open his hand, but he can't bear to let go. He rants and raves until he's exhausted, and then he's captured."

Great, so now I'm a stupid monkey.

Serrano smiled gently at me. "How about you concentrate your crime-solving skills on the actual murder that just took place?"

I narrowed my eyes at him. I wasn't done yet, not by a long shot, but I'd play his little game for now. "Okay, Detective, maybe the culprit was a jealous spouse from the way the photographer carried on. From what I'm hearing, it sounds like he was down at the pub with a different woman every night."

Eleanor nodded. "Sounds like he's boinked just about every woman in this village under the age of forty."

"But why go to the extreme of killing him?" I mused. "Why not just beat him up? A jealous husband wouldn't trash all the stuff in the studio either."

"Maybe he would," Eleanor said. "Depends what's on the film."

Serrano nodded. "Good point, E."

"Plus, he didn't just go to the pub." She took a long swig of her black coffee. "I heard he stopped in at the Raven Lounge a time or two."

I sucked in a breath. The motorcycle gangs that hung around that biker bar would not appreciate the way Roos strutted around like a bleached-haired peacock, mouthing off his West Coast expressions and liberal ideas. "Yes, someone might have taken exception to a guy like him coming into their place."

"A guy like him?" Serrano leaned forward, intent on me.

I shook my head. It was true that Alex Roos was almost androgynous, but I didn't think he was gay.

"Methinks he didst protest too much, though?" Eleanor's whisper seemed to echo my thoughts as I suddenly had a picture in my mind of watching Roos, hard at work flirting. Had he been trying *too* hard? Had there been a run-in with some real homosexuals, or had he made a pass at someone in the Raven?

I frowned. "The fact that Roos's cameras were stolen from the carriage house suggests he may have captured something incriminating on film. A bribe, a drug deal, perhaps. Maybe it wasn't a straightforward robbery after all. What was so inflammatory in his photos that someone, maybe in politics or some other high position in society, would want covered up?" I almost didn't realize that I'd spoken aloud.

"Good." Serrano nodded at me in approval. "I like the way you're thinking now, Daisy. You need to keep your mind open to all possibilities." He drained his mug and set it on the counter. "Hungry, Eleanor?"

"Yes, ravishing. I mean, ravenous."

He grinned at her. "Want to grab a bite at the diner?"

Eleanor nodded and bestowed her best cat smile on him. Serrano took her arm, and they turned to leave.

"Wait!" I said. "So, did you manage to get the, um, body out of the attic?"

Serrano raised his eyebrows. "Yup. But as Angus had predicted, it was a helluva job. Not a pretty sight."

I shuddered as I tried not to imagine the scene.

"One good thing was he was wrapped in a drop cloth before he was spray-foamed, though. We still may be able to get some clues."

"Do you know if he was dead before he was made part of the attic?" Eleanor asked.

"Not yet."

Even if Martha had brought some treats, I'd have lost my appetite by now.

"Someone must have driven the truck loaded with drums of the stuff over from the construction site. There's a limited number of people who would know how to operate that truck and know where the keys were kept. That's why my number one suspect is our favorite builder."

"Beau Cassell? But why?" I asked.

"Because he doesn't have an alibi for the night of the murder. And because he's an arrogant bastard. That always gets my attention."

"So are a lot of people I could name."

The corner of Serrano's mouth quirked up slightly.

"But why rush up into the attic and expose a body that you know you just hid up there?" I said. "It doesn't make sense."

"The arrogance that makes him think he can't be caught. And apparently if that high-density closed-cell foam is applied too thickly, the way it was, it creates intense heat within its core. It's like the molten center of a volcano. Cassell *was* right to alert everyone that it was a dangerous situation. The whole thing could have exploded."

"Is that what someone *wanted* to happen? A massive explosion that burned the house to the ground, taking the evidence with it?"

Serrano glanced at Eleanor. "Ready, Ms. Reid? Where's your coat?"

"Didn't wear one."

He shook his head as he slipped off his jacket and wrapped it around her. I pictured the residual heat of his body in the silk lining warming Eleanor's slim frame. "See ya, Daisy. Thanks for the coffee."

They hurried toward the door, his hand against the small of her back.

I threw my hands up in the air. *Great.* Like a dog that loses interest once it knows the bones are gone.

"Is that all they want me for, Alice? Martha's treats? And without them I am nothing?"

I'd been sitting on the stool behind the counter, and now I slipped to the ground, letting my vertebrae fall back into place before I attempted to move.

I was still grumbling to my mannequin about the total cupboard love on the part of Serrano and Eleanor when I realized I wasn't alone.

Mary Willis was in the corner, looking through a selection of vintage snaps and fasteners still on their original cards. My signature "new" old stock. She looked up at me, her worn Persian lamb coat hanging haphazardly on her thin frame because she'd missed a button. "Oh, that's all right, dear, I still talk to my Fred, and he's been gone almost a year now."

When Mary's husband had died, she'd brought in a bunch of exquisite linens to sell. I'd given her a fair price, and it had worked out well for both of us.

I smiled, hoping my face wasn't as red as it felt. When she came over to the counter, I rang up her purchase of two dollars and slipped one of Laura's bookmarks into her bag as a treat. "Have a great day, Mary."

After she left, I held up a hand to Alice. "Don't say it, okay? No comments from the peanut gallery."

Alice smirked at me, but stayed blissfully silent, so I set about refreshing the store for the next wave of customers. Merchandise was selling quickly in this holiday season, and I added more linens, glasses, and tableware to the front window.

Even though I didn't have the patience for needlework, I could spend hours crafting a beautiful display, or hot-gluing pods of star anise over a Styrofoam ball. I took some balls I'd already made, stuck some whole cloves into any empty spaces, and then added them to a platter with pinecones, fresh greens, cinnamon sticks, and a scattering of tiny gold ornaments.

"I think we could put a price tag of at least twenty dollars on this. What do you think, Alice?"

Fabulous.

I lit four candles on a brass Swedish angel chime. As the heat of the candles rose, it made the paper-thin angels spin, gently ringing the Christmas bells.

Who *was* that guy on the street with Ruth? I knew the look of people who had been intimate, their heads a little closer together than normal. How long had this been going on? And had Ruth really killed Stanley to get him out of the picture?

My mind was in a whirl, like the angels wafting in a circle. Trying to ignore my growing conviction that Ruth had something to do with the death of her husband, I focused on what I knew for a fact.

The memories of our years of friendship infused with her glamour and warmth and his intelligence and sense of humor. Stanley and Ruth were one of the nicest couples Joe and I had ever known. They fit together. They were always talking about what they would do when he retired. The trips they would take to South Africa, to Australia, to Greece.

I blew out a heavy breath. I'd bet when Ruth pictured her golden years, it didn't involve taking care of a terminal patient who didn't even know who she was.

I was suddenly glad Joe had pushed me to take early retirement. I wasn't sure how I'd felt about it at the time, leaving the excitement of New York, but our life in Millbury really was a dream come true. I had a business that I adored, and Joe was happy puttering around the yard, or fixing up treasures we discovered at yard sales. Not to mention, his honed cooking skills were to die for. I bet he could enter one of those cooking contests and . . .

Focus, Daisy.

I glanced over at Alice. "Sorry."

The door to the store opened, and it wasn't a wave of customers, but a tsunami in the form of PJ Avery.

I quickly made a fresh pot of coffee.

"Saw Martha outside," she said, in her abrupt way of speaking. "Putting up flyers all over town. Advertising for Cyril Mackey like he's a missing cat."

"Oh, dear."

PJ had recently come into a sizable inheritance, but it hadn't changed her lifestyle much. She still worked at the newspaper every day, and her wardrobe was still retro Army Navy store. A pack of cigarettes poked out of the pocket of her safari jacket.

"You should quit smoking, young lady."

"Oh, gimme a break. You're not my mother."

"I know," I said, my smile fading as I wished for the hundredth time that I could somehow fill that gaping hole in her life.

"Hey, Daisy, it's cool. Lighten up. I'll quit when I'm ready." She looked over at the counter where the coffeepot hissed as it brewed.

"Before you ask, no, there are no treats today."

She shrugged. "That sucks. Anyways, thought you'd want to know something. That photographer, Alex Roos? He called me the day before he died to say he was working on 'something big.' Said he could use my help."

"Really? Did you let Detective Serrano know this?"

"Yeah, but that's all I could tell him. Roos and I never met up, so Serrano didn't seem too interested."

"Never mind about him." I poured us both some coffee. "*I'm* interested."

"Did some digging into the dude's background. Turns out he's actually from this area originally and was some kind of radical photojournalist, back in the day."

PJ paced up and down in front of the Welsh dresser.

Cyril would have said she had ants in her pants. I'd learned that I couldn't watch her when she did this or I'd get slightly seasick.

"Pretty badass, actually. He took on the tough stories; hell, he even took on the Philadelphia unions, and trust me, that's playing with fire."

I frowned. Had all that flamboyance on Roos's part just been an act?

As if reading my mind, she said, "Different guy from the one we thought we knew, right?"

"It's quite a leap, isn't it, PJ? From investigative reporting to fashion photography?"

She snorted. "Yeah. How the mighty have fallen. Who knows, maybe some jerk from his past caught up with him and he had to make a quick getaway."

"Did he ever have a run-in with Beau Cassell?"

"Not that I know of, but maybe he stumbled on something that Cassell wouldn't want to be made public knowledge."

"Like what? A shady real estate deal? I wonder if he involved Cyril in whatever it was." I blew out a breath. "And either Cyril is dead, too, which I refuse to think about, or he's hurt or injured somewhere."

PJ rocked back on her heels. "Wouldn't last long in this weather. Hey, perhaps he's in hiding. Could he be staying with someone to fly below the radar? Like Martha, maybe?"

I shook my head. "No, not Martha. She's dramatic, but I don't think she's *that* good of an actress. Regardless, we need to make a plan to find him. And soon."

"Assuming he's still alive, where would he hang out? What did he like to do?"

"Apart from give me a hard time, I don't really know. I usually only ever saw him at the salvage yard." Cyril and I had understood each other on some elemental level. We'd never had the need for the usual small talk—we just got

right to the heart of whatever it was we wanted to discuss—
and as a result, I didn't know much about his past. All I
knew was that he had once been a miner in Western Pennsylvania before he ended up in Millbury.

"He went to the auction once in a while, and he liked to
fix things, but I don't know of any other hobbies. I never
saw him at the grocery store, although I suppose he had to
go there sometime. I never saw him on the streets of Millbury or Sheepville, either. He didn't have a washer and
dryer, though, so he must have gone to the Laundromat now
and then."

"How about the pub? I'll check there." She waved a
hand at me. "You can do all those other boring places."

Early on Sunday morning, I made my usual pilgrimage to
the salvage yard to feed the cat. I hadn't slept well at all,
tossing and turning for hours. Finally, at 5 a.m., I decided it
was useless to try anymore and I slipped out of bed, not
wanting to disturb Joe. I drank several cups of coffee while I
tackled the fiendishly difficult *New York Times* Sunday crossword puzzle, cursing editor Will Shortz even as I admired
him, and waiting for daylight.

As I poured kibble into his bowl, the little black cat rubbed
his way around my ankles.

"You don't seem overly concerned," I said to him,
yawning. "You think he's coming back, too, don't you?"

I listened to the sound of dry cat food crunching.

"See yon lantern?"

My heart skipped. I could almost hear Cyril's voice echo
in the kitchen, and I looked over to where he had been
pointing that day he'd told me a smidgeon about his past. A
battered black iron and brass lantern stood on a shelf over
the doorway into the living room.

"That's a miner's lamp. I keep it there to remind me of

all that I went through to get to this place. How lucky I am to be done with that kind of life."

I sucked in a breath. Cyril had worshipped Martha, and told me he'd never been happier. To a loner and an outsider like him, she represented a warm, happy home. Something he'd never had.

And yes, he was a tad resistant to her busy social calendar, but he still went to everything with her, didn't he? He could have refused, could have stayed in his trailer. But he didn't. He loved her so much that he suffered through those swanky occasions just to be with her.

There was no way that he'd disappeared of his own accord.

I said good-bye to the cat, hurried up the lane from the junkyard, got changed, and headed for church.

Our little community church was situated not far from Glory Farm, surrounded by open fields with an ancient graveyard in the back. It looked like an old-time picture postcard, painted white, with its bright red door and bell steeple, where bells rang every hour on the dot. We were so far out in the sticks and buried in the past that we still had live bell ringers instead of automated electric ones.

When I arrived, I was surprised to see Eleanor standing outside.

"What are you doing here?" I asked. "I've never really seen you at church, unless it's for a wedding or a funeral."

"I'm here for moral support." She nodded to where Martha, dressed completely in black and wearing an enormous black hat with black netting, was making her way over to us.

"Oh, dear," I said.

"It may as well be a funeral," Eleanor murmured.

The only spots of color on Martha were her chestnut hair and the redness around her eyes.

"What are *you* doing here?" she also demanded of Eleanor when she had given us both a hug. Or as much of a hug as she could manage due to the constraints of the hat. "I thought you didn't believe in organized religion?"

Eleanor shrugged. "I live my life so I can look at myself in the mirror every day and be proud of the person in the reflection. That's enough for me and my God. *She's* okay with it."

Martha just rolled her tear-puffed eyes at me. "Do you guys believe that someone took my flyers down last night? Every single one. Who would do such a thing? How can people be so mean?"

"Never mind about that now," I said. "It's freezing out here. Come on. Let's go in."

Inside the church, Joe sat on my left, Eleanor was on my right, and Martha sat on the other side of Eleanor.

As the reverend asked us to pray for the recently departed, tears pricked my eyes and I felt as though I could almost see Alex Roos's spirit winging its way up into the rafters of the beautiful old church. I prayed for a sign that Cyril was okay and touched the pack of cigarettes in my pocket like a talisman. A wave of desperation threatened to sweep me under, and I prayed for the strength to continue to believe he was still alive. To not give up hope.

My lack of sleep was catching up to me, the effects of early-morning caffeine were long gone, and I breathed in several deep breaths, trying to suck in more oxygen to clear my head. Eleanor was busy pulling tissues out of her bag as fast as she could and handing them to Martha.

Althea Gunn led the chorus in her usual wobbly contralto. The rest of us were used to the racket, but Eleanor looked at me wide-eyed, and in spite of my sadness, I had to smile at her shocked expression.

"Holy Toledo. Is this for real?" she whispered. "She sounds like a ghost. No, wait, a constipated phantom." She moaned, fluttering her hands in front of her. "Or one that's laying an egg."

"Stop it," I hissed.

"Woo-hoo-ooh!" Eleanor moaned again, a little louder this time, the sound almost drowned out by Althea's out-of-tune but resolute singing.

The wailing vibrato grew in intensity, like someone was doing karate chops on Althea's back. I could feel the shaking of silent laughter where Eleanor's arm touched mine, and I struggled against the hilarity bubbling up inside.

"Hey, Daisy, remember that scene in *When Harry Met Sally*?" Eleanor wiggled her eyebrows suggestively. " 'I'll have what she's having.' "

"You are *evil*."

The more I knew I shouldn't laugh, the more I wanted to. Joe looked over at us and simply shook his head. I cupped my hands like blinders around my streaming eyes so I couldn't see her, but at that moment Althea hit a high note.

Eleanor grabbed the pew in front of her and threw her head back, as if in the throes of the greatest climax she'd ever experienced.

That did it.

I jumped up, slid quickly past Joe and the couple next to him, and practically ran out of the church with a hand over my mouth before the geyser inside me could explode.

I ended up in the graveyard and collapsed on a nearby gravestone, where my wild howling and choked laughter were enough to wake the dead. I laughed and laughed until I couldn't laugh any more.

"I'm glad our sermons are so entertaining, Daisy Buchanan." I looked up to see Father Morris standing over me. He had a light Irish accent and a melodious voice as rich as heavy cream.

I couldn't think of an appropriate explanation. I felt as though I was ten years old, not fifty-eight. What the heck was the matter with me? "Sorry, Father. It's not that, it's just . . ." Suddenly I realized I was sitting on a gravestone, too, and I jumped to my feet. "I'm so sorry." Not only had I left the service prematurely, I was laughing like a fool and being disrespectful of the dead.

"It's all right. When Patrick Carney was alive, he never minded a beautiful woman sitting on his lap, especially one in such a good humor. I'm sure he wouldn't mind now."

I sighed. "Oh, Father, there's just been so much going on lately, what with Stanley dying and then the murder of Alex Roos, and now I'm worried sick about Cyril. I'm a little emotional. I guess there's a fine line between laughter and hysteria."

"Everyone needs to let the steam out of the pressure cooker now and again." He smiled gently at me. "Good to see you, Daisy."

"You too."

As he turned to leave, I called out, "Father? Could I ask you something?"

He raised an eyebrow in question.

"Do you think it's possible to feel as though someone is still alive? Even though you don't know for sure?"

Again, that gentle smile. "Our loved ones always live in our hearts and in our memories."

I stared up at him, his figure backlit by the colorless sky. Were the souls of Stanley Bornstein and Alex Roos restlessly roaming this earth, or were they at peace?

After he left, I kept Patrick Carney company for a few moments longer while I watched a red cardinal flit across the graveyard.

Chapter Nine

"I could really go for some gingerbread, or maybe a banana pecan muffin." Eleanor gave Martha a gentle poke with her bony elbow. Usually a special request for one of Martha's baked goods was an instant call to action.

I'd managed to catch the end of the sermon, thankfully, and now we were milling around at the coffee social.

"I couldn't *possibly* think of food at a time like this. I'm distraught that Cyril wasn't even mentioned in that service." Martha's mouth drooped. "Maybe if someone would find my soul mate, I might be more inclined to cook. Maybe if I could get some *help* from this village instead of being sabotaged or ridiculed at every turn."

My heart was breaking, and I hugged her as tightly as I could. "Don't lose hope, Martha."

"I can't. It's all I've got." She dabbed at the corners of her sore eyes.

"Look, Cyril is a Yorkshireman, and as stubborn and

ornery as they come. If anyone can survive and land on
their feet, it's him."

"Yep. Old birds are the toughest!" Eleanor said, and
then she lowered her voice to a murmur. "Speaking of
which, these dry-as-dust brownies of Sally McIntire's are
definitely for the birds."

At that moment, there was a commotion near the doorway and I looked up to see the unfortunate Sally being led
out of the room by her husband, who seemed to have a
tight grip on her arm.

Dottie Brown came over. "Did you see how red her eyes
were? Apparently she's been crying for days, grieving over
that dead photographer." After Martha, Dottie was the
town's second most reliable resource for sizzling gossip.

It was true that Sally had hung around on the set every
day, giggling and making eyes at Roos.

Dottie lowered her voice. "And on the afternoon of the
Bornstein funeral, Jim McIntire was scouring the town for
his wife, who was *not* where she was supposed to be."

"Really?"

"She used to complain that he called her fifty times a
day—to check up on her, asking her what she was doing,
even if she was just out with a girlfriend for lunch." Dottie
pursed her lips. "If she turned her phone off, he'd show up
at the restaurant. Total control freak."

"Guys like that have a lot of repressed anger," Martha
said. "It wouldn't surprise me at all to find out he was the
one who killed Roos."

Eleanor nodded toward Althea Gunn, who was man-
handling a trestle table across the room by herself. "By the
pricking of my thumbs, something bitchy this way comes."

"Excuse me," Althea snapped as she passed us, the table's
legs screeching against the floor.

I hurried to help her, but she'd already swung it into

place. I walked back to my compatriots, raising my hands in the air.

"All that religion, but I can't see as how it's done her much good," Eleanor muttered. "I don't think I've ever met such a miserable person."

"Someone tried to rob her house once," Dottie said. "She tied him up and beat the crud out of him before the police got there. The guy told one of the officers he'd never been so glad to see anyone in his life."

After church, I told Joe I had some errands to run. Time to put my plan into action to see if I could find any trace of Cyril. I headed over to Sheepville and went to all the places I could think of—the supermarket, Laundromat, library, bank, and hardware store. It was sunny, but frigid. So cold that taking a breath of air hurt the back of my throat.

I'd brought a notebook with me, and for a while I diligently noted who I spoke to and the date of the last sighting, but it didn't take long to realize I was following in Serrano's footsteps. For as much as Serrano had seemed nonchalant about this whole situation, it was obvious he'd done his homework.

After an hour or so, I was dragging, so I stopped in at Jumpin' Java Mama, a coffee shop on Porter Street near the library. On a chilly day like this, I wasn't the only one with a yen for a hot beverage, and the little café was doing a roaring business. I claimed a cozy spot near the windows by slipping my coat over the back of one of the mismatched yellow-painted chairs. The round table was decoupaged with old postcards and bathed in the weak rays of the afternoon sun.

There were works from local artists for sale on one wall, and an antique coffee table with a chessboard sat in

front of a sofa stuffed with yellow-and-red batik pillows.
People were busy on their laptops, and a couple of kids
were squeezed into one of the large armchairs, contentedly
sipping hot chocolate.

I went up to the counter, where a sign said SAVE THE
DRAMA FOR YOUR MAMA. The cheerful steel drums of Carib-
bean music mixed with the buzz of conversation and the
laughter of the young hippie-type baristas. I could picture
Eleanor being right at home working in a place like this in
her day. I ordered a latte and was tempted by the Rocket
Fuel Brownies, but I decided I'd save room for dinner. I'd
just sat down at the table and was about to take a sip of the
frothy concoction when I looked up to see what I was sure
was the back of Cyril Mackey as he slipped out of the shop.

I banged the cup down on the table and scrambled out
after him onto the sidewalk. I stood there for a minute, heav-
ing for breath, looking up and down Porter Street in both
directions, but he was gone.

I trailed back into the café, my heart racing, my body
still shaking from adrenaline.

Was it really Cyril, or just wishful thinking on my part?
And if it *was* him, why the hell didn't he stop to talk to me?

*Oh, Daisy, it could have been any other guy with long
gray hair. You only caught a glimpse.*

In my current emotionally wrung-out state, I had to agree
with my inner voice. I wasn't sure what I'd seen. Or if there
had actually been anyone there at all.

I sighed and picked up my latte, and then just as quickly
set it down. A newspaper on my table was open to the *New
York Times* Sunday crossword puzzle.

I frowned at it and tried to remember. It hadn't been there
when I hung my coat on the chair, had it? No, because I'd
admired the vintage postcard from Greece and another
from Ibiza clearly visible on top when I first chose this table.

I grabbed the newspaper again, held it up to the light,

and scrutinized it. Both Cyril and I were crossword fanatics, and I was sure I recognized his spidery capital letters.

Seeing as I'd already solved the puzzle at home, I suddenly saw that one clue was deliberately filled out incorrectly to say *canary* instead of *yellow*. Why did he fill it in that way? Was there some kind of clue in the *clue*?

Was Roos a whistleblower, like a canary signaling the presence of methane in a mine, for something unsavory that was going on in Millbury?

I was relieved to think that Cyril was alive, but why was he hiding?

On Monday morning, when I set out with Jasper for our walk, it was still cold, but it was a bracing, energizing cold, not the biting chill of the past week.

Jasper and I walked down the length of Main Street and then headed south on Grist Mill Road, past the church, toward Glory Farm. I tried to imagine what this road approaching Millbury would look like with the fields gone, the country lane widened, the earth churned up, and a slew of ugly Cassell townhomes replacing the unspoiled vista.

I paused while he peed against a pile of snow pushed to the side of the road by the plows, the wavy yellow slash looking a bit like the mark of Zorro.

He was experiencing snow for the first time this winter. Earlier this week, I'd laughed at his look of surprise when he took his usual launch from the back step and landed in the unfamiliar stuff. He recovered quickly, though, burying his face in it and eating it.

I'd slept well last night. Catching a glimpse of Cyril had helped ratchet the pressure down a notch. I was still worried, but there was hope. I hadn't told Martha that I thought I'd seen Cyril in town, though. Perhaps Serrano's mantra of verifying cold, hard facts had worn off on me, but before

I toyed with Martha's emotions, I wanted to be absolutely sure.

A red fox ran onto the road in front of us, and I held my breath at the unexpected sight. Jasper nearly choked himself to death on his leash trying to pull me closer, but the fox paused for a moment, staring at me.

"Go! Go! Don't get run over," I urged.

He disappeared through the undergrowth into the unmown fields. I kept him in sight as we walked along the side of the road, watching as he leapt, almost rabbitlike, as he toyed with some small prey in the grass.

After we passed the farm, we veered off the road onto a path that led toward the woods. The landscape was a rusty patchwork of orange and brown splashed with yellow, and sunlight falling on the leaves of trees made them almost glow.

I let Jasper off the leash and threw snowballs that he dove for and came up puzzled at their disappearance, his nose covered in snow. Blood surged through my muscles, and I almost felt like I was a teenager again, tramping over the fields, cheeks flushed, strong and confident, my whole life ahead of me. When I got home, the aches and pains of an older body would set in, but for right now I didn't care.

"Let's go, boy!" I yelled and broke into a run, laughing with the sheer joy of being alive. Jasper danced alongside me, catching my mood, his eyes bright and mouth open in delight

We passed a waterfall and I stopped to catch my breath, watching the water rushing around and over the stones. Like the ebb and flow of life.

Memories flooded in of me with my childhood dog. What a great dog he was, so smart and well-trained. I wasn't sure I could say exactly the same of Jasper, but he was sheer unadulterated fun and pure endless love. I bent down and hugged him tightly.

* * *

Later that morning, as I hung another antique sampler on the wall at Sometimes a Great Notion, I reflected that my business was about selling memories. The handmade samplers, folk art, quilts, books, furniture, and linens all told a story of past lives. I was simply the caretaker of these treasures to pass along to another generation.

What would my daughter's generation hand down to their children? People didn't even print photos anymore. Everything was on their phones. How would they ever preserve the past? I smiled as I thought about Sarah, who, as a kid, never liked having her picture taken. Now one of her favorite things to do when she came home was to go through the old albums.

I read again the verse so carefully stitched by a young girl over a hundred and twenty years ago:

> *Let them see the error of their ways*
> *Confess their sins to heaven*
> *Accept the light of holy truth*
> *All wouldst be forgiven*
> *Let me not wail and weep*
> *'Tis clear where my path must lie*
> *Now with eyes that see*
> *I follow humbly the heavenly light*

Eyes that see. The eyes of a child. The eyes of God.

There was also the eye of a camera. I was sure Alex Roos had captured something on film that someone wanted to keep quiet, but without his cameras, how would we ever know what it was?

I walked over to the counter where I was putting together a couple of glass jars filled with notions for an interior designer who had requested accent pieces for a shelf in her client's study. I slipped some wooden bobbins into each, together with rolled pieces of tatting lace and spools of white and cream thread.

"I'll tell you what, Alice; I'm still wondering about Ruth and what her story is."

I pictured standing on the driveway that night in the falling snow and looking back up at the main house and the master bedroom window. Did Roos see something incriminating the night Stanley died? Threaten to expose her affair? Who knows what he might have seen. After all, he was living in her carriage house, and with a powerful telephoto lens . . .

Thought that Roos said he hadn't slept at home that night.

I stared at Alice. "Darn it, you're right. He couldn't have seen what happened."

Some customers came in then, and for the next few hours it was a steady stream of business. For a favorite customer, I gift wrapped a lacemakers' box, which was a workbox fitted with essential tools—a pillow, patterns, scissors, pins, and bobbins. Another woman purchased a rare tatting shuttle case of mother-of-pearl with an abalone inset, made in England in the 1850s.

When I had time to catch a breath, I filled in some spaces in the display in the center of the store with a selection of crochet hooks and darning eggs, made of silver, wood, and Bakelite. I set an emery in the shape of a tomato next to them. It was like a small pincushion containing polishing powder. Pins and needles could be thrust through to remove rust and rough patches. Actually, I thought it would make a nice little thank-you gift to Althea for her help with the sampler pricing, so I set it aside.

It was almost five o'clock when the phone rang.

"I have some intel," a hoarse voice whispered. "Can you meet me at the pub? Don't wanna discuss over the phone."

"Okay, PJ," I said, smiling. She was taking this investigative reporting thing very seriously. "Be there in a few."

I called Joe and told him I'd be home in about an hour. He said he was still busy with a furniture piece he was working on, so I promised I'd pick up dinner from Pop's Pizza.

The Sheepville Pub was about half a mile past Backstead's Auction House, and another half mile before the center of town. There was usually a startlingly eclectic collection of cars outside, and tonight was no exception. From BMWs, to a plate glass truck, to a Harley. I parked next to PJ's light green Fiat, the only thing she'd splurged on since her windfall.

She was sitting at the bar, nursing a bottle of Rolling Rock and chatting with Vikki, the bartender. The pub wasn't a fancy place, with its dark wood paneling and ancient jukebox in the corner, but the burgers were tasty and the beer was cold. There were multicolored lights hanging above the rows of bottles, although not in honor of the upcoming holiday. It looked like this year-round.

Vikki grinned at me. "Hi, Daisy, what can I get you?"

"Glass of chardonnay, please." I slid onto the stool next to PJ and ran my fingers over the scarred oak top worn smooth as shellac. "So? What's up?"

"I've uncovered more information about the night of the photographer's disappearance." She nodded toward Vikki, who was uncorking a fresh bottle. "According to Vikki here, Roos stopped at the pub after the shoot."

"On his way to the funeral?"

Vikki shook her head as she set the drink in front of me. "I think his exact words were, 'I don't really do funerals, man.' But he *was* planning on going to the shivah. Said he needed a stiff one before he went, pardon the pun." She chuckled. "Sorry. Just can't get those damn leather pants of his out of my mind."

She hurried down to the other end of the bar to wait on

someone else, and PJ pointed the tip of her bottle at me. "And get this. *Cyril* was here with him."

I choked on my wine. "Really?"

"Yeah. But he suddenly rushed off to the bathroom and never came back, leaving Roos without a ride."

"That doesn't sound like Cyril. Why on earth would he do that?"

She shrugged. "No idea, but sounds like Roos had to walk the rest of the way home." Suddenly PJ nudged my elbow. "Yowza. Check it out."

I glanced over to where Nancy Fowler was dancing to the jukebox music, surrounded by a crowd of interested men. She wore a red dress with a handkerchief hem that flounced up as she moved, showing her long legs. Her milquetoast husband, Frank, hung back with a benevolent look on his face.

"Look at her. Shakin' the moneymaker." PJ snickered. "She knows how to move her hips, that's for sure."

Vikki came back over to us and stuffed some dollar bills into her tip jar.

"I didn't know the pub had live entertainment," I said, nodding toward Nancy Fowler.

Vikki smiled as she poured tortilla chips into a couple of plastic bowls. The pub handed out free chips and a salsa so fiery that it made for some substantial beer consumption. "She acts like a party girl, but she doesn't even drink. Natural endorphins, I guess."

"And her husband doesn't mind that she dances with other guys?"

"He seems okay with it. A lot of men wouldn't be, though."

Did Nancy Fowler have a fling with Roos, and Mr. Meek and Mild over there had finally had enough? Or had Alex snapped a photo of her in a compromising situation? For a politician, the wrong picture at the wrong time could destroy a career.

PJ consulted her notepad. "Oh, and one of the regulars saw Roos taking shots along Grist Mill Road that day."

"Before he met up with Cyril? I wonder if he was using the vintage camera that he got from my store."

Vikki shrugged. "Beats me. But you know, it's strange. The guy always seemed stone-cold broke whenever he came in here. Women were buying *him* drinks."

I turned to PJ. "We should tell Serrano all of this."

"Oh, I already did, honey," Vikki said. "By the way, what's going to happen with your calendar now?"

I took a swallow of my wine, as if it could wash my frustration away. Obviously Detective Serrano had not seen fit to share this news with me. Guess our information-sharing was a one-way street. What the hell was the matter with him lately?

"Eleanor's trying to talk the guys into reshooting, but we'll also need a photographer to work for free, and time is running out to get it done before Christmas." I gave a heavy sigh. "Think I might go have a chat with Mr. Cassell. See if I can get him to listen to reason."

Vikki grinned as she wiped down the bar. "Good luck with that, honey."

The next morning, I drove over to Sheepville to the development where Beau Cassell was still building, hoping to present the case of the Historical Society and our village in a calm fashion, away from the overheated atmosphere of the zoning meeting.

It was a peaceful drive along curving River Road, where it ran parallel to the Delaware River. In the summer, the trees would form a green canopy, but now leaves were falling, exposing the view of the water and the Victorian and Tudor houses perched along its banks. Bucks County was idyllic, with its narrow country roads, creeks running through quiet woods, covered bridges, old mills, and stone barns.

When I neared the town, open fields appeared, bordered by thick forests in the distance. Farms that had been worked for centuries had crops that came right up to the road with hand-lettered signs that offered eggs and milk for sale.

As I passed the bakery on Sheepville Pike, I suddenly recognized Stanley's old nurse, Jo Ellen, coming out of the shop.

Seeing her reminded me that I was also supposed to be on the lookout for evidence on Stanley Bornstein's death. Most people thought it was a blessing that he was gone, but I still clung to the memories of my cultured, intelligent friend and I felt I owed it to him to make sure justice was done.

I drove past her for a half a block or so, swung the car into the first space I could find, hopped out, and then nonchalantly strolled back in her direction.

"Hey, Jo Ellen! What a surprise. How are you doing?"

She frowned, a wary look in her eyes.

"I'm Ruth's friend. I met you the night that, well, you know . . ."

Finally her broad face cleared. "Oh, that's right. Now I remember you."

"I—ah—didn't see you at the funeral last week. I must have missed you in the crowd."

She stared at me for a moment, her dark gaze assessing me. "I didn't go. I'm not comfortable with all them high society folks." She pursed her full lips, made fuller by a mahogany lip gloss. "I had a long, long time to say goodbye to that man. I figured I can honor him in my own way."

I swallowed. I wasn't a particularly consistent churchgoer myself. Like Eleanor said, it was more important how you lived your life day in and day out. This woman had cared for him through the most difficult period of his existence.

"It must be hard for you, though, being out of a job all of a sudden."

"Miz Bornstein gave me a nice severance. I'm doing fine."

"It was such a shock. I mean, I talked to him that night, and the next day he was gone."

Jo Ellen shifted the large white box she carried to one hand and wrapped her orange scarf tighter around her neck with the other. "I seen it before. I knew he was near the end. The body just starts shutting down and there ain't nuthin' anyone can do."

"It seems as though Ruth tried to provide all the latest medicine and treatments for him."

"Miz Bornstein did everything she could. Drove me crazy sometime, but you had to admire her devotion to that man. I never seen anyone more devoted."

And with that, she walked away, apparently done with me and our conversation.

I continued my fake stroll toward the bakery, but when I glanced over my shoulder and saw her getting on a bus, I hurried back to my car.

Cassell's current development was off Sheepville Pike, which ran parallel to Grist Mill Road. It was a huge sprawling conglomeration that covered a couple of hundred acres. As things stood now, there was no way for the residents of Millbury to get to Sheepville other than go the long way around. North on Grist Mill, across on River Road, and south on Sheepville Pike, for a five-mile trip. If the builder won the parcel on Grist Mill abutting the top end of his development, it would provide access for people to cut through to Sheepville. I could see why some people were for his proposal, and if I was completely truthful, I had to admit it would be convenient, especially in the winter months, but it would destroy the dreamy old-world approach to our village.

I found Beau Cassell standing next to a construction trailer, smoking a cigar. He wore jeans and work boots, but the jeans were a pristine dark blue and his gold watch glittered in the sunlight. Sort of like a gentleman farmer from days gone by.

When I suggested that he step out of the bidding on Glory Farm for the sake of historic preservation, he laughed so hard, he choked on his cigar smoke.

"You've got to be kidding, lady. That farmland in Millbury is prime real estate. Not only that, do you have any idea of how much money I've spent already on engineering? On plats and surveys, and now for a goddamn traffic study? This is *business*."

I bit my lip. To invest his own funds to that extent, he must have a reasonable assurance he would get the variance approved.

A crane swung a roof-truss system into place over one new home. Down the block were units in various stages of development, some with their frames of prebuilt wall panels already standing, some with poured basements waiting for their wooden skeletons. Workers were yelling indistinguishable instructions to one another over the cacophony of the pop of a nail gun, the beeping of a truck in reverse, the clang of metal meeting metal.

"And what are you bleeding hearts going to use it for?" He held up a hand. "Wait, don't tell me. Whatever it is, it's a waste of good ground."

"A community center for the children," I said, raising my voice above the din while struggling to hold on to my temper. "Perhaps a battered women's shelter, too."

"Oh, that's just *great*. Bringing in delinquents who'll cause no end of trouble? That'll go over big with the Board of Supervisors."

"Those women are trying to get away from trouble! They're not delinquents, they're victims." I took a deep breath. "Look, what about all the beautiful open land in Bucks County that's disappearing with this type of development? Don't you *care* about the environment?"

Cassell pointed the glowing stub of his cigar at me. "People always blame the builder, but these townships only have themselves to blame. They're the ones who mandate huge lots and frontage. Buyers these days insist on having their one acre, or more, for their custom builds. I'm proposing a cluster of townhomes that not only provides affordable housing, but also makes the most efficient use of the land."

Time for plan B. Seeing as the society's hopes of being able to buy the land were dwindling anyway, perhaps I could convince him to at least leave the old farmhouse standing.

"Okay, so how about gifting the house and a couple of acres to the Historical Society? Think about the enormous goodwill you could curry in the community with such a gesture."

He laughed again. "Get out of here, Ms. Buchanan. I have a business to run." He tossed his cigar stub into the muck, got into a dented white truck, and drove off. I had to jump back to avoid getting spattered.

"I should have realized it's a waste of time appealing to your better nature, because you simply don't have one!" I yelled after him as the truck careened into the distance.

The same little man who had appeared on the day poor Alex Roos was found scurried over to me. "You see how he is, don't ya? You should hear some of the stories about the way he operates, from sabotaging his competition to poaching workers from their sites. He's a ruthless bastard."

I stood there, still shaking with fury. A chain saw whined in the distance, cutting down trees and chewing up the scenic backdrop of our lives.

Was Roos planning some kind of exposé on Beau Cassell and his substandard building practices? Was he threatening to ruin him and that's what got him killed?

"He's a cheap so-and-so, too," the old man continued, his eyes bright. "Makes his poor secretary sit in that trailer with no heat or air-conditioning. Never lets her take a day off. And that pip-squeak foreman of his is a real prize."

I looked around, but I couldn't see any sign of the taciturn Randy.

"I've given that son of a gun my punch list a million times, but he ignores it. And I moved in two years ago." He sidled closer to me, so close that I could smell the musty odor of his clothes. "Cassell doesn't even live in one of his own houses. What does that tell ya?"

I shrugged and smiled, backing away ever so slightly and wondering how to make a polite getaway.

He tapped his forehead. "I just remembered something. Something I forgot to tell the cops. But you seemed pretty chummy with that one detective. Perhaps you could mention it to 'im." He paused, enjoying the drama of the moment.

I held my breath, nodding for him to continue.

"I saw a flash of light out of the bedroom window of that vacant house the night the photographer guy was killed. What do ya suppose that means?"

"I don't know. But I'll pass it along. Thanks." I got back in my car and promptly drove over to the vacant house.

Screw Serrano.

There was a lockbox on the front door, so I hurried around to the back. The window in the basement was still broken, and it would be easy enough for me to slip inside.

I blew out a breath and gingerly kicked out the rest of the jagged edges of glass. I wasn't a particularly athletic person, but Angus had made me clamber up enough ladders into precarious old barns on our picking adventures that I knew what I was capable of. I put my gloves on, held on to the top of the window, slid my legs inside as low as I could go, and then dropped to the floor.

The house was even more hostile and soulless than I remembered.

Just hurry up and get this over with, Daisy.

I ran up the stairs and into the master bedroom to where the window faced the street. I looked out across the rows and rows of houses that all pretty much looked the same, trying to see what Alex might have spotted from his vantage point. Who was he spying on? Cassell? Or someone else?

A board creaked. I held my breath, but there were no more sounds. No human footsteps, anyway. Perhaps it was the tortured ghost of Roos, still trapped in this hellish place.

I gritted my teeth. Well, if it was, he wouldn't want to scare me. I was here to try to find out who did this to him.

I went out of the house through the front door, turning the lock on the doorknob and pulling it shut behind me. I drove over to the parallel street in the development and glanced up at the house I estimated to be directly across from the vacant one.

Sally McIntire was standing at the uncurtained bedroom window, staring out with a numb expression on her face, wearing nothing but a bra and underpants.

Chapter Ten

That afternoon, I called Ruth. Maybe I'd been too hasty to judge, and maybe there was a good explanation for the encounter I'd witnessed in town. She sounded receptive on the phone, so I told her I'd come over after work and bring dinner.

Joe was taking a jewelry-making class on Tuesday nights. Recently he'd gotten into making miniature dollhouse furniture, and apparently this would help improve his skills. He said he'd grab something to eat at home before the class.

I picked up a broccoli-and-cheese stromboli from Pop's, together with a green salad and a couple of iced teas.

When Ruth answered the door, I had to stifle a gasp. She looked like she'd been crying for hours. Her perfect eyeliner had run down her face, making her look like one of those Pierrot clowns with crosses for eyes, and her hair was sticking up as if she'd run her fingers through it a thousand times. I set the bag down on the foyer floor and folded her into my arms.

"Oh, Ruth, I'm so sorry about Stanley. This must be such a terrible time for you."

"It's not that—I mean, it *is*—but something else has happened. Something even more terrible."

She was shaking so badly that I helped her into the expansive light-filled living room and onto one of the silk chairs near the fireplace. The room was so massive that there was space for three couches in the center, each holding rows of perfectly primped pillows in a muted mix of yellow and cream plaids and florals. A square glass coffee table holding a Chinese vase and a stack of oversize books sat on a pale yellow wool rug, and sage-and-white striped silk drapes adorned the tall windows.

I knelt down in front of her and took her hands in mine. "Ruth, what is it? For God's sake, what's happened?"

"I'm ruined. Completely ruined!" She sank her head back against the chair. "Oh, Daisy, I've been such a foolish woman. So gullible."

Was she talking about her reputation? Had someone else besides me seen her in town?

"Look, Ruth, I don't quite know how to say this, but are you referring to the man you were walking with in Sheepville the other day? I—um—couldn't help but notice you."

She nodded miserably. "He wasn't just my lover, he was my financial planner. Edward Flint. The creep who's run off with most of my money!"

Her lover?

I got up, painfully, my knees cracking as I did so. Wow. If she did kill Stanley for his money, the irony was that now it was gone.

"And that's not all," Ruth moaned. "I invested the Historical Society's money in the same damn fund." She broke down sobbing again.

"What?"

Now I had to sink into a chair. Ruth was a brilliant

fund-raiser, and we'd entrusted her with the treasurer duties. "Are you *sure* the money has disappeared? That there's not just some accounting mistake?"

Ruth nodded miserably. "I'd recommended Edward to my friends, too. This afternoon I got a call from one of them. He was getting a bad feeling that something was not quite right about the quarterly reports, and so he went over to Edward's place to talk to him. It was completely cleaned out. His office, too. And, of course, all of our accounts. We called the police, but who knows if they'll ever find the creep? He could be in Nicaragua by now. The last time I saw him was that day in Sheepville."

I closed my eyes briefly as I tried to control my anger, my disappointment. She needed my love and support now, not recrimination. "I need to let the members know," I told her. "I'll be right back."

With an effort, I stood and walked out into the foyer, where I made a call to Eleanor that we had to have an emergency meeting of the Historical Society, and gave her a brief run-down of the catastrophe. She said she would round up as many members as she could and meet me at Ruth's house. I also left a message for Joe with the news, saying I might be home late.

I walked back into the living room. Ruth hadn't moved from her prone position on the chair. "Ruth, the society members should be here soon. Are you hungry? I brought some dinner."

She shook her head of spiky hair. "Sorry, but I don't feel like eating. You go ahead if you'd like."

"I think I lost my appetite, too. How about an iced tea?"

She wiped at her eyeliner-smudged cheeks. "Actually, I'd rather have some coffee."

"Come on, let's go into the kitchen." I put an arm around her, led her into the kitchen with its long stainless steel table, much like a prep station in a restaurant, and handed her a box of tissues. I put the stromboli and salad away in the fridge that was already packed full of food. Probably leftovers from the shivah.

Stanley had been an enthusiastic cook, and this addition to the house was a real chef's kitchen. In contrast to the rest of the elegant old house, it was super modern, with light cabinets, yards of gleaming stainless, tons of gadgets, a commercial stove, and two dishwashers.

The coffee machine itself was a fabulous affair, capable of producing cappuccino and espresso as well as regular java, and I stared at it for a moment to figure out its bells and whistles.

"That's when I first realized something was wrong with Stanley," Ruth said as she watched me grind some Kona beans. "He was standing in front of that coffeemaker one Saturday morning, just staring at it. I asked him what was wrong, and he said he couldn't remember how to do it."

I glanced over my shoulder at her.

"I was in denial for such a long time. I told myself it was just senior moments. I mean, we all have those, right?"

"Oh, sure," I said as I filled the filter. "Heck, I often go upstairs and then wonder what I went up there for."

"It's so hard to wrap your mind around the fact that things have changed, and they're never going to get better. *He's* never going to get better." She plucked another tissue out of the box and wiped at the streaks under her eyes. "It's the shame, Daisy. It takes so long for you to get past that, to say you need help, and by then it's too late."

A troubling thought popped into my mind. Joe was often forgetful and sometimes did quirky things. Should I be watching him for subtle signs? I took two blue china mugs out of the cupboard and hunted around for the sugar.

"Stanley and I did everything we could. We did exhaustive research on the disease, we got him the best doctors, the best medicine. Because he'd worked for a pharmaceutical company, he was still in touch with people who were on the cutting edge of research. He even tried an investigational drug that kept him stable for a while."

I sat at the table across from her. "Did he know what was happening to him?"

"Yes—that's the awful part about Alzheimer's. It doesn't take away your intelligence. He said he could feel himself changing bit by bit, like another tiny piece of his brain was being pared away. He started using the wrong words for things because he couldn't remember the right one. We made jokes of it, because it was easier to laugh than cry."

On the wall next to the steel baker's rack behind her, I could see a black-and-white photo of Stanley standing with his research team as he accepted an award for his latest breakthrough.

"Some days he seemed so rational that I'd lull myself into a false sense of security, and then one day I found him out in the garden, because he couldn't find his way back inside. From our own garden! After that, he became afraid to leave the house." Tears fell from her eyes.

I wanted to comfort her, but I sensed that it was more important to let her talk. The coffee finished brewing, and I took some milk out of the fridge.

"He'd go into his office every day, as if he was still working. I guess he felt like he was doing something useful, but all he did was rearrange his books and leave them scattered over the floor. It drove me insane. I'd yell at him, and he'd look at me with fear in his eyes. Finally I realized that all I could do was go with the flow and give him my love and my kindness as much as I could during that long good-bye."

"Like dogs do. Live in the moment, I mean."

Ruth gave me an odd look. "Yes, I suppose so." She took the mug of coffee from me and drank it black. "And of course, the sex was the first thing to disappear. The medication shut

that side of our life down immediately. That's when I met
Edward."

I squirmed on my chair. How long until everyone from
the Historical Society got here?

I couldn't exactly condone Ruth's transgression, but I'd
learned over the course of my almost six decades on this
earth not to judge people too harshly. She'd had a heavy burden to bear, and it must have been a lonely and painful existence for her to watch her beloved husband fade away. Could
I really blame her for seeking a little romance and attention?

She stood up and went over to the French doors that led
out to the garden. "There was one violent episode. We'd
recently changed his meds, and suddenly he lost it and came
at me with a knife." Her back was toward me.

"My God, Ruth. I can't believe it. Stanley was always
such a peaceful, gentle man."

She sighed. "He didn't remember it, but *I* did. Then he
became convinced that giant lab rats were taking him out of
the house in the middle of the night, testing drugs on him. You
wouldn't believe the gruesome things he told me. That they
removed his eyeballs and put cameras back in where his eyes
had been so the rats could watch what I was doing to him."

Ruth wrapped her arms around herself, and I could see
the sharp angles of her shoulder blades.

"It was like his brain scattered in all directions. We
adjusted the medication and he became docile again, but
then he went into a dark place where I couldn't reach him
anymore. He was absolutely terrified. Nothing I could say
would reassure him. God, he didn't even know who I was."

She came and sat back at the table and drained her coffee in one gulp.

"Oh, Ruth, that must have been so hard."

She nodded. "I had to keep reminding myself it was the
disease talking. I guess if I was in a place where I didn't
know anyone or where I was, I'd be scared, too."

I saw for the first time just how much she'd had to deal with. I knew that Alzheimer's was a terrible disease, not only for the person afflicted, but perhaps more for the families involved, but I hadn't visualized what life was like day-to-day. Now I was ashamed I'd ever suspected her of murder.

"Ruth, I wish I could have helped you more. You could have leaned on me, and your other friends." Although as I got up and poured us some more coffee, I reflected that I would probably have been the same way. Trying to control everything myself and too proud to ask for help.

She trailed the spoon through the bowl of sugar, making dunes of white crystals. "I pictured Stanley and me spending the rest of our lives together. All the times we shared, those trips we took. Now it was only me that remembered them. And the bad experiences do a great job of replacing the good memories.

"If you think about it, Daisy, that's all we are: a collection of memories. Once that's gone, who are we? Other people live in ours, whether living or dead. In turn, our actions and words take up a place in their hearts and minds. Alzheimer's is so cruel because it steals them. The great memory thief."

I desperately searched my mind for some stories of our time together. "Hey, remember that dinner we had out on the patio that one summer? When Joe and I came over and we cooked steaks and lobsters on the grill?"

Her mascara-smudged eyes brightened a little. "Oh, what a feast that was. What a great evening. Joe even made a tarte tatin on the grill for dessert. That was amazing."

"And Stanley always made the best coffee," I murmured.

Ruth gave me a sad smile. "I begged the doctor for better medicine, more medicine, to prolong his life as long as possible. The doctor asked me what it was exactly that I wanted to prolong. That's when I realized how selfish I was being. I had to watch my husband slowly fade before my eyes, like a Polaroid photo in reverse."

I pictured Joe's well-built body wasting away, the anguish I would feel if he didn't know who I was. My eyes were brimming now, and I grabbed a tissue out of the box. "Jeez. I'm supposed to be comforting you. Not doing a very good job, am I?"

"Yes, you are. It's such a relief to finally tell someone." She sighed heavily. "Life has been so manic. I missed my friends. I missed my *life*. I was looking forward to some peace, some sense of control again. And now this."

A few minutes later I was relieved to hear a knock on the door. I hurried to answer it, and Martha and Eleanor came rushing into the house, followed by Debby Millerton, the librarian, and Annie Sparks, who owned the herb shop. I led them into the kitchen, where Ruth dissolved into tears again at the sight of the members of the Historical Society.

"My God, what have I done?" she wailed. "I'm so sorry, everyone. I'm so embarrassed."

They crowded around her, making murmurs of condolence and reassurance, while Ruth moaned and kept repeating how sorry she was. Above the babble, I noticed Eleanor hanging back, white-lipped and silent. I drew her into the living room.

"E, are you mad at Ruth?" I whispered.

She ran a hand through her hair. "Yes. No. Oh, hell, I don't know. I'm just as mad at myself, I suppose. As president, I should have had better procedures in place. There should have been two signatures required on checks, that type of thing. But it seemed as though Ruth was so good with money, and I trusted her . . ."

"We all did. Turns out she was good at raising money, but maybe not so good at managing it."

We glanced toward the kitchen, where Ruth was taking great gulps of air. "Of course, I'll have to lay off my cleaning service," we heard her sob. "Kathleen won't be happy, but what can I do? I'm not even sure where she keeps the vacuum!"

Eleanor rolled her eyes at me. "And now we don't have the resources to hire another photographer, or get the calendar printed. *Damn* it."

"Come on," I said, taking hold of her arm. "No use crying over spilt milk."

"Can we think of some other ideas to make money?" Debby was asking the group as we walked back into the kitchen.

Eleanor sighed. "We've been through this before. The calendar was the best idea we ever came up with."

"And I already tried to reason with Beau Cassell," I said. "That was a complete dead end."

Eleanor folded her arms across her chest. "There is no more mercy in him than there is milk in a male tiger."

"How about the farmer who owns the land?" Debby handed Ruth another tissue. "Can we appeal to him?"

"Old man Yerkel hates Cassell, which is why he's been stalling on selling him the farm," Martha said. "However, he doesn't give a hoot about historical preservation. Mrs. Yerkel did, but she's gone. They moved to the Outer Banks for her health, but she died this summer, and he now needs the money for her massive medical bills."

"Why did they leave all that stuff in the house?" I remembered peeking inside the kitchen and seeing the table, dishes, and paintings on the walls.

"She was too sick to pack it up, and he didn't care."

"It's all rotting away in there," I said. "It's criminal."

"Yes, it's a shame," Debby said. "My sister said Mrs. Yerkel had some beautiful samplers."

My ears pricked up. "Samplers?"

"Oh, no, those she donated to the Historical Society," Martha said. "In fact, Althea Gunn restored some of them for us."

"It looks as though Cassell will win the farm after all. There's no hope now." I felt sick.

"That's assuming he gets the zoning change. It's not a

done deal yet." Eleanor turned to Ruth. "The more imme-
diate problem is that you have no money. Was everything
tied up in this fund?"

Ruth ran a hand through her hair, leaving it sticking up at
a new angle. "We never kept much in our checking account—
only a couple of thousand—the rest was in the money market
fund, and we moved it over when we needed it. All I really
have left is this house."

"How about an estate sale?" I suggested. "Do you have
any items you could get rid of for some ready cash?"

Ruth brightened. "Oh, yes. There are so many books,
Stanley's clothes, his skis . . ."

"I'll help," Martha said.

I smiled at her. Martha was great at organizing large-
scale events, and a project like this would be good to keep
her busy and take her mind off her troubles.

"Me too," Eleanor said.

"Don't you *ever* work at your store?" I asked.

She shrugged. "Only when I feel like it. Which isn't
very often."

Ruth jumped up to consult the calendar on the wall.
"We can hold it this weekend. The following weekend is
Thanksgiving, which is no good, and then people will be
rushing around for Christmas. I think the weather forecast
is good for Saturday."

"Is that enough time to get ready?" I asked.

"I know what to get rid of," Ruth said, a firm note in her
voice.

The conversation swirled around me as I struggled to get
my thoughts together. Stanley was gone. There was nothing
more I could do for him.

Let go of the green banana, Daisy. I pictured pulling
my hand out of the hole and found myself rubbing my
wrist. Cyril was another story, however. I'd never give up
on him.

* * *

When I got home, I found Joe in his favorite place, the kitchen. He was cooking a spinach frittata, and the toasty smell of eggs and cheese bubbling together suddenly made me realize how hungry I was.

"I figured you might not have had a chance to eat, so thought I'd whip up some comfort food."

"Did I ever tell you I love you, Joe?"

He frowned, spatula in hand, gazing up at the ceiling as if pondering a difficult question. "Hmm, once or twice? I dunno. Maybe you need to tell me again."

I threw my arms around him and hugged him. When he would have normally pulled back, I held on, unwilling to let go. "I love you," I whispered against his faded denim shirt, drinking in the comfort of his familiar body against mine.

Joe tipped my chin up and kissed me. "Love you more. Now, come, sit. Tell me what's going on."

He handed me a well-deserved glass of wine, and I sank down at the butcher block table while he put the pan under the broiler for a minute to finish the frittata.

The story of the night's events poured out of me, and Joe let me talk without interruption. One of the reasons he'd been so good at his job as a negotiator for the electricians' union was that he was a great listener.

Joe set a plate in front of me, and I dug in to the meal, murmuring in delight. Once I'd taken the edge off my hunger and sat back in the chair, exhausted, he smiled at me. A strange smile, as if drinking in every detail.

"What is it?"

"You're so beautiful."

"Me? This gray-haired old lady?" I laughed. "Have some more wine, Joe."

"No, I mean it."

I blinked against the prick of tears. God, what would I

do without him? I tried to count my blessings every day, but sometimes it didn't feel like enough. One of my favorite Winnie-the-Pooh quotes ran through my mind. *If you live to be a hundred, I want to live to be a hundred minus one day so I never have to live without you.*

Jasper laid his head on my knee as if sensing my mood, and I stroked his silky head. One of the cruel realities of being human is that we are aware of our mortality. We know how long we are expected to live, but dogs have no concept of days ticking by. They get up in the morning, ready to enjoy whatever today has to offer. I wished I could be more like Jasper, instead of worrying about things that I couldn't control.

On the table was a grouping of the latest models off Joe's production line of miniature dollhouse furniture. One of his best-selling items was a replica of an old steamer trunk, much like the one that had inspired me to open my store.

Customers loved the story of that trunk, as well as Joe's exquisite handiwork, and I filled the finished chests with tiny strips of lace and ribbon. It was a popular giveaway to people who signed up for the mailing list as well as a door prize at open houses.

How would I know if my dear love was going down the same road as Ruth's husband?

I decided that the miniatures would be my clue. As long as he could do this kind of intricate, challenging work, he must be okay.

Joe ducked his head to meet my gaze. "Earth to Daisy? What's going on? I can see the smoke coming out of your ears."

I pushed my worries away and smiled at him. "I'm just glad we have our health and each other."

"Amen." Joe clinked his glass against mine.

And in the quiet of the kitchen, gazing into the eyes of the man I loved, with our beloved dog dozing at our ankles, it was as good a prayer as any I'd ever heard.

Chapter Eleven

My morning routine used to be that I would stop by the diner, pick up some coffee, and go to the salvage yard to see Cyril before work. But Patsy wasn't waitressing at the diner anymore. And Cyril was gone.

Now, after I fed Cyril's cat, I drove to Sheepville, stopping at Jumpin' Java Mama, checking every table for the newspaper and inspecting the crossword puzzle, but there were no more clues. Maybe it hadn't been him after all.

When I headed down to Sometimes a Great Notion, carrying a bag from the bakery, I saw Eleanor sweeping the sidewalk in front of her shop.

"Hey, did you get a new car?" I called, gesturing at the broom.

"Very funny, Daisy." She spotted the bag full of pastries. "It's come to this, has it?"

"Sadly, yes."

Eleanor stomped the broom on the sidewalk. "This is

ridiculous. We're grown women. We should be able to bake
our own treats without expecting Martha to do it all the
time. How hard can it be?"

I shrugged and waved good-bye and opened the door to
Sometimes a Great Notion. The vigorous holiday sales
meant that I had to restock the displays more than usual,
and I needed to get to work. I'd decided to expand on my
dinner table theme and was setting up a new display using a
classic Provençal tablecloth of yellow and blue when the
owner of the cheese shop next door came in.

"I've brought you a bribe," she said. "Some Humboldt
Fog for some of your delicious coffee."

I eagerly accepted the wrapped package of mold-ripened
goat cheese. "Deal, although I think I'm getting the better
end of it."

"Ooh, how much is that tablecloth?" she asked.

I smiled, refolded it, and sold it to her at cost. After she
left, I put the cheese in the fridge and started over. I discovered I had a good collection of scissors, including one with
its bows fashioned to look like pheasants and the shanks
like roosters. I added a Victorian brass butterfly that held
two needle packets under each wing, some W. Avery & Son
brass needle cases from the late nineteenth century, and a
wooden machine bobbin.

I'd just stepped back to assess the arrangement when
the doorbell jangled again and Serrano strode in.

I glared at him. "Well, well, well. Look what the cat
dragged in."

Serrano raised his arms in bewilderment. "How come
it's colder in this fricking shop than outside?"

"How come *you* expect me to tell you everything I know,
and you don't bother to return the *favor*?"

"Daisy." He sighed, and I gritted my teeth as I saw the
patient look spread across his face. "Relax. Remember I'm
the detective in this scenario, okay?"

I was about to tell him to take a long hike off a short pier when he grinned.

"In fact, I did come to give you some news."

He looked hopefully at the counter where I'd set out some chocolate croissants from the bakery.

"Bribery will get you everywhere, Detective." I poured him a cup of coffee and put a croissant on a plate.

"Autopsy results came back on Alex Roos," he said. "You know, the way that guy was killed—being spray-foamed in the mouth—sounds a lot to me like a message for a traitor to shut up."

"How awful." I pressed a hand to my own mouth, images of how Alex Roos must have suffered coloring my mind red. "Can forensics estimate the time of death?"

"Tricky one. You should see what fifteen-hundred-degree heat does to a human body."

"Okay, okay. I know I asked for information, but maybe not that much."

Serrano licked some of the chocolate out of the flaky pastry. "There were rope fibers on the corpse. He was probably tied up for a while before they killed him."

"They?"

"Could be. To manhandle a guy into an attic and spray-foam him into the rafters would take a strong man, possibly two."

"There's something else," I said. "One of the neighbors in the Cassell development saw a flash of light out of the window of the vacant house that night. The McIntires' house is directly across from it. Jim McIntire might have gone storming over there if he thought the photographer was taking pictures of his wife."

Serrano was focused on savoring the last piece of croissant. I wasn't sure he'd even heard what I said. I almost felt like snapping my fingers to get his attention.

"I don't suppose you found a camera near the body?"

He shook his head. "No. Why?"

"I gave Roos a vintage camera that he said he planned to use for the shoot with Cyril. If he had it with him that night, where is it now? If we can find that camera, it might hold the clue to the murder."

"He coulda left it in Cyril's truck while they went in the pub."

"Oh, you're probably right." I sighed, feeling deflated. Now that I thought about it, Alex wouldn't have schlepped his stuff into the bar, because he would have assumed that Cyril was giving him a ride home. "Speaking of Cyril, though . . ."

I told Serrano about the crossword puzzle in the newspaper, but before I was even halfway through the story, it sounded like a stretch, even to me.

He placed his mug and napkin neatly on top of the plate. "Daisy, you need to keep a clear head on this one. You can't let your emotions and panic about Cyril cloud your thinking. As a matter of fact, I'd rather you stay far away from this case. Whoever did that to Roos is a ruthless bastard. If Cyril Mackey *did* see what happened that night, he's lying low for a good reason."

After he left, I logged on to the Internet and did some research on Beau Cassell, looking for news articles. Not surprisingly, he'd had run-ins with residents of other townships. I found plenty of angry bloggers who'd purchased Cassell homes complaining about the quality of the build. In fact, one group was involved in a lawsuit against him about a mold issue and how he'd failed to properly remediate the problem.

I sucked in a breath as I saw a name and face I recognized. Terri Jones. The woman with the bad cough from the sampler group. I might have to stop by another class and have a chat. Had Roos reverted to his photojournalist roots and that's what triggered his demise?

I stood and stretched my back. And what had Cyril meant by the canary clue?

"Come on, Cyril," I said out loud. "I need more of the story. Why don't you show yourself? Why not come home and let Serrano protect you from whatever's going on?"

So not only did I talk to mannequins, but now I was talking to a guy who wasn't there and could quite possibly be dead.

Stop it. Don't talk like that. Alice was glaring at me.

"You're right." Even if this was a psychotic episode, there was no sense thinking that way. I had to cling to the belief that Cyril was out there, somewhere.

"Who are you talking to?"

I'd been so wrapped up in my thoughts that I hadn't heard the front door open again. Eleanor stood there, staring at me.

Oh, the hell with it. "I was talking to Alice," I said with as much dignity as I could muster.

To my surprise, Eleanor didn't snicker. "Bet she's a good listener." She walked past me toward the kitchen in the back. She was carrying a bulging grocery bag.

I scurried after her.

"I thought we should try to make some cookies," she said. "They may not be as good as Martha's, but what's the worst that can happen?"

"Isn't that what the victim always says before she enters the dark house alone in those B movies with a serial killer waiting in the basement?"

Eleanor smirked as she pulled out a bag of flour and some sticks of butter and smoothed a crumpled piece of paper onto the counter. "All we have to do is follow this recipe and we'll be fine."

"What are we making?"

"I call them Kitchen Sink Cookies."

We set to work. Eleanor measured out the ingredients

while I mixed. Rolled oats, walnuts, sugar, and three eggs went in after the flour and butter.

"Wait—there's no coconut in this recipe," I demurred as Eleanor dumped in half a bag of shredded coconut.

"I know, I like it, though." She followed up with a mountain of chocolate chips, popping a handful into her mouth.

I peered at the paper again. "And no chocolate chips, either."

"Details, details." Eleanor waved a hand in the air. "Everyone knows that chocolate makes everything better."

The batter was so heavy by this point that we had to take turns mixing it by hand because it was too dense for the beaters.

Eleanor peered at the recipe again. "Ah, rats! I knew I'd forget something. The vanilla! Never mind, I have bourbon. Should work just as well." She pulled a flask out of the back pocket of her jeans and sloshed a glug into the bowl.

We dropped it by huge clumps onto baking sheets and slid them into the oven. Soon a wonderful aroma wafted through the store.

"This should entice the customers," I said, breathing in deeply. "Even if they don't taste good, they smell great."

I was just taking the first batch out of the oven when the doorbell jangled and Martha swept in.

"Uh-oh, caught in the act," Eleanor muttered.

"What on earth are you two doing?" Martha took a small piece off one cookie and bit into it gingerly while we held our breath. "Amazingly good. I think you two should make *all* the treats from now on."

"Now look what you've done," I said to Eleanor. "This is why I pretend not to know how to fix the garbage disposal at home."

Eleanor didn't answer. She was too busy finishing her first cookie and reaching for another. She drank like a fiend and ate whatever she wanted, but her body was lithe and fit, and the energy fairly sparkled from her. There were laugh lines around her eyes, her hair was completely white, but her skin was luminous with hardly a wrinkle.

Martha shook her head sorrowfully. "There's no justice in this world. Look at her, Daisy. And she never goes to the doctor either."

Martha's physician saw her more often than he did his own mother.

"If I'm going to take my clothes off in front of a man, I need more of a payoff than a chit to pick up some pills." Eleanor licked melted chocolate off her lips. "My arteries are all clear, anyway. Those lipid thingys don't stand a chance against high-octane vodka. And I run five miles every day."

I nodded. I knew she did yoga, too. "I walk Jasper a lot and I think the crossword puzzles help keep my brain active. How about you, Martha?"

Eleanor snorted. "The only running she ever does is to the shoe sale at Macy's."

Martha tossed her mane of vibrant red hair. "Oh, and by the way, Ms. Reid, did you hear that your little barber friend had a date with Ronnie the psychic the other night?"

"What?" Eleanor paled.

"You heard me. Took her to the Bridgewater Inn and wined and dined her all night long. Bet she's a happy medium now."

Martha and I laughed uproariously, until Eleanor started banging the used beaters and bowls into the sink.

"What are you so upset about?" I asked. "You didn't want him, anyway."

Martha placed her hands on her hips. "Yes, if you've finally decided you like him, why not ask him out? Forgive me for saying this, but you're too old to be subtle."

Eleanor scowled. "I've got two words for you, and they're not *Happy Birthday*."

* * *

The next day, I drove over to Sheepville to catch the Thursday morning sampler class. On the passenger seat next to me, in one of my signature shopping bags, was the emery I planned to give to Althea, along with some vintage needle cases.

I'd already sold two of the samplers to a collector from Maryland for a great price. The profit would cover the store's rent for the next couple of months. I was debating keeping my favorite for myself, the one with the house like Claire's painting.

When I arrived, the class was about to start. I slipped the bag under Althea's nose and mouthed the words "thank you." PJ and Liz were already there, and I found a seat next to them.

Althea peered over the tops of her bifocals at me as she pulled the items out of the bag. She held up one of the needle cases. There was the merest breath of a smile on her face.

"Remember, class. You need to choose the right size needle to make a hole in the fabric just large enough for the yarn to pass through. If the hole is too small, it will spoil the thread. Too large and it will show on the finished work." She mumbled something else to herself as she put the things back in the bag.

"I think she said 'thanks,'" PJ whispered to me.

"Consider the natural properties of the stitches and use these to achieve the effects you want. Do *not* force cross-stitches into elaborate curves, for example, but rather exploit their intrinsic zigzag quality."

"Then you won't come undone," I snickered. Althea fixed me with a stern gaze.

What was I doing? I should know enough about being a teacher not to be the difficult student sitting in the back with the bad kids.

"Today, class, we're going to learn fancy herringbone," Althea boomed. "At first sight, it might look complicated, but it's quite easy."

"Easy for her to say," Liz muttered.

"Using a foundation of ordinary herringbone, space your stitches widely apart. Next, work Saint George cross stitches over the top and bottom crosses of the herringbone row. On the third journey, run a thread through the horizontal bars of the previous stitches without picking up any ground fabric."

My head was spinning. She'd lost me at *Saint George*.

"Could you repeat that?" Liz asked, her hand in the air, but PJ was already hard at work.

I was amazed at the multitude of different stitches and how Althea could remember them all, let alone the variations on each name. It seemed like each stitch had three or four other monikers. It reminded me of Eleanor, who knew the Latin names for all the flowers in her garden, as well as the common garden varieties.

However, even though this was only my second class, I was actually starting to recognize some of the stitches. At least enough to know that Althea's sampler featured some incredibly difficult ones, but there were a few of those on PJ's, too.

"If you paid attention, Mrs. Gallagher, instead of chatting with your *friends* here, you might learn something."

I slid farther down in my seat. Althea began to make her rounds, and her first stop was at our table.

"Can you teach me the Catherine wheel?" PJ asked.

"That might be a little advanced for now, Ms. Avery."

PJ's mouth set in the familiar stubborn line. "I just want to know which are the hardest stitches. Those are the ones I want to use."

"As I've mentioned ad nauseam, you should use the stitch that is appropriate for the *design*, regardless of difficulty." But even as she chided PJ, I could see a grudging admiration on Althea's dour face. She showed her protégé how to work a large circle of blanket stitches, work a second row inside and spokes throughout, all the while without picking up the fabric. PJ followed her directions, creating something that looked a bit like a complicated flowery starburst.

I got up and did my usual walkabout. It was interesting what everyone decided to include on their samplers, especially Althea. Hers were all about atoning for past sins. I couldn't imagine that the grim woman had much of a wild past, with how holier-than-thou she was.

I lingered next to Terri Jones, the woman with the incessant cough. "Hi, Terri, I'm Daisy. That's a beautiful pillow."

She coughed again, covering her mouth.

I couldn't think of a good transition, so I just jumped right in. "I—um—was researching Cassell-built homes for a friend of mine, and I came across the story about the mold in your house."

Her lips thinned into almost a snarl. "My little girl nearly died from a case of severe asthma, and I'm always sick. I can't prove the house caused it, and we may never win our case, but you should tell your friend to stay far, far away from anything that man has touched." The quiet demeanor was gone, and I unconsciously took a step back from the savage anger in her eyes.

Could this woman have gone so far as to try to frame Cassell for murder? I could almost hear Serrano's voice in my head, mocking my wild suppositions, but I knew the power of motherly love. The most meek and mild of women could turn into demons to protect, or in this case avenge, their children.

"This should interest you, Daisy Buchanan, if you ever have the urge to duplicate an old sampler, like Iona here." Althea's booming alto brought me back to reality. "Linen is essential for heirloom pieces. It's also better to use dark brown than black thread. Most of the colors on antique samplers are faded now, of course, but it's clear that the shades were delicate from the first."

I nodded, grateful for the advice, however hard-won. I couldn't exactly say that I liked Althea, but I loved to watch an expert at work

"It's sad that so many people today feel that they must rely on another's design, instead of creating something entirely their own." Althea thumped on the table for emphasis. "The secret of the old samplers was their individuality, their personal character. That is the only principle you need to remember."

"Oh, but I like working on the kits," Abigail Weller said cheerfully.

A hush fell over the room.

Althea took a deep cleansing breath. "With a good command of stitches—and that means not just the ability to produce a stitch, but to know the effect it will have on different fabrics and threads—it becomes possible for the embroiderer to produce truly original designs. Trust me, you will thank me later."

I could see her point. Give a man a fish and so on. The class could certainly aspire to master the kind of breathtaking work stretched out on the frame at the front of the room.

Although Althea was stilted in normal social interaction, she was a good storyteller, weaving in facts effortlessly. A walking textbook of knowledge about her craft.

Grace Vreeland leaned over to me. "Good teacher, isn't she? I always said she missed her calling. Should have pursued her dreams, instead of going to work for that no-good builder."

"What?"

"Oh, yeah, she was Beau's secretary for ages. She only just retired a couple of years ago. How she put up with that bastard for so long, I'll never know. It's not like he paid her well, neither."

"She's such a competent, take-charge woman," I murmured.

Grace snorted. "She had to be. Years of working in a construction office with Cassell and his men. She had to hold her own."

I moved around the class, deep in thought. I found myself standing behind Iona, the woman who had been working on the embroidered purse in the last class and was now copying an antique sampler, a family record originally sewn by one Catherine March in the nineteenth century. It was a delight to watch Iona's slim fingers work the threads, so slim that her simple gold wedding ring was slipping off her fingers.

Dottie had also come over to take a look, and we read the poignant verse together in silence:

> *Peace is the gift I leave with you*
> *My peace to you bequeathe*
> *Peace that shall comfort you through life*
> *And cheer your souls in death*
>
> *This work in hands my friends may have*
> *When I am silent in the grave*
> *O Jesus, keep me in thy sight*
> *And guard me through the coming night*
>
> *Let no fond love for earth exact a sigh*
> *No doubts divert my steady steps aside*
> *Nor let me long to live, nor dread to die*
> *Heav'n is my hope and providence my guide*

"The verses seem somewhat grim, don't they, for such a young girl?" Dottie asked Althea.

"Children were much more conscious of death in those

days, and how precious life is. Infant mortality was high, and they probably experienced the loss of at least one, if not several, of their siblings. You can see that this poor child lost four small brothers and sisters—all gone in five months."

"Iona hopes she can finish in time," Dottie murmured in my ear. "Lung cancer. She's asked one of the ladies in the class to fill in the date after she's gone."

I sucked in a breath. It was rather morbid, but I understood in some strange way. I guess when your days were numbered, you didn't need to stand on pretense, but I hated to think of this gentle woman gone from the earth.

People always said they would want their doctors to tell them if they had some incurable disease, but was it better not to know? To enjoy your days in blissful ignorance until the end? I shook my head. One of those conundrums that made my head ache and my spirits sink.

After the class was over, I stood at the register with Dottie and watched as Althea Gunn strode off down the street, wearing a long black coat and a man's trilby hat.

"She lives very frugally. I think she furnishes her wardrobe from the church's annual jumble sale. And she doesn't drive anymore," Dottie said. "Donated her car to charity and walks everywhere. She's probably fitter than a woman half her age."

Althea would certainly be familiar with Beau's underhanded business practices. Was it Beau's sins she was atoning for? Did she suspect that he'd killed Alex Roos? How blind was her loyalty to her former employer?

Dottie counted some bills out of the register and put them in an envelope. "She told me to give her earnings from teaching these classes to the community garden project. You know, Althea's a pain in the butt sometimes, but she donates an awful lot to charity, often anonymously, and devotes much of her time to the church, free of charge."

"Everyone has a saving grace," I murmured.

Althea's sanctimonious attitude still got on my nerves, but I thought I understood her a little more. I'd been trying to learn this lesson for fifty-eight years, but I was reminded of it yet one more time.

Never judge a book by its cover.

On Friday morning, I drove over to Cyril's trailer as usual. I'd asked Ronnie the psychic to meet me there. I knew it was a long shot, but I was getting desperate. Everyone else thought she was a little kooky, but I understood the feeling of the connection to the past, to the energy in the universe, to the memories a place could contain, and I was hoping she could give me something, anything, in the way of reassurance.

Ronnie got out of her VW Beetle and teetered through the salvage yard on spiky boots that were laced halfway up her plump legs. She was wearing black skintight leggings, topped off with a short skirt. She also wore a neon-pink down vest, about a dozen necklaces, and gloves that left her fingertips bare. It was an outfit a Goth teenager would love.

Stone the crows! Cyril's voice was so clear in my ear that I turned, half expecting to see him there. *Talk about mutton dressed as lamb.*

"See a spirit?" Ronnie grinned at me. Her platinum blond hair was stuffed under a Greek fisherman's cap, the kind John Lennon might have worn.

I smiled shakily. "Something like that, I guess."

A shadow flitted across the top of a pile of iron radiators, and she nodded wisely. "Signals from the unknown. They're all around us."

I didn't want to tell her it was probably Cyril's cat.

She surveyed the yard with its mountain of truck tires, old brass bed frames, rusty automotive signs, broken bicycles, and the odd porcelain toilet.

"Sweet suffering Jesus."

"Don't worry, he keeps it nice on the inside." I opened the door to the trailer and we walked in. I was on high alert for anything that was different from the last time I was there and I left Ronnie in the kitchen while I wandered into the living room.

I glanced back and saw her trailing her fingers across the kitchen counter, the plant in the corner, the newspaper recycle bin. I could just picture Serrano's reaction if he knew I'd brought a psychic here. *You don't really believe in that crap, do you, Daisy?* He dealt in cold hard truths, but we were both truth seekers in a way. We just went about it differently.

As if reading my mind, Ronnie said, "It's not always facts, and it's not always scientific. Sometimes youse just gots to believe, Daisy."

Finally she stopped pacing and stood stock-still in the center of the kitchen. "Oh, he's alive, I'm sure of it now." She sounded so confident, relief flooded through me.

I hurried over to her side. "How can you be sure he's not passed on?" I whispered.

She closed her eyes for a moment as if channeling his spirit, and then opened them and winked at me. "Just joshing with ya. The stove's still warm. He probably recently made a cup of tea, or at least someone did." She nodded toward the Boston fern. "Good to see you've been watering this, too."

"But I haven't. I forgot. I've only been feeding the cat."

She smiled her enigmatic smile. "Betcha if you go in the bathroom, you'll find that he zipped home for some fresh clothes, got washed up, and went on his way again."

I ran into the bathroom. The toilet seat was up now, while I was sure it wasn't before, and I spotted a few water droplets on the tiled wall.

I went back into the kitchen to find Ronnie taking a

newspaper out of the recycle bin. "Today's date," she said as she handed it to me. "You know, even if there weren't all these obvious clues here, there are still vibrations in the universe you can sense if you stay open to them. Like dogs who know when you're coming home."

I smarted a little at the word *obvious*. Had there been other signs on my earlier trips and I'd missed them? Also, we were assuming it was Cyril who had been here, but what if it was the killer, toying with us?

I ripped the paper out of her hands and flipped to the crossword puzzle. The clue was *Easter visitor*, and instead of *bunny rabbit*, Cyril had written *bonny castle*.

I knew he'd taken a huge risk by coming home, so it must be important, but I was stumped. What did *bonny castle* mean? Was it a reference to Beau Cassell, perhaps? *Beau* as in *beautiful* or *bonny*? *Cassell* for *castle*? Why the hell did Cyril have to be so cryptic?

"I could do with a little more information here, Cyril," I muttered, and then I explained to Ronnie about the previous clue in the paper at the café.

"No one else knows about this?" Her kohled eyes were suddenly shrewd.

"I told Serrano, but he really didn't take me seriously."

"Good. Now, you need to meditate on what this means." Ronnie hitched up her bra straps and twitched her short skirt down an inch. "Cyril is obviously depending on you to figure it out."

I watched, almost mesmerized, as she twirled her necklaces around one finger. I wondered if she and Tony Zappata were getting serious. Martha had lost her true love, and now it looked as though Eleanor might lose a chance at romance, too, if something was going on between Ronnie and the Millbury barber. I was bursting to ask her about it, but couldn't think of an appropriate segue.

"Ah, Daisy, I wondered when you were going to get around to that."

I jumped. Had I spoken aloud? I really needed to stop talking to Alice in the shop. I wasn't even aware of when I was doing it anymore.

Ronnie laughed. Actually it was more of a raucous chuckle. "Eleanor Reid weren't a bit interested in him before, was she?"

I stared at her.

"Don't worry, there's nothing going on with me and my good friend Tony. We go way back to growing up together in Northeast Philly. Just helping out a pal. Jealousy's a powerful emotion, ain't it?"

I laughed. "So this is simply a ruse to get Eleanor to see the light?"

Ronnie grinned and tapped the side of her nose. "Only the spirit knows."

When I got home, I took Jasper for a walk, and suddenly spotted a black shadow darting through the yards, always keeping us in sight.

"Hello, His Nibs."

The cat was an odd little character, just like his owner. I wondered what to do with the latest clue Cyril had left, like a trail of mysterious bread crumbs. He was counting on me to help, but did I have the right stuff to figure out this deadly puzzle?

Chapter Twelve

It was Laura's day to man the store, and when she arrived, we chatted about the next open house that would be coming up after Thanksgiving. Sometimes a Great Notion was a bit off the beaten track, but luckily much of my business came from interior designers looking for unusual or antique accessories, bedspreads, and linens. Not to mention the collectors and dealers who came from miles away.

We decided to serve mulled wine and prepare some spicy pecans in vintage Ball jars as takeaway gifts. I asked Laura if she could work tomorrow as well so I could help out with the estate sale at Ruth's. She eagerly agreed, saying she could use the extra money.

I headed for Sheepville and the town hall. In addition to my other duties, I was conducting some research for the Millbury Historical Society on the Underground Railroad.

Pennsylvania had been an important thoroughfare to carry slaves north to safety in Canada, and there were already several houses or "stations" in the township on the National Register of Historic Places. Of course I knew something about the railroad from my years as a history teacher, but now I was delving deeper into the stories of Millbury and its environs.

I parked in the lot and walked up Porter Street to Jumpin' Java Mama. I ordered a small coffee and did my usual routine of checking each newspaper on every table for the crossword puzzle. The laid-back baristas didn't even glance my way or comment on my behavior, content to live and let live.

Sally McIntire strode into the shop, wearing formfitting Capri pants, a tight aqua tank top, and a Lycra jacket. It wasn't really warm enough for that kind of outfit, although I vaguely remembered that she was some kind of personal trainer. It certainly showed off her toned body to perfection.

She ordered a smoothie in her singsong voice, requesting one with spinach, banana, pineapple, Greek yogurt, and coconut oil. I went over to her as she dropped into a graceful lunge, using the counter as a ballet barre.

"Hi, Sally. Wow, that sounds like a healthy breakfast."

"I'm on my way to work out with a client." She looked up at me and a dazzling smile transformed her face. "I have to set a good example, and this gives me all kinds of powerful antioxidants and fiber."

"I should try it sometime. You certainly seem full of energy."

She paid for her drink with a credit card and grasped the cup with manicured aqua-colored nails that clicked against the plastic.

"Are you doing okay?" I asked. "I know you seemed— um—rather upset at church."

"Oh, yeah. Poor Alex." The sun went behind the clouds for a moment, and then she brightened again. She sipped

the concoction through a straw, her eyes as wide and disin-
genuous as a child's under her cap of blond hair.

Guess Roos is yesterday's news.

"Can I ask you something, Sally? A friend of mine is considering buying a Cassell-built home." I mentally crossed my
fingers at the white lie. Patsy *had* been considering one
before we found a dead body inside it. "But I've heard of
people having lots of problems with the quality of the build."

Sally bounced in place, as if she might burst from too
much energy. She sucked down more of the smoothie in
one long voracious suck.

"Yeah, we've had stuff go wrong with our house, too.
Luckily, my hubby, Jim, is very handy. He used to work in
construction before he sold insurance, so he was able to fix
a lot of things. He even spray-foamed our attic himself."

It wasn't just her smile that was dazzling. Her wedding
ring was a huge emerald-cut diamond. Jim McIntire must
be doing very well in his insurance business.

"Okay. Gotta go. 'Bye, Daisy." She wiggled her fingers
at me and pranced out of the café just as Liz Gallagher
walked in. They sidestepped each other, and it would be
hard to miss the look of disgust on Liz's face.

Liz shook her head as she came over to the counter and
ordered a cappuccino.

"I take it you two know each other?" I asked.

"She used to teach aerobics at my gym, but now she's
doing one-on-one training." Liz lowered her voice. "And I
hear that there's more than dumbbell flys happening on
that weight bench."

"Really?"

Liz chuckled. "You should have seen the scene in the
gym one day. Her husband was convinced she was screw-
ing one of his clients and screaming that he wouldn't be
made a laughingstock in this town. Ha! We didn't want to
tell him it was too late."

"Apparently he was going crazy looking for her on the night of Roos's murder," I said. I could see why stodgy Jim McIntire could feel insecure, wondering if he was man enough to satisfy his hyper bombshell of a wife.

I finished my coffee, said good-bye to Liz, and walked back to the town hall.

I found Constance Banks in the Parks and Recreation department on the fourth floor. Constance had been a big help to me with my research. I'd gone through the census records, church and cemetery records, and local archives, but she had an ancestor, Rufus Banks, who'd actually traveled the thoroughfare.

It was so hard to uncover information, as not much was written down for safety reasons. Constance had promised to show me some family records today—photo albums, diaries, and the like. She didn't want to lend them out, but said she was willing to let me take a look in person.

I sat in the file room and pored through the gold mine of information, especially Rufus Banks's diary. There were some references to places in the area that were known "safe houses," and I drew a little map for myself.

It must have taken incredible courage to be an abolitionist in those days, let alone a railroad conductor. Some slaves came directly from the slave states of Delaware and Maryland, across the Mason-Dixon line, and into Chester and Lancaster counties.

It was something of a myth that the railroad was a highly organized operation, at least not when the runaways first made their bid for freedom. They would receive help when they crossed the border into Pennsylvania, and be given food and clothing and sheltered in barns, spring houses and attics. Even sometimes in warehouse bins along the Delaware Canal. It was also a myth that many escaped. It was really only a handful compared to the millions in captivity.

I could almost hear the voice of Rufus Banks as he talked about how slaves had to go everywhere with a pass, that slave marriages had no legal standing and could be broken up at the owner's will, and how, after working on the plantation all day, he'd worked on his own meager garden patch by the light of the moon. I felt the familiar anger burn through me at how inhumanely these people had been treated. Stories of overseers who would whip a slave's back in one direction and then turn the lash so the skin fell apart like a ripped checkerboard. And, as if that weren't enough, they finished by putting salt in the wounds.

The spirits of those who had gone before me seemed to be with me in that room.

Parents separated from children, husbands from wives, complete families destroyed. The few who did manage to escape were hounded by slave catchers, who stopped at nothing to take them back, dead or alive. The terror of being recaptured and 'sold to go far south' was palpable in the memoir. How much interminable heartache and suffering had these people endured?

I sighed and tucked the map into my pocket. I went back to the front desk and handed the papers back to Constance, too overwhelmed to say much.

"Thank you very much, Constance. See you soon?"

She looked up at me with her world-weary but kind brown eyes. "If God is willing and the creek don't rise."

The elevator in the Sheepville Town Hall was small and badly in need of renovation. It shook alarmingly as it started, and I gripped the rail on the wall, staring at my blurred reflection in the dented metal sides.

I was toying with the idea of getting out on the next floor when it stopped and Beau Cassell's new foreman got

in, wearing a crumpled raincoat. He bashed the buttons for
the lobby and the door closure repeatedly, and the doors
finally creaked shut.

I closed my eyes and concentrated on my breathing. I
knew I should have taken the stairs.

Serves you right, lazy Daisy.

I stole a quick glance at the foreman, who was staring
straight ahead. His coarse black hair stuck up in several different directions, as if it was too much for a regular comb to
keep straight, and his heavy eyebrows gave him a perma-
nently dour expression. Cassell was such a preening peacock.
Somehow I didn't see the connection between these two.

Suddenly there was a distant thud, and the car stopped
with a jerk.

I looked at the floor buttons in panic. The number *3* was
still lit up. We must be stuck somewhere between the third
and second floors.

I heard a deep moan, sounding very loud in the enclosed
space, and I realized it had come from my own throat.

The foreman looked at me, but I was too busy fighting
panic to care, despairing as the familiar wave swept over
me anyway, leaving a flotsam of cold sweat, racing heartbeat, and shaking legs in its wake.

How far was it to the ground floor? What if the cables
snapped on this thing and we went plunging to our deaths?
The metal walls closed in on me, and I couldn't help but let
out another moan.

"Jesus, lady, are you all right? Here, why don't you sit
down." He helped me to the floor and peered at me in concern. With one arm he reached up and pressed the alarm
button. "Don't worry. Take a deep breath."

I stared at his ravaged face, the lines of a hard life probably aging him beyond his actual years. He also looked like
he needed a shower with his rumpled wardrobe and disheveled hair, but he didn't smell, even in these close quarters.

"Come on. Breathe," he urged.

I took a few deep gulps of air. "I'm so sorry about this. I've always had a thing about small spaces."

"Understood. I've had to get used to it myself over the years."

An image of Cyril popped into my mind. "Hey, were you a miner?"

His expression changed, and he stood up and pressed the alarm button again in one long ring. "Is anyone out there?" he yelled. "There's people stuck inside. Come *on!*"

I heard an answering shout, and seemingly a lifetime later—although it was probably only a few minutes—the car began to move.

When the elevator finally stopped and the doors opened to reveal the lobby, I stumbled out on trembling legs, almost bumping into Frank Fowler, who was carrying a stack of posters. He caught my elbow with one hand as I swayed.

"You look like you've had quite a shock, Ms. Buchanan," he said.

The foreman pushed past us both and headed for the lobby doors without a backward glance.

I sucked the deepest breath I could manage. "I certainly have, Mr. Fowler. Can't our taxpayer dollars pay for a new elevator?"

He smiled faintly. "Not in the budget this year, I'm afraid."

"Just glad I wasn't alone in there." I nodded to where Beau Cassell's foreman was walking out onto the street. "He helped calm me down."

Fowler's expression hardened. "Well, he doesn't do much for *my* blood pressure. He's always skulking around here, trying to push Cassell's interests with the board. Constantly hassling me and my wife."

As one of the three commissioners for Bucks County, Nancy oversaw the Planning Commission, among other departments.

He held up the posters he carried, with his wife's picture splashed across them and the slogan NANCY FOR GOVERNOR. She had the kind of face that the camera loved. The wide-apart eyes, the large mouth, almost Jackie Kennedy–esque. I remembered hearing the gossip that her ambitions ran way beyond county commissioner, although it was a big leap to governor.

"What a magnificent woman she is." Frank sighed, a smile curving the edges of his pale lips. "I'd do anything to protect her, you know."

Methinks thou doth protest too much. One of Eleanor's favorite phrases popped into my head. The foreman might be a bit off-putting, but he wasn't *that* scary. He'd been courteous, even kind to me in my moment of need.

Fowler seemed as though he was going over the top to cover up any kind of association with Randy. Was our township attorney actually in cahoots with Beau Cassell, perhaps taking bribes in the form of campaign contributions? How far would he go to ensure a victory for his beautiful wife?

Maybe the "big thing" Roos was working on had something to do with Nancy Fowler, and not Beau Cassell at all.

On the day of the estate sale, I dressed in an old plaid shirt and jeans. My usual wardrobe at Sometimes a Great Notion wasn't much better, but I'd dressed down even more today, planning on moving boxes and furniture around and generally ready for a good workout.

Joe was pouring a cup of coffee and he looked askance at my wardrobe. "Are you going to the store?"

"No, it's the estate sale for Ruth. You know, to raise some cash because she's flat broke. I told you about it."

"Oh yeah, I forgot."

I frowned at him. "You *do* remember that the new mattress is being delivered today, right?" Our daughter, Sarah, was coming home for Thanksgiving, and I'd ordered a new mattress for her room. Joe had to stay home to accept delivery, which was why he wasn't coming to help out, too. He looked puzzled, and I felt a quiver of unease. "Joe, now you've got me worried."

He leaned back in his chair and raised an eyebrow. "Seriously, Daisy? You think *I'm* losing it? You're the one who has conversations with inanimate fiberglass dress forms!"

I hadn't realized he knew about my unconventional relationship with Alice. "Touché. Okay, I'm sorry." I kissed him good-bye and drove over to Martha's because I'd promised to give her a ride. She drove an old Lincoln Continental, and her tank of a car was terrible in the snow. Like a giant toboggan.

When I walked into her house, my spirits soared as I smelled the aroma of buttery goodness.

Martha was back!

I rushed into the kitchen, anticipating a smorgasbord of baked goodies on the counter, but there was only a scented candle burning, labeled *SUGAR COOKIE*. Martha was dressed in a sober black shirt and pants instead of her trademark voluptuous flamboyant colors.

My heart sank as quickly as it had risen, like a soufflé brought out of the oven too early.

However, when we arrived at Ruth's, I could see that Martha had done her usual stellar job of organization. There was a sign with balloons at the end of the driveway, and there had been directional markers on every turn we'd made from the main road.

Outside the front door, rows and rows of borrowed picnic tables were groaning under the weight of stacks of books, piles of clothes, DVDs, blankets, sheets, and curtains. Pairs of skis leaned against the wall next to a set of expensive luggage.

Inside the house, the living room, dining room, and study

had been turned into staging areas. The kitchen and other rooms were roped off, but more signs directed customers upstairs to various rooms where Ruth was selling off bed frames, bedspreads, dressers, and chairs. I'd advised her to contact a dealer for the paintings and Stanley's rare and first edition books, and to schedule an auction with Angus for some of the better furniture.

I eyed the dinner service sitting on the dining room table. "Are you sure about this, Ruth?"

"Yes, I'll keep my everyday china. That's good enough for me. And for my friends when they come over."

I hugged her. "You're being very brave. It's usually so hard for people to let go of things."

"You know, Daisy, while it's true that the house is paid off—and thank God, because it's all I have left—this place is far too big. I can't even afford the upkeep on it, let alone the taxes. I plan to sell it and buy a place in the city. Heck, I won't even need a car. In the meantime, I'm going to close up those rooms upstairs." She opened a drawer in the china cupboard and took out a crystal vase. "I'll use the study for my bedroom. It's a lot warmer down here, and I won't have to heat the house as much."

Martha swept in. "No time for idle chitchat, now. Let's man our stations!"

We obediently headed outside to our assigned posts. Angus was here today, too, lending muscle to move furniture, and Eleanor had insisted on managing the cashbox.

On one of the tables were stacks of beautiful hardcover cookbooks.

"You're selling these for three dollars each?" Martha asked in disbelief.

"Yes, Stanley did the cooking, and then Kathleen prepared dinners for us to freeze when she was here on her cleaning days. I won't bother to cook for myself."

Martha stared at her. "You're rail-thin now. You need to eat." She shook her head as she gathered stacks of books into her arms and headed for Eleanor at the checkout.

I could see that feeding Ruth would be her next project.

"A Waring blender! Best blender ever made," Angus said to me as we inspected the kitchenware table.

I looked at the price tag on the retro black-and-silver appliance. Twenty-five dollars. I thought it might make a nice housewarming gift for Patsy. I added a set of margarita glasses and a glass pitcher.

I also found a yellow slicker that had belonged to Stanley. Even though he'd been a small-framed man, it was huge on me, but after my experiences of rain jackets that promised to be waterproof and were not, I thought it might be good for walking Jasper in drenching rain.

A stack of books on antiques and a brand-new set of grilling tools for Joe, and I was ready to pay close to a hundred dollars for my haul. If no one else showed up, Ruth might still do all right from her friends alone. But I didn't have to worry. Soon there was a steady flow of people throughout the house, and we were kept busy, bringing more items out to replenish the tables, sometimes pricing on the fly.

Almost everything in the study was for sale. I stood by and monitored the transaction as Stanley's gorgeous desk was negotiated until I was satisfied Ruth got a reasonable price. As Angus helped the buyer take the desk out to his truck, Ruth grabbed my arm in delight.

"A thousand dollars, Daisy! Can you believe it?"

"It's worth it. It's real mahogany."

Other buyers were admiring the souvenirs from the Bornsteins' trips abroad: a silk kimono, a lovely humidor from one of their visits to Paris, some tribal artifacts.

A few hours later, Ruth and I ended up in the kitchen at the same time for a much-needed break and a cup of coffee. Stuff had been flying out of the house. We'd lucked out with the weather, which had stayed sunny and dry. Ruth had priced everything well and she seemed to have no qualms about haggling to move merchandise. The study was practically empty now, and the tables outside were surrounded by eager buyers.

"I must say, you're being very practical about this whole deal," I said.

"Don't have much of a choice, do I?" Ruth gave me a wry smile. "But you know, Daisy, it's cathartic. It feels *so* good to be doing something. I felt like I had no control over my life for the longest time." She ran a finger over the edge of a nearby photo frame. "Plus, I can't complain. There are people who have been left far worse off than me, with absolutely nothing. I let my emotions rule my head. It's my own stupid fault."

I stared at her in admiration. I'd always thought of Ruth as this perfectly manicured, perfectly cosseted woman who had no more pressing worries than where to make the next dinner reservation or who should be on the guest list for her next soiree. She was handling this far better than I ever would have imagined.

I walked outside to see Serrano inspecting a pair of skis, and Eleanor eyeing Serrano.

"What's up, Eleanor?" I deliberately stood in front of her.

She craned her neck and smiled her cat smile at me. "Just admiring the view." Serrano bent to pick up another ski, his faded jeans a perfect fit.

Eleanor made a sound that could have been mistaken for a deep purr. "You know that book that talks about a thousand things to do before you die? *That* man is top of the bucket list. And after all, who could possibly deny a dying woman her last wish?"

I sucked in a breath. "Wait a minute. What are you saying? Are you *dying*?"

"No." Eleanor crinkled her nose. "But I might use that line. Worked on you, didn't it?"

I leaned across the cashbox and gave her a playful shove.

"Find a man your own *era*, never mind your own age," Martha hissed from her position behind a neighboring table.

I wandered over to Serrano. "What are you doing here, Detective?" He didn't exactly strike me as the yard sale type.

"I had a few more questions for Ruth." He eyed the skis in his hand. "And then I saw these."

"Ha! Bitten by the yard sale bug!" I didn't want to get too personal, but Serrano was a well-built guy, and Stanley had been much slighter and shorter. "Um, are you sure they'll fit you?"

"I'm thinking they'd be good for my nephew. I'm heading to New York for Thanksgiving. Perhaps he and I can hit the slopes together over the holidays."

He'd never talked about his family much, and I greedily stored away this morsel of information.

He set the skis against Martha's table and picked up one of the hardcover books. "My brother is into history. Anyone know anything about these?"

Debby Millerton came over to us, her eyes shining.

"Well, Detective, it just so happens that we have a librarian in our midst," Martha said, winking at me.

I saw Debby's cheeks flush, and my heart ached for her. Serrano was the stereotypical unavailable male. Not only that, but I knew he had a dark past. How dark, I wasn't quite sure, but he was a big challenge for any woman. I'd never seen him check out any of the attractive single females in town. In fact, he seemed to spend most of his time avoiding them, holding himself in his usual tight control.

Although there was a glimpse of a smile now on his face as he looked at Debby. He was unfailingly courteous, but I wondered what went on in that shadowed psyche.

* * *

Around four o'clock, Martha declared the sale was over, so we boxed up what was left, folded the tables, and stacked them against the side of the house. Darkness was falling as we traipsed inside, satisfied that Ruth would live to fight another day.

Serrano was sitting at the long kitchen table with Ruth. She looked tired, but peaceful.

"Ah. Bliss. To finally sit down. It's the simple pleasures in life." Eleanor stretched her arms over her head.

"Hey, Serrano, any news on the investigation into Alex Roos?" I asked.

"I've interviewed the women who dated our victim, and anyone else who had any contact with him. The funny thing was that all he wanted to talk about was the history of Millbury, not how he could get them into bed."

Martha sniffed. "That's very well and good, but what, may I ask, are you doing about finding my dear Cyril?"

"We've checked out his salvage yard and his known whereabouts on the day of the murder, but there's no sign of him or his truck. I've issued a BOLO for the vehicle. What else can we do?"

She heaved a sigh of exasperation. "Organize a manhunt—get the dogs out—call the FBI. I don't know. Do *something*!"

Serrano shot me a helpless look.

"Martha, I think the police are doing everything they can. Come on. I'll walk you out, Detective."

He gathered his skis and books with alacrity.

"We found Edward Flint's car," he said in a low voice once we were safely standing on the gravel outside.

I glanced at him in surprise. *Unsolicited information, eh?*

"At a shopping center under construction. No sign of him, but if he met up with the same guys that found our friend the photographer, let's just say he's part of the parking lot by now."

"Ew."

"Apparently he was using contributions from later investors in his fund to pay off the earlier ones and so didn't rouse suspicion until now. I'm going to do a little digging to see who else invested with this same guy."

I nodded, my mind in a whirl. "Do you suppose the death of the photographer had anything to do with Flint's disappearance? Had Alex found out what he was up to and confronted him?"

Serrano shrugged. "Sheer speculation. But I *can* tell you that one of the bar patrons recalled seeing Beau Cassell's truck heading away from the pub just before 6 p.m. on the night of the funeral. It stopped to pick up Alex Roos on the road. It was dark so they couldn't see who was driving, but they think it was a tall guy. I'm bringing Cassell in for questioning, and we'll test the truck for forensic evidence." A hint of a smile appeared on his face. "I think we've got our man."

I flashed back on the huge tool chest in the pickup bed. It would certainly be big enough to hide a man's body.

But then I remembered seeing Cassell walking up the driveway to Ruth's house. "Sorry, Serrano, but I distinctly saw him here right around that time, and he was driving his Mercedes, not a truck. I remember the egotistical license plate—*A1-BLDR*."

How ironic was it that I was providing the obnoxious builder with a great alibi?

Serrano sighed and shifted the skis in his grasp. "Daisy, I know you've been upset with me, thinking I'm being tight-lipped and keeping you out of the loop. The thing is, I *have*. I really don't want you involved in this one."

"But I feel like Cyril needs me and—"

"Look, I don't mean to be brutal, and I would never say

this in front of Martha, but the odds are that Cyril didn't make it."

I swallowed against the acid in the back of my throat, knowing there was a chance he might be right, but resenting him for saying it.

"I gotta tell you, I wouldn't hold out much hope. But if he *is* still alive, he obviously feels the situation is dangerous enough to stay underground. You should, too." Serrano's voice rose. "I'm serious, Daisy, this might be some heavy shit. I know how you like to barge in on everything . . ."

I took a deep breath, half-annoyed and half-ready to try to convince him I had an important part to play, when he leaned the skis against his leg and took hold of my hands. Suddenly all I could feel was the electrifying, thought-stopping warmth zinging between our fingers.

"Daisy, I care about you." He squeezed my hands briefly. "Do me a favor. Please. Let me handle this one alone."

He swept up his purchases, stalked down the driveway to his car, and threw them into the backseat.

I stood there watching as the taillights of the Challenger sped away, finally remembering to breathe, my heart racing as if I'd swum the length of an Olympic-size pool underwater.

Chapter Thirteen

I walked back inside to the exhausted but exhilarated group lounging around Ruth's kitchen table.

"What a day! I'm starving!" Eleanor announced. She was busy straightening a massive stack of dollar bills so that they faced the same way.

Martha rolled her eyes. "Imagine my shock and surprise."

"Actually, I'm feeling a little hungry myself," Ruth said.

Annie nodded, rubbing a smudge on the stainless steel table with the arm of her crocheted sweater. "Mm. Me, too."

Martha swept over to the fridge. "Say no more, people. Leave it to me."

I smiled at Eleanor, reading the same pleasure in her eyes as we watched Martha bustle around, pulling out various covered dishes onto the counter.

"Ruth, we'll need to do a final tally, but I'd say you made well over seven thousand dollars today." Eleanor smoothed the last bill on top of the stack.

Debby clapped her hands. "Really? How on earth did we make so much?"

I sat next to Eleanor on one of the Swedish design chairs. "There were some big-ticket items in the mix. Stanley's desk, lots of other furniture, the artifacts."

"I can't believe it," Ruth said. "Thank you all so much for your help. It will certainly keep me going for a while." A shadow crossed her face. "Oh, but I should really give this money to the Historical Society to make up for losing—"

"No," Eleanor said firmly. "You need it to live. The society will regroup to fight another day."

I nodded. "The real money will come from your artwork and the rare books. Let's see how that goes first, and then we can talk. In the meantime, you need the wherewithal to hold on to this house until it's sold."

Martha was rummaging around in the vegetable drawer when she suddenly let out a loud gasp.

"What is it, Martha?" I wondered if she'd cut herself on something.

She turned to us, a smile spreading across her face, holding up a handful of rolls of undeveloped film.

"Hey, that's the same kind of film that Alex used!" I jumped to my feet and rushed over to inspect the find. "Wow. I bet it's the photos from the calendar shoot."

"Apparently, Ms. Bornstein, you are not a very healthy eater and you never go in your vegetable drawer." Eleanor smirked at Ruth, who grinned sheepishly.

"But that's fantastic! There's still a chance to finish the calendar as long as we can raise the money for the printing," Annie said. "We just need to find another Mr. March."

Debby bounced in her seat. "What a stroke of luck!"

Martha's lip quivered. "How can you all even consider replacing Cyril?"

We sobered up and exchanged glances.

"Of course not; it's out of the question," Ruth said. "What were we thinking?"

"On that note, I need a damn drink. Ruth, where do you keep your wine? Never mind, I see it." Martha marched over to the baker's rack and extracted a bottle of cabernet sauvignon. "You don't mind, do you?"

Ruth shook her head meekly as Martha opened the wine and set out a bunch of balloon glasses.

Eleanor rolled her eyes at me. "Yikes, look out."

"Oh, let her have some fun," I said. Both Ruth and Martha were doing what they had to do to survive. "But just club soda for me. I'm driving."

Martha poured five healthy portions, which drained the bottle, and threw it into the recycle container with a crash.

"I can't wait to see how these photos turn out." Eleanor took a sip of her wine, and her eyes lit in appreciation. Stanley was not only an enthusiastic gourmet cook, but an avid wine connoisseur. "Tell you what, I never realized what a nice ass the butcher had hidden under that apron. Or, dare I say it, the postman, probably from walking up all those hills in snow, rain, heat, and gloom of night."

As if on cue, a crash of thunder sounded outside, and the wind jangled the hanging chimes out in the garden. Soon we heard the drumming of heavy rain on the roof.

"Where did you find Alex Roos, anyway, Ruth?" I found an open bottle of club soda in the door of the fridge and poured myself a glass.

"Actually he approached *me* in the first place. Said he'd heard about the calendar project and that he'd been wanting to visit this area anyway. He even offered to pay his own ticket to come from California and work for a cut-rate price. It seemed like a gift from heaven at the time."

I sliced a piece of lemon into my soda. "Don't you think that's a bit odd?"

"Poor Alex." Debby set her wineglass down, her bottom lip trembling. Her eyes looked suspiciously bright.

"Okay, look, let's change the subject," I said. "How's your book coming along, Debby?" She had been writing a romance novel in her spare time for the past five years, and I was pretty sure Serrano was her muse. Although Alex Roos may have provided some inspiration, too.

Eleanor took another bottle of wine out of the rack. "Yes, when are you going to let us read your chef d'oeuvre?"

Debby blushed. "Not sure I will ever be brave enough to let anyone do that."

"Her shay what?" Martha frowned at Eleanor as she chopped up some salad greens. "For Pete's sake, speak English, woman."

"She means her masterpiece," I said.

Debby laughed. "It's just a little romance."

"Everyone needs a little romance in her life sometimes. Oh, and by the way, Eleanor, I'm giving you a ride home. There's no way you're riding your Vespa in the rain, especially after a glass of wine. Or two."

"Or three. Aye, aye, cap'n."

Martha waved her chef's knife in the air. "I love romance novels. I can't read those highfalutin literary books. Give me an enjoyable story that takes me away and doesn't give me nightmares. God knows, real life is scary enough."

"Speaking of romance, Sarah and Peter are coming home next week." My daughter had fallen in love with a film producer who sounded like he might be The One. Joe and I really liked Peter and hoped this relationship might last longer than the usual six-month time span of Sarah's affairs. "Hey, I have a great idea! Why don't you all come for Thanksgiving dinner?"

"Aw, thanks, I'd love to," Debby said, "but I'm going to my sister's."

Annie shook her head. "Sorry, but I'm with family, too."

"How about the rest of you?" I looked at my single friends. Ruth, who lost her husband and her boyfriend in the space of a few days. Eleanor, who lost her beau at the end of the Vietnam War and never quite got over it. I hoped that one day she would give love another chance. And, of course, there was Martha, despondent over Cyril and doubly upset by the gossip saying he was tired of her controlling ways and that's why he had disappeared.

"Sounds like a party," Eleanor said, splashing more wine into her glass. "I'm there."

The rain that lashed down all evening had turned to treacherous ice overnight, and Joe drove carefully down Main Street toward the community church on Sunday morning. The roads had been barely salted, and the church parking lot was not much better.

Martha met us as we walked up to the front doors. The familiar brightness was back in her eyes, and an excited pink warmed her freckled cheeks. Working on the estate sale had done her a world of good.

"Daisy, I've decided I'm going to help out at the soup kitchen this week, and on Thanksgiving morning, too, cooking for those poor, starving people. Don't worry, I'll still come to your dinner, but I think this will help keep my mind off my troubles."

"That's a fantastic idea, Martha. Good for you." I gave her a big hug.

Thinking of the soup kitchen reminded me of the community garden at Glory Farm, where a group from our congregation grew produce to donate to food programs for the hungry. Beau Cassell would put an end to that, too.

Again, it made no sense that Althea would support Cassell, and then donate her needlework class earnings to the volunteers who worked the land he wanted to take away.

Eleanor joined us a few moments later, just as Frank and Nancy Fowler were walking up the steps.

"Back again, Eleanor?" I grinned at her.

"I'm only here for the entertainment, er, I mean, the singing."

Nancy missed her footing slightly on the slippery stones, and Frank caught her elbow to steady her.

"Did you hear the news?" Dottie Brown came bustling over to us. "Althea Gunn was the victim of a hit-and-run while walking along Sheepville Pike on Saturday night."

"Oh my God, is she dead?" I said.

"She's alive, but barely."

A chill ran down my spine, especially as I had recently been reflecting how fragile life was. "Any witnesses?"

Frank Fowler paused and glanced in our direction, his face visibly paling at the news, until an insistent call from his wife summoned him into the church.

"What was Althea doing walking along that road in the dark?" Joe asked. "Was it just an accident or did someone deliberately try to run her over?"

Dottie shrugged. "She was at a church meeting earlier in the evening, but that's all I know. She's in a coma, so she can't be questioned."

Martha frowned. She took her role as Information Central in Millbury quite seriously, and lately Dottie had been intruding on her turf.

"I can think of plenty of reasons for Beau Cassell to be a victim," Eleanor said, "but why Althea? Yes, she was bossy and intimidating"—and here she looked over at Martha—"but so are some other people."

"And she gave a lot to charity, *and* she was a good teacher." I'd seen from the sampler class that the women respected her. They might not like her, but I didn't think anyone hated her enough to try to kill her. "It must have been an accident."

"Well, she'll be missed at church, seeing as she's the lead bell ringer," Dottie said.

Eleanor smirked. "Never send to know for whom the bell tolls; it tolls for thee."

"Knock it off, Eleanor." Martha gave her a shove. "I don't know, it's like the wrong people are getting hurt or killed lately. What the heck is going on?"

"There's bad luck hitting this village." The talkative little man from the Cassell development was suddenly at my side. "I'm writing to the paper about that road where Althea Gunn was hit. There're no streetlights, and there've been lots of accidents. Disgraceful. The township should do something."

"And why didn't the driver stop?" I wondered. "Perhaps it was someone driving drunk, or someone with a suspended license."

"Or someone who was up to no good." The old man winked at us.

A woman who was even shorter than him came up and gripped his arm. "Maybe it was *someone* who should give up driving because he can't *see* properly anymore and refuses to go to the optician to get his eyesight checked?"

"Ah, woman, leave me be." He struggled against her grasp. "You're always nagging." He winked at us again. "I haven't talked to my wife in three weeks. I didn't want to interrupt her. Bada-bing!"

She marched him up the steps into the church and they disappeared inside, but we could still hear the sounds of her berating him echo around the hallowed space.

"See, that kind of behavior is why I'm glad I'm still single," Eleanor said.

"Oh, but I loved being married." Martha's eyes filled with tears.

Joe cleared his throat. "I expect the police will look for paint chips from the car at the scene," he said quickly, with

a worried look at Martha. "You know, some of those for-
eign makes would be a dead giveaway. Glass from headlights can often help, too." He loved to tinker with old cars,
which was a good thing, considering that our Subaru had
almost two hundred thousand miles on it.

After the service, where Eleanor miraculously behaved
herself this time, we headed outside again. Perhaps it
wasn't such a miracle, but rather that she was slightly hungover from the amount of wine consumed at Ruth's.

Suddenly there was a yell behind us, and I watched in
horrified slow motion as Grace Vreeland slipped on the top
step and came crashing down the whole flight, landing
with a thud on the ice at the bottom.

I hurried over to her. "Oh, God, Grace, are you okay?"

Grace moaned. "My ankle. I think it's broken."

I reached down to try to help her into a sitting position,
but she waved a frantic hand. "Don't move me. Aargh."

Martha was already on her cell phone calling 911. Joe
ripped off his coat and slid it under Grace to protect her
from the cold as much as he could without jostling her.

"The ambulance is on its way," he said.

She moaned, and I knelt beside her. "I was going to go
and look after Althea's cat today," she whispered, grimacing
in pain. "But I won't be able to go anywhere for a while.
Could you do it for me?"

I eagerly agreed. None of us had ever been inside Althea's
house. "Do you have the keys?"

"No. Strange, isn't it? Seeing as we are cousins and all.
But there you are."

I gasped. "Wait, you're Althea's *cousin*?"

My face must mirror every thought in my head. In spite
of her agony, Grace gave me a wry smile. "It's family, Daisy.

You don't get to choose. I know Althea's an odd one, but she's my only living relative. I'm stuck with her."

"But how were you going to get in to feed the cat?"

"I was going to ask the police to give me the keys out of her bag at the hospital." She gritted her teeth against the pain. "I also wanted to pick up some of her personal items to make her feel more comfortable there while she recovers."

I quickly scrambled for a pen and scrap of paper in my bag and wrote down the list of items Grace dictated to me until we heard the whine of a siren.

"Don't worry about a thing," I said. "I'll take care of it."

As the ambulance men loaded poor Grace into the vehicle, I saw the Fowlers slide into a black sports car and speed away.

I called Serrano and explained what had happened and that I needed to check on Althea's cat. He agreed to get hold of the keys and said he'd meet me there in an hour.

Althea lived in a Federal-style house that was about two hundred years old. It sat right on Grist Mill Road, just past the church, at the last bend before the intersection with Main Street in Millbury. Again, I wondered why she hadn't been rooting for the Historical Society to win Glory Farm. Anyone who lived in a house this old must have a real love for architecture and a respect for the past in order to be able to stomach the upkeep. A ladder was propped up against one wall. I'd bet anything that Althea had been cleaning out her gutters and I shuddered at the thought.

Serrano zoomed up a minute later and opened the front door. We walked into a formal parlor that held one armchair with a lace antimacassar over its back. Next to it was a simple gateleg table holding a black leather Bible, but nothing else. Then into a stenciled living room with Prussian blue–painted woodwork and a nonworking fireplace, where everything was also fanatically spare and neat. The only hint at décor was the samplers hanging on every wall.

The bulging horsehair sofa wasn't exactly made for comfort, but the gigantic orange cat lounging in the middle of it didn't seem to mind. He purred at the sight of us. A very loud, throbbing purr.

Serrano laughed. "Hey, buddy. You haven't missed too many meals, have you?"

The cat jumped down from the sofa with a thud and wound his way around our ankles.

I smiled as I bent to scratch his ears. As formidable as Althea was with people, she'd obviously adored and spoiled her pet. The purring increased threefold, and Serrano chuckled again.

"You're a funny guy." While he took his turn at petting the friendly feline, I took a peek at the nearest sampler. Even though the verse was old in style, I recognized Althea's expert needlework and spotted her stitched signature in the bottom right-hand corner.

Give me a house that will never decay
For this is where I lost my way
Confessed not my sins or troubled mind
Instead made haste away

A man convinced against his will
Is of the same opinion still
E'er you remark another's sin
Bid your own conscience look within

In the House of the Lord this day
Let us build a new foundation
The guilty will see the error of their ways
Bring upon themselves swift destruction

I shook my head. *Jeez, Althea.* Why was all her work so grim? I wondered what had happened in her life to give her such a dour outlook, until I remembered she'd worked for Cassell for years. That ought to do it for anyone.

Serrano and I wandered into the kitchen, and I fed the cat and put down fresh water. There was a litter box in the powder room that looked relatively clean.

He took out his cell. "I gotta call Animal Control and get this guy picked up and into foster care."

"Please, can't you leave him here?" I begged. "I'll look after him. I could come every day and feed him."

"Sorry, Daisy, no can do."

"Look, he's an old cat," I said, scrambling for the right words. "It would stress him to no end to take him out of his environment. He'd be much happier here in his own home. You let me take care of Cyril's cat, didn't you?"

"That's different. Besides, I don't think you'd be able to resist the urge to snoop around this poor woman's house. Why do you think I met you here, instead of sending one of my officers?"

I resisted the urge to stick my tongue out at him.

"We need to make sure he's safe until the old girl comes out of the hospital." Serrano brushed some orange fur off his pants. "If she ever does," he finished darkly. "It's not looking too good right now." He jerked his head toward the stairs. "Go get her stuff, and let's move."

The master bedroom was barely the largest of the three modestly sized rooms upstairs. In the way of old houses of this period, there were no walk-in closets, only a narrow one-door affair that held a meager handful of clothes. It wasn't hard to find the robe that Grace had described, and I folded it into the shopping bag I'd brought, wrinkling my nose at the sickly sweet smell of mothballs.

On the bed was an immaculately white matelassé coverlet, and there was another Bible on the bedside table.

There was a small fireplace in this bedroom, too, with the same grayish blue–painted trim on the mantel, as well as on the windows and doors.

I wandered over to the opposite wall to admire an antique sampler with a tree of life design and quirky folk art animals. There was even a rooster in the branches of the tree! From the faded condition of the threads, I knew it was genuinely old, not one of Althea's recent creations.

Son of God thy blessing grant
Still supply my ev'ry want
Tree of Life thy influence shed
With thy sap my spirit feed

Tend'rest branch alas am I
Wither without thee and die
Weak as helpless infancy
O confirm my soul in thee

All my hopes on thee depend
Love me save me to the end
Give me the continuing grace
Take the everlasting praise

Another had a series of names stitched into panels. I remembered Althea saying in class that one very interesting type of nineteenth-century sampler was the family record. The best had pillars on each side, an arch across the top, and were decorated by garlands of flowers.

This must be Althea's family. I traced the names inscribed with my finger. A little bell rang in the back of my mind, but for the life of me I couldn't figure it out.

"Come on, Daisy, let's go!" came the impatient call from downstairs.

On impulse, I snapped a photo of the sampler with my

cell phone and tossed the rest of the requested items to take to the hospital into my bag: Althea's Bible, some toiletries, and her pillow. I hurried back down the stairs. Grace had asked me to bring an unfinished sampler that was in the living room, too. I thought this might be a bit ambitious seeing as Althea was in a coma, and who knew how long it would be until she could tackle something like this again, but I dutifully packed up the embroidery hoop.

We walked back onto the street, and Serrano locked the front door. I stared up at the bedroom window, that little bell clanging again in the back of my mind.

Suddenly I remembered where I'd seen a sampler like the one in her bedroom. I thrust the bag into Serrano's arms. "Got to go, Detective. Talk to you later."

I jumped in my car and tore off, leaving Serrano standing on Grist Mill Road with a bemused expression on his face. I knew exactly where I was headed.

The one-room schoolhouse that served as the Historical Society's headquarters.

Chapter Fourteen

Now that I was a member, I had my own key, and I opened the door with shaking fingers. Along the left wall sat a row of the original student desks. In the center was a long table where the society held meetings and where we displayed informational brochures for the public. Portraits of some of the founding members of the society lined the opposite wall.

I hurried toward the back of the room where, amid yellowing maps and various black-and-white framed photographs of Millbury from a hundred years ago, a few samplers hung on the wall. I wondered if these were the ones that had come from Glory Farm. Of course I'd noticed them before, but with more of an antiques shop owner's eye for the overall pleasing quality rather than studying them in detail.

One was a family record, very similar to the one in Althea's bedroom, but it was much larger in size and more extensive in scope. In some of these small communities, there were only a handful of families who originally owned all the land, and I could clearly see the branch for the Gunn family.

I yanked out my cell phone, opened the photo, and began comparing the names. In the quiet of the room, which at one time must have resounded with children's laughter and chatter, I went back and forth. From present day back to the past, one by one, until the names suddenly stopped on the society's sampler.

What the heck? I leaned closer to the sampler on the wall until my nose was about two inches away from it. Upon careful inspection I saw where the top corner was re-darned, and if I wasn't mistaken, it was with a difficult darning stitch that Althea had shown PJ.

I zoomed the picture on my phone as large as I could go and continued up the tree until I gasped as one name jumped out at me. Otto Gunther. A famous ruthless slave catcher mentioned in Rufus Banks's diary.

Althea's ancestor.

I sank onto the tiny wooden seat of one of the desks, my legs weak. I traced the scarred surface with my fingers, my mind in a whirl. The family must have shortened their name from Gunther to Gunn at some point, hoping to erase the past. The sampler in her house was so beautiful that she couldn't bear to get rid of it, in spite of the damning tale it told.

Okay, think about this carefully, Daisy, before you jump to any conclusions.

Serrano had said that Roos was asking all kinds of questions about the history of Millbury. Was this the story he was working on? If he planned to reveal her shameful family record, I knew now why Althea would have had reason to kill him.

My heart raced faster. *She* was the one who stole Cassell's truck that night and picked up the photographer as he walked along Sheepville Pike. Althea would know where the keys to the vehicles were kept from years working as the builder's secretary. Probably in the construction trailer, and heck, she might even still have a door key. Althea was a tall woman, and she wore a man's trilby hat. The witness could have easily mistaken her for a male driver in the dark.

Maybe she picked up Roos just to talk to him, to try to convince him to change course, much the same as I'd done with Cassell. But when he refused, she panicked and killed him to keep him from exposing the truth. She tied a spare bell rope around him to drag him up the stairs into the attic.

Not only could old samplers tell tales about the past, but in this case, they provided clues to the present story.

I called Serrano, bursting with my news, but he was in his cold, distracted zone again and said it was merely circumstantial. Besides, he didn't see how an elderly woman could drag a full-grown man into an attic.

"You should have seen her move that trestle table at church!" I practically yelled. "And she's a *bell ringer.* They're in the process of replacing the ropes at the church with new ones. Serrano, it all fits! I'm convinced Althea is the killer."

Abruptly he said he had to go and hung up.

However, instead of being irritated, I smiled to myself. Let him run around, wasting his time. I'd sit back and wait for him to see that I was right.

Yet again.

Thanksgiving was fast approaching, and I had my hands full readying the house for Sarah and Peter's arrival, plus the busy days at the store. I'd broken the news to Joe

right after the estate sale about our expanded list of dinner
guests, hoping he wouldn't mind, but he was delighted. He
suggested inviting Angus and PJ, too, and we'd made it an
even ten by inviting Mary Willis, the lovely widow who'd
sold me so many wonderful linens. I hated to think of her
being alone at the holidays.

Joe had spent every night since then poring over cookbooks and planning his menu.

I called Martha. "Why don't you stay with us for Thanksgiving? Don't just come for dinner. Sarah and Peter will be
here, and it would be fun. The store will be closed on Friday,
and you can hang out for the whole weekend if you want."

She readily agreed. "I can help Joe with preparing the
meal, too. I'll be done at the soup kitchen by noon, and I'll
head right over."

I didn't ask Eleanor to stay, as I knew she would prefer
to be in her own bed. Eleanor was a lone wolf who valued
her privacy, but Martha hated being by herself.

With Sarah, plans were always fluid until she actually
showed up, but she arrived on schedule on Wednesday
night, together with her boyfriend, Peter. Eleanor stopped
over after work, eager to see my daughter, and we assembled in the kitchen, chatting excitedly about the latest film
that had just wrapped in Spain and exclaiming over the
gifts Sarah had brought for us. Sarah told Eleanor how
she'd refused to go to a bullfight, and Eleanor nodded
approvingly. My daughter and Eleanor had worked together
on many of the same film sets and they always enjoyed
swapping old war stories.

"I'm so happy you're here for the holidays, darling. You,
too, Peter." I smiled at the dark-haired gorgeous young
man at my kitchen table. I'm sure he had his faults, but I'd
never seen Sarah so happy, and for that, I adored him.

"Thanks for having me," he said with a smile. Joe handed
him a beer, and the two men clinked bottles.

"Oh, I love Thanksgiving. It's my favorite!" Sarah exclaimed. "Are you making your special stuffing, Mom?"

I glanced at Joe, and he hid a smile. I didn't want to tell her it was doctored Stove Top, to which I usually added some cranberries, celery, and chopped pecans.

"No, um, actually Dad is making the traditional version this time with celery, carrots, onions, sage, and browned sausage."

"Want to see the menu?" Joe had a shy smile on his face.

"Of course, Daddy, but I already know it's going to be *awesome*."

"Martha's making the desserts," he said, "but the rest is on me."

He handed her a sheet of paper in a festive orange design that would be displayed on a stand in the study during cocktail hour.

Joe and Daisy's Thanksgiving Menu

APPETIZERS

Parmesan Cheese Straws

Antipasto Platter

Pâté de Campagne with Cornichons and Crackers

STARTER

Margarita Lime–Grilled Shrimp Cocktail

DINNER

Roast Turkey with Bourbon Maple Glaze

Sausage, Chestnut, and Sage Dressing

*Butternut Squash–Cheddar Gratin
with Rosemary Bread Crumbs*

Mashed Potatoes and Sweet Potatoes

Roasted Balsamic Cipollini Onions
Green Beans Amandine, Sweet Corn, and Brussels Sprouts
Cranberry Sauce
Turkey Gravy
Buttermilk Biscuits

DESSERT

Pumpkin Cheesecake
Fig Pecan Pie
Chocolate Mousse

"Yowza," Sarah said. "How many people are coming to this shindig?"

"Leftovers are the best." Eleanor sipped her martini. "Don't worry about it, kid."

Martha arrived as promised the next day, around one o'clock. Joe had been up early that morning, preparing the dishes that could be made ahead of time. Martha rolled up her sleeves, and I offered to help, too, but Joe was one of those people who liked to have room to maneuver in the kitchen, and one extra body was enough.

I took myself off to the dining room and unwrapped my Limoges dinner service. At each plate I set a mini pumpkin as a placeholder, with the guest's name lettered on the side. Along the middle of the table I'd created a rustic arrangement of bittersweet branches wrapped around white pumpkins, sitting on a bed of pinecones and oak leaves with votive candles staggered in between.

I was happily polishing the silverware and about to set out my best wineglasses when I heard the sound of raised voices coming from the kitchen. I tossed my towel onto the table and hurried toward the commotion.

"Oh, I always stuff *my* turkey," Martha was saying. "That's the *only* way to do it."

Joe exhaled. "Well, I like to cook the dressing on the side in a casserole dish. Not just for safety reasons, but I think the turkey cooks more evenly that way."

Martha sniffed. "I'm telling you, it tastes so much better with the juices from the bird."

Joe shoved a pile of cut up onions, celery, parsley, and thyme into the body cavity with such vigor, it was a good job the poor fowl couldn't feel a thing. He threw the neck, liver, and gizzards into a pan where butter was already sizzling. "*This* juice will add flavor. Trust me."

She peered over his shoulder. "I always cover my turkey with a wet buttered cheesecloth, too. Do you have a cheesecloth here, Joe? If not, I can always run home and get one. There's no need to baste, and it cooks perfectly."

I winced. One of Joe's favorite parts of the operation was basting the turkey. My husband, who was normally so even-keeled that nothing could rock him, was looking a little flushed.

"Hey, Martha, how about a glass of champagne?" I suggested. "And I could use your help in the dining room, if you have a minute."

I'd never seen Joe open a bottle so fast.

Martha and I finished setting up the dining room, and then I enticed her into a game of cards in the living room. Eleanor showed up an hour later, and together with Sarah and Peter, we switched to Pokeno, one of my favorite vintage games, sort of a cross between poker and bingo. While we played for stacks of pennies, the enticing aroma of roasting turkey wafted through the house. Jasper enthusiastically huffed the air, almost choking on his own drool and alternating between keeping an eye on the kitchen and fixing me with a pleading stare.

"You're a dog," I told him as I shuffled the cards. "Dog food is good for you. Not turkey."

"Oh, and I suppose fatty cheese and large quantities of chardonnay are good for you," Eleanor said.

Sarah snickered.

I leaned down to pet him, and Jasper gave a little jump up and kissed me on the mouth.

"Ew, Mom, how do you know he didn't just lick his privates?"

Eleanor roared as I wiped my lips.

"His mouth is cleaner than yours, in more ways than one, young lady."

PJ was the next to arrive. "I brought a bone for the dog, too," she said gruffly as she handed me a bouquet of yellow chrysanthemums, orange roses, sunflowers, and eucalyptus.

I hugged her. "Thank you for the beautiful flowers, and the bone is a fantastic idea. It'll keep him busy while we eat dinner and stop him from bothering the guests."

Jasper danced around so hard, he almost fell over backward. PJ laughed.

"Go ahead," I said, "you can give it to him now if you'd like. Be his best friend."

As the dinner hour drew closer, we moved to the study for drinks and appetizers. Martha opted for more champagne, Eleanor had her usual vodka martini—shaken, not stirred—and Peter opened a bottle of Washington State chardonnay for the rest of us.

Sarah flicked her long blond hair over one shoulder and munched on a cheese straw. "How come you didn't invite Patsy and Claire, Mom?"

"They're spending the holiday with Patsy's sister and her family."

Joe popped his head into the study, holding a potato

masher. "Anyone want to work out their aggressions on the mashed potatoes?"

Martha jumped up and whipped it out of his hand before anyone else could even open their mouths. "I'll do it. I'll need butter, milk, sour cream, and plenty of pepper," she ordered as she marched out of the room.

Eleanor, Sarah, and Peter followed with alacrity. They'd been in the film business long enough to know when a pivotal scene was coming up, and they were eager to see how it would play out.

PJ nodded toward the doorway. "So what's the deal with Eleanor?"

"What do you mean?" I spread a dab of pâté on a cracker.

"Why didn't she ever marry? She's a successful businesswoman, she's a lot of fun, and she still looks great for her age. I mean, she's a little *different* and everything, but you know . . ."

I exhaled. It wasn't my place to reveal Eleanor's secret pain. Her fiancé had been killed in combat right at the end of the Vietnam conflict, and somehow she'd never quite recovered, not even after all these years.

How to explain to a twentysomething that life's twists and turns sometimes took you on a path not of your own choosing? How the option of getting married might seem like such a given at that age, but it wasn't always so easy.

"Sometimes it's hard to find the right one," I said carefully. "Joe and I are very lucky, but it's not always such a smooth path for everyone."

The rest of the guest list—Angus, Ruth, and Mary Willis—arrived within minutes of one another, and I scurried to take coats and fill drink orders. Angus, ever kind, had given both ladies a ride in this snowy weather. Soon the house was full of the sounds of laughter, chatter, and the clink of toasts being made all around.

"Where's the rest of the gang?" Angus asked.

"In the kitchen," I said. "Come on, let's go check out our own version of *Iron Chef*."

"Stop her before it's mashed potato soup," Eleanor murmured to me as we entered the room. I gently took the bowl from Martha's hands.

Joe had brought the turkey out of the oven to rest, and we all oohed and aahed at the golden brown skin.

"You can never have too much gravy," Martha declared as she moved over to the drippings pan. She added some stock and began to stir up all the tasty bits into bubbling brown delight.

I slipped my arms around Joe, and he looked down at me with a rueful smile. "Just surrender to the inevitable," I whispered. "I love you."

Peter asked how he could help, and I directed him to open the bottles of Beaujolais nouveau and pinot noir in the dining room. Everyone else took a dish and carried it in, and soon the old table was groaning under the weight of the feast.

The moment everyone was seated, Joe said a prayer. I silently gave my own prayer of thanks for the glorious sight of my family and friends gathered together in our home. I wished that Cyril could have been here, but wherever he was, I sent a fervent message out to whoever was listening up above to keep him safe and warm.

As we said amen, the lights suddenly flickered and went out. The only illumination came from the votives flickering among the white pumpkins.

"Joe, did we blow a fuse?" I gasped.

"It's circuit breakers now," he reminded me, "and no, I don't think so." He glanced toward the window. "Looks like the whole street is out. The weight of the snow and ice must have brought down some power lines."

"Don't worry, everyone, I have more candles." I pulled

a bunch of candlesticks out of the drawer on the sideboard, and soon the room was filled with a magical glow.

"Thank goodness the dinner was cooked first," Joe said. "Let's have a toast. Happy Thanksgiving, everyone!"

"I think we should toast the chef, too," Martha said. "Outstanding job, Joe."

Amid the chorus of agreement and praise, I smiled at my husband and raised my glass in a loving salute.

We began passing dishes around, and I didn't have to ask anyone twice to dig in. Angus piled his food so high, it was touch-and-go if it would stay on the plate, and Eleanor's meal wasn't much smaller.

"Did you ever have this butternut squash casserole before?" Angus asked her.

"No, but I'll try anything twice."

"Daddy, you might need to open some more champagne," Sarah said as she took hold of her boyfriend's hand. "Peter and I have an announcement to make. We're getting married!"

Tears sprung into my eyes, and in the hubbub that followed, I managed to hug both Sarah and Peter before I was enveloped in Martha's arms and thumped on the back by Angus.

"This is the perfect romantic atmosphere, with all these candles," Sarah exclaimed. "We couldn't have planned it better."

"Speaking of planning, did you set a date yet? Where are you going to have the wedding?"

Jeez, there was so much to prepare. I'd need to nail Sarah down on a date soon. She wouldn't realize that these things could take months, a year, to plan, let alone trying to book a church and a venue.

"Mom! Just enjoy the moment, okay?" She smiled at me. "Don't start making yourself crazy yet."

I nodded even as I was forming a guest list in my mind. Joe's mom had passed away a few years back, but his dad would come, if we could drag him away from fishing off the Florida Keys. My parents, of course, would make the trip for a wedding, even though they weren't good at traveling anymore. And our friends from Millbury . . .

Sarah nudged me, and I chuckled. She knew me too well. "Okay, okay. I'll worry about it later."

While we ate, we took turns at bringing Sarah and Peter up to date on recent events. Jasper sprawled across PJ's feet under the table and never left her side for the whole meal, ever hopeful for tidbits that I strongly suspected she slid to him every now and then.

"It's amazing that such a quiet little village has so much drama and violence going on," Peter said as he sipped his pinot noir.

"Ain't it just?" Angus took another buttermilk biscuit out of the basket and stuck it in his pool of gravy. If Eleanor had been counting on leftovers, she hadn't counted on Angus's mountain-man appetite.

I told them about the neighbor in the Cassell development seeing a flash from the window of the vacant house, and said perhaps Roos was taking photos of someone across the street.

"Or maybe there was a tryst going on *inside*, and he was doing erotic shots of Sally McIntire?" Eleanor suggested.

But Sarah, who was an avid photographer, threw cold water on that theory. "At night he wouldn't have used a flash, but a big aperture on low speed."

"Did you ever think that maybe he was signaling for help?" Joe said, his dark eyes solemn.

We looked at each other, and I swallowed some more wine to ease the tightness in my throat. "Well, with all the busybodies in that development, it's a shame that no one answered his plea."

"It's so hard to believe that Althea Gunn is a murderer. She's such a God-fearing woman," Mary Willis said, making the sign of the cross.

"Her evil ancestor made money off people's misery," I said. "That knowledge must have haunted a person like Althea, who was always so worried about appearances."

Eleanor snorted. "She was so busy telling other people how to live, she forgot to figure out the right way for herself."

"So she steals this guy's truck," Peter said, ticking off plot points on his fingers as if going through his latest script treatment, "knowing where the keys were kept in the construction trailer. She picks up the photographer on the road and drives him to the site. Did she somehow get him into the house, and *then* he signaled for help?"

"Seems like a long shot," Joe said. "Don't think I would sit still long enough to be tied up and spray-foamed if I were him."

"Maybe she killed him somewhere else." Eleanor took another helping of Brussels sprouts. "Then she went back and trashed the studio to make it look like a robbery."

"Good God, woman!" Martha said. "Do you have worms or something? That's your third helping tonight!"

"Why don't you just f-f-fade away?"

Sarah grinned at Eleanor. "The Who, right?"

Eleanor nodded as she dished another mound of stuffing onto her plate.

As I looked around the table, I realized we had a lot to be thankful for. Our freedom, our health, one another. "Enough of this sad talk," I said. "Let's have another toast to Peter and Sarah."

Mary shyly raised her glass. "Well, dears, I hope you'll be as happy as me and my Fred. We were together almost forty years before he passed."

"Yeah, the old married couple is something of a rare treasure these days," Angus said, "whether by divorce or, at our age, death." He raised his glass. "Best of luck, kids."

Ruth sighed. "I don't suppose I'll ever have another chance at marriage. I *would* have been a good catch if I hadn't made such a stupid mistake. I'd be a wealthy widow now. You wouldn't believe how many people want nothing to do with me anymore because I can't go out to expensive dinners or invite them to a fancy party."

Sarah raised an eyebrow at me, and we shared one of our rare moments of perfect understanding. "Hey, Mom, I just thought of something. I could take the last model photo for free if we can find another guy. I have all my camera stuff with me."

"Yeah, and I could spring for the costs of the printing." PJ looked up from handing tidbits to Jasper.

"Thank you both, that's a wonderful offer, but let's discuss it later, okay?" I glanced at Martha. The fizz had completely faded from her. I bit my lip, wondering again if I should say something about seeing Cyril in town and the crossword clues. Even though I was pretty sure he was still alive, if he was staying hidden, there must be a very good reason.

No, I decided, I couldn't tell Martha, who had never been able to keep a secret to save her own life.

A fter dinner, we said good-bye to Mary Willis, Ruth, PJ, and Angus, and Joe pressed big bags of leftovers into their hands. The rest of us assembled in the kitchen to help clean up.

Eleanor scraped mashed potatoes into containers and grinned at Peter loading the dishwasher and Joe slicing up the rest of the turkey. "Ah, my fantasy. Two men. One to cook and one to clean."

"Joe, why don't you leave the rest to me?" I said. "You've done more than enough for one day."

He didn't need a second invitation, and he, Sarah, and Peter headed for the living room to watch the game.

"How about a nightcap, girls?" Eleanor looked at me and Martha after we'd put the food away and the kitchen was sparkling clean again.

Martha shook her head. "I'm exhausted. I've been on my feet since 5 a.m."

"I laid out towels for you on the guest bed, and there's an extra comforter in the closet," I said. "Make yourself at home. I won't be far behind." I hugged her. "Good night."

Eleanor and I repaired to the study, and I poured two glasses of port.

"Congratulations again, Daisy," she said. "That's wonderful news about Sarah and Peter."

I grinned. I felt like I'd been doing a lot of that this evening. "It certainly is. I'm glad that Sarah finally gave this relationship a chance." As I put some more logs on the fire, I thought about Ruth and Stanley, Martha and Cyril, me and Joe, Eleanor and her lost love. The couple who fought in that vacant house, and the anger and bitterness they must have felt. Jim and Sally McIntire, and the jealousy over her supposed affairs. Angus getting divorced from Betty after all those years. My daughter and Peter just starting out in their new life together. How hard relationships could be, but how rewarding if one was prepared to put in the effort.

"How about you, Eleanor? Would you ever consider opening up to love again?"

She snorted. "A lot of good it did Martha."

Jasper rested his head on Eleanor's knee, and we were quiet for a few moments as we sipped our drinks and enjoyed the warmth of the flames. The power was still out, but there were so many fireplaces in this house that we should survive the cold night.

"You know, he lives in my dreams, still," Eleanor murmured, startling me out of my reverie. "Sometimes they're so real that I wake up disoriented, and it takes me a while to adjust to the fact that he's gone. The dream world is so much happier than this one."

I sipped my port and just listened. We'd been friends for a long time, but she'd never talked about this before.

"I often have the same dream. We're sitting on a park bench together and I can hear his voice, clear as day. We laugh and talk, and then I look back and he's fading away, until I realize I'm alone on the bench."

Jasper heaved a sigh and she stroked his head. "I want to be a dog in my next life. Humans always live in some abstract notion of the future, or the past, but we don't really enjoy life the way we should. Look at this guy."

He opened his mouth in a wide grin and swished his tail.

"You know what, you're right," I said. "Instead of constantly worrying about what's going to happen, or looking back in longing, we should enjoy this moment, right now. After all, you can't live in two places at once. And Jasper is probably the happiest . . . being I know."

Eleanor grinned. "You were going to say *human* being, weren't you?"

I nodded, but I wasn't about to lose the thread of this particular story. "What did he look like?" I asked softly. "Your beau?"

She smiled wistfully. "Oh, he was beautiful, Daisy. Tall, dark-haired, with a smile that could make me melt. A bit like a younger Serrano, as a matter of fact."

I struggled to find exactly the right words. "You know, Eleanor, you realize that you're in love with the memory of a beautiful young man, but you're comparing him to guys our age, and that's not really fair because they'll always come up short. I mean, Tony Z might have been pretty cute in his day. Heck, he's still cute." I had a soft spot for the little barber, who kept a jar of dog treats for the dogs who passed by his store on Main Street.

"Yeah, but Tony Z *is* short."

"Everyone comes into your life for a reason, Eleanor. Maybe Serrano is playing the part of the prince coming to wake Sleeping Beauty."

Eleanor chewed her lip thoughtfully. "You mean, to make me realize that those feelings still exist, somewhere deep down?"

"Exactly. Sort of like Cyril did for Martha. And in turn, she brought the light back into his life."

"More like a klieg light. The kind that turns night into day on a movie set." She grinned at me, and then her expression turned serious again. "Do you think Cyril's alive, Daisy?"

"I think he may be in real trouble, which is why he's gone underground and can't contact her. Look, promise me you won't repeat this to anyone?"

Eleanor rolled her eyes.

"Okay, okay. I don't know why I said that." If anyone could be trusted to keep a secret, it was the dark horse sitting next to me, so I told her about the crossword clues, and the fact that I thought Cyril had stopped home at one point and then vanished again. "Eleanor, it's eating away at me. I feel like such a heel about keeping this from Martha, but—"

"He's obviously trying to protect her," Eleanor said firmly. She tossed back the last of her port. "That man adores her and he's depending on you to keep her safe. End of story."

I exhaled. "Thanks, E."

After Eleanor left, struggling a little under the weight of her to-go bag, I said good night to the group in the living room and headed up to bed, Jasper at my heels. The electricity suddenly came back on, and the old heating system roared as it powered up again.

As I passed the guest room, I could hear soft sobs inside.

I knocked gently. At a murmured "Come in," I opened the door. Jasper barreled in ahead of me and leapt up onto Martha's bed. He licked the tears from her face until she gave a watery laugh, and then settled himself against the length of her body with a grunt. Martha threw her arm around him. "Oh, Jasper is just the best therapy in the world. What's better than hugging a fuzzy warm animal when you're feeling low?"

I smiled and sat on the edge of the bed next to them. This had been Sarah's old room, until I'd recently redone another one down the hall in a more elegant style for when she came to stay. This one was painted a powder blue, there was a light blue comforter on the bed dotted with white daisies, and some of Sarah's childhood artwork was framed on the walls.

Martha sniffed. "In a way this is worse than when Teddy died. At least I knew what happened to him. The not knowing about Cyril, it's so awful."

I touched her cheek, feeling the trace of a tear that Jasper had missed.

"And I'd gotten used to being alone. I didn't always like it, but I was used to it. On an even keel, as it were. Now I'm all messed up."

The angst about keeping this secret from her ripped away at my heartstrings again. How much of the game could I give away and still protect the end zone?

"You know, Martha, I feel like Cyril is out there, alive, somewhere. I don't know how I know. Sometimes there are feelings that you just can't explain." I kept rambling on, not really knowing what I was saying, but stroking her hair until I felt a sigh escape her. "Don't lose faith, okay?"

"This is nice, Daisy," she said in a sleepy voice. "Thank you." Some of the tension was gone from her face. "I feel so safe here." I hoped she would sleep. She certainly looked exhausted. I tucked the covers around her, like I'd done for Sarah when she was a child.

The next morning, when I woke up, I had to blink at the alarm clock several times. Maybe it was wrong because of the power outage. There was no way it was 10 a.m. I peered at my cell phone and gasped. I threw on my robe and hurried downstairs to find Joe and Martha in the kitchen.

"I can't believe I slept so late," I said as I slid an arm around Joe.

He held a finger to his lips and pointed toward the tiled floor of the pantry, where we kept a dog bed. Our ungainly puppy was curled up in it, and His Nibs was snuggled up in the curve of Jasper's tummy.

"How the heck did he get in here?" I whispered to Joe.

Jasper looked up at the sound of my voice, but didn't get up, merely thumped his tail gently. Usually he was raring to go for his breakfast and walk, but he must have been worn out from the excitement of the day before, plus still full of the treats from PJ. The cat slitted an eye and closed it again. Jasper probably felt like a giant electric blanket.

"I saw the little guy hanging around the yard when I let Jasper out for the last pee of the night," Joe said with a chuckle. "It was snowing like the dickens, and he must have slipped in without me noticing."

"Never mind," I said. "I'm glad he's here."

Martha was busy flipping crepes onto a plate and sprinkling them with vanilla sugar. Sarah and Peter trailed into the kitchen a couple of minutes later, and I sipped my coffee in pleasure. Our huge sprawling house had come alive with all our guests.

After we gorged ourselves on crepes, brandied apricot jam, whipped cream, and toasted pecans, plus fresh fruit and gallons of coffee, Martha announced that she and Sarah were going Black Friday shopping at the Montgomery Mall. "Want to come, Daisy?"

I shuddered. "No, thanks." While I could putter around a flea market for hours, shopping for clothes, especially in a huge shopping center, wasn't really my thing.

Joe leaned back in his chair. "I'm going to put up the Christmas lights with Peter's help." He smiled, obviously relishing the idea of having a new son-in-law to do "guy things" with on holidays.

Every year at this time, there was a grim competition with the neighbor across the street to see who could string them up first.

"We usually hang icicle lights along the edge of the roof between the pillars and greens wrapped with light strands along the top of the fence," Sarah said to Peter.

"And this year, for the front door, I thought I might make a wreath out of wine corks," I said. "We have almost enough left over from last night." Everyone laughed as I nodded toward our recycle container.

But when we went out onto the porch with the battered cardboard boxes we'd retrieved from the basement, the Victorian across from us was already lit up, with every gable, window, door, and stick of picket fence illuminated.

"I don't believe this!" Joe exclaimed. "I thought I might beat him this time. He must have been doing it at midnight, the bastard. Come on, son, we've got to get to work."

Peter grinned at me and downed the rest of his coffee. "I'll get up on the ladder, Joe. You can hand the stuff to me."

"Are you inferring that old people should not get up on ladders?"

Peter's smile grew wider. "Certainly not, sir."

I left them to their male bonding. I fed the cat a can of tuna fish, but when I opened the back door to take Jasper out for a walk, His Nibs slipped out and was gone.

Jasper and I met lots of other people out walking their dogs on this holiday morning, where the snow-covered village seemed to have its faults filled in by the smooth layer of white. Like a celebrity in the glow of a spotlight, with her lines softened and wrinkles washed away.

Eleanor's comment about dogs living in the present echoed in my mind. You only had to watch Jasper diving in the snow, shaking it off, and doing it again to realize that, whereas my mind was already bounding ahead.

When we got home it would take forever to dry him off. I hoped I'd left a stack of old towels in the pantry near the back door and—

I stopped stock-still on the street. I wasn't really present in this beautiful scene, right here, right now. I stared up at the sky that was so bright, it was almost painful to look at, feeling the bite in the air that said more snow was on the way. I made a snowball and threw it for Jasper, laughing as he dove after it. Out of the corner of my eye, I caught a glimpse of a black shadow skipping through front yards, following his own path, but never far behind us.

After I brought Jasper home, I decided to go to Cyril's trailer and pick up food for the cat. If he was going to hang out at our place for the time being, I'd need to keep some of his kibble on hand.

I opened the door warily, but the trailer was quiet and untouched. This time, I wasn't about to leave any stone unturned. I touched the stove, which was cold, and the plant in the corner, which felt a bit dry. I filled the kettle and poured some water into the hanging basket.

There were no new papers in the recycle bin and no food gone from the cabinets. I scooped a few meals' worth of kibble into the plastic bag I'd brought and locked up the trailer again.

How on earth was Cyril coping in this weather without a home? It made me think again of the journey of the slaves to Pennsylvania and what they must have endured. Some without proper clothing or shoes, traveling cold and scared in their desperate bids for freedom.

Why the heck was he still hiding? If Cyril had been reading the local newspapers, Althea's hit-and-run was front-page news. He should know it was safe to come out now.

I couldn't stand the bitter cold for more than a few minutes, even with my gloves and boots, and I couldn't wait to get back in the car and turn on the heat. I set the cat's food on the passenger seat and was about to leave when it occurred to me that I hadn't checked out the back of the salvage yard on my recent visits. I blew on my fingers, got out of the car again, and trudged around behind the trailer, where there was a veritable graveyard of old automobiles.

In the middle was a rusty Ford pickup truck that had sat there as long as I'd known Cyril. In the summer it would become almost completely overgrown with masses of purple morning glories clambering over its roof and through its windows. Now it was a white skeleton, but the classic shape was still recognizable.

I shivered and squinted at the landscape littered with truck caps, grappling hooks, and oil drums, willing my intuition to guide me to the right spot. I'd sat at Cyril's kitchen table and stared out at this view enough times that I should be able to spot something different.

Suddenly the weather vane popped into my mind. Were its arms pointing in a different direction today? I ran back inside the trailer and stood next to it, raising my own arms in the same way, trying to imprint the angle in my mind. I hurried back outside again, and suddenly I saw it. I ran over to a towering pile of tires and sheet metal, peered through a gap, and underneath was Cyril's truck.

Frantically, I pulled away some tires so that I could squeeze through a gap. When I yanked open the driver's door, on the front seat was the old camera I'd given to Alex Roos.

Chapter Fifteen

I picked it up with shaking fingers. I couldn't quite tell in the dim light inside the cab, but it looked like there was a roll of film inside the camera. There was something else on the seat, too, and as I touched it, I realized it was a CD. I didn't know if it was important, but I stuffed it in the pocket of my jacket anyway, slung the camera around my neck, and got out of the truck. I rearranged the tires as best I could around it and hoped that the next snow forecast for tonight would erase any footprints.

Once I was safely back in my car, I cranked up the heat and, with my teeth chattering, drove to Sheepville and the police station. I knew Serrano was in New York with his family for Thanksgiving, but I called his cell anyway and left a message about my discovery. I gave strict instructions to the officer on duty that there might be critical information contained on the film and to get the pictures developed as quickly and carefully as possible.

When I got back in the car, something in my pocket jabbed me in the hip as I fastened my seat belt. I pulled the CD out of my coat pocket. *Van Lear Rose* by Loretta Lynn. As far as I knew, Cyril wasn't a fan of country music. If he listened to music at all, it was usually blues.

Why this one?

I slipped the disc into the player, and country music with garage rock overtones resonated in the car. As Loretta belted out a duet with Jack White about getting drunk on pitchers of sloe gin fizz, I sucked in a breath. Loretta Lynn. *The coal miner's daughter.*

The canary in the mine. Was *bonny castle* also something to do with mining?

I raced back to Millbury, or rather, drove as fast as I could given the condition of the roads. The store was closed today, and after I opened the door, I locked it behind me, not turning on the lights. Before I could switch on my computer, my phone rang.

It was Serrano. "Got your message. We're getting those photos developed as we speak."

"Thanks, and I honestly can't wait to see them, but you didn't have to call me back. You're on vacation, after all."

He grunted. The detective was the type who couldn't ever really relax. He was happiest when he was working. "By the way, Daisy, you can eliminate Jim McIntire from your list of suspects. We brought him in for questioning as to where he was on the night of Roos's murder. He's in the clear. Works a second job as a night security guard. He clocked in and out, plus there's the camera surveillance."

"Poor man," I murmured, remembering Sally's massive diamond ring. "He must be exhausted from working two jobs."

"Yeah, sounds like his wife is an expensive proposition. Oh, and someone matching the description of Flint the finance guy got on a plane to Belize several days after the funeral. We're trying to track him down now. Gotta go. I'll be back in town tomorrow, and I'll come see you then." He was gone before I had a chance to say good-bye.

I turned on the computer and ran a search for "bonny castle." In between the references to towns in Kentucky and Canada, I finally found a Bonny Castle Mine in Cambria County, Pennsylvania. It was shut down now, mainly due to the fact that years ago, there had been a tragic roof collapse. Eight miners were trapped inside, and two of the men died. I stared at the photos of the rescuers with grime-covered faces and resolute expressions standing outside the mine shaft.

I scoured the Web for more stories, reading one newspaper account after another. The owner was fined heavily for repeatedly ignoring safety warnings from his engineer and for pushing the men to keep drilling.

I felt the familiar zing down my spine as I unearthed the next article. "And guess who the attorney was who represented that owner, Alice?"

Alice looked at me, but didn't try to guess.

"Frank Fowler! The plot thickens, eh?"

I kept reading. Stories from long ago about mules, women, and children pulling loads of coal out of the mines. It seemed as though people were expendable, but if a mule died, there was hell to pay. Mules were expensive.

My blood chilled as I came across a photo of a child worker, a packet of chewing tobacco in his top pocket. The pictures of men going into the dark opening of the entrance made a light prickle of sweat break across my forehead. There was no way I could do that job, not for a million dollars. Even the thought of going underground into a long black tunnel was enough to set off a panic attack.

How brave was Cyril to do that kind of work, day after day?

I looked away from the screen and wondered what he

was trying to tell me. And why mention a coal miner's daughter? Did the mine owner have a daughter? I spent the next hour searching, but came up short.

On a whim, I pulled up Nancy Fowler's bio. It was the most generic summary of any politician I'd ever seen, and nothing in any press release said anything about her early years or where she was from.

I called PJ Avery and brought her up to speed.

"Think I'm gonna take a road trip out to Western Pennsylvania to see what I can dig up in person," PJ said. "There's only so much you can find out online."

Outside the windows of Sometimes a Great Notion, large flakes of snow were swirling down. "I don't think you should be going anywhere in this weather, young lady."

There was a long sigh on the other end of the line. "Daisy, you worry too much."

"Look, please be careful," I begged. "And not just with the driving. I haven't figured out what the heck is going on here, but whatever it is, one man is dead, another is missing, and an elderly woman is fighting for her life over at Doylestown Hospital."

I bit my lip as I hung up, wondering if I should have kept my mouth shut. PJ was a lot like me in many ways—barreling ahead on her own agenda, throwing caution to the wind, with scant regard for her own safety.

I locked up the store and walked back to the house. Sarah and Peter were leaving in the morning, and we'd planned on one last special dinner. The snow was quickly accumulating. There was about a two-inch layer on the cars along Main Street already, and it had only been snowing for half an hour. When I got to our house, Joe had come outside to make a start on shoveling the sidewalk.

"Why don't you wait?" I said. "We'll only have to do it again later."

"I know, but this way it won't be so heavy."

Peter came down the front path. "Here, let me do that, Joe," he said as he took the shovel from my husband's hands.

Joe winked at me. "There is *some* benefit to getting old, eh, Daisy?"

I laughed. "I think I'd better take Jasper out now, instead of after dinner."

"Don't go too far. This stuff is coming down fast."

I hurried inside, clipped a leash on the dog, and slipped on the jacket of Stanley's that I'd bought at the estate sale. It was much too big on me, but the way it hung down past my knees meant that I should stay pretty dry. I rolled up the sleeves a little, put on my gloves, flipped up the hood, and headed out into the storm.

The creeping greenery along the fence looked like funnel cake dusted with confectioner's sugar. As we walked down Main Street and headed south on Grist Mill Road, I heard the far-off sound of church bells ringing "O Holy Night."

No footsteps had marred the pristine surface of the road near Glory Farm. Mine and Jasper's would be the first. I stood in the middle where no cars were traveling and the snow made everything still. I caught my breath at the black-and-white wonderland. From the largest bough to the thinnest twig, all had a dusting of snow, outlined in white as if by some meticulous artist.

Again, I knew what Eleanor meant. You didn't have to be in a physical church to experience this overwhelming sense of peace and awe at the beauty of the world.

We turned around and headed for home, the snow falling harder now, and the temperature plummeting with every step. My gloves were getting wet, so I pulled them off and put my chilled hands deep in the pockets of my jacket, searching for warmth.

In the left-hand pocket, my fingers brushed against a piece of paper. Probably an old shopping list or something.

When we reached Main Street, I moved into the shelter of the canopy over the bike shop and pulled it out.

As I read the amorous words on the paper, signed by someone named Anna, I realized with a sinking heart that this was an old love letter to Stanley Bornstein, written to him by someone who was obviously his long-time mistress.

I refolded the paper with fingers that were shaking, and not just from the cold. I exhaled against the ache in my chest at the realization that dear, gentle Stanley was apparently not the guy I thought he was.

The snow floated down like silver glitter in the glow of the streetlamps. The vicious little pricks stung my face, almost itchy against my skin. I wiped at them angrily and hurried the last few hundred yards to our Greek Revival, the candle lights in each window calling me home.

I went around the back of the house and came in through the kitchen door, kicking off my snow-covered boots on the tiled floor and hanging the now hateful coat on the hook next to Jasper's leash. I slipped the paper into the pocket of my jeans and toweled the dog dry.

Sarah and Peter were at the butcher block table, and Joe was at the stove. In between his Christmas decorating, my amazing husband had found time to make one of his specialties: crab cakes with a lobster risotto and snow peas.

"How are the roads outside, Daisy?" he asked.

"It's getting really bad, and I didn't see a salt truck yet."

Joe nodded. "It's snowing quicker than they can plow. They'll wait 'til morning to tackle this one. You young people may have to get a later start than you planned."

Sarah took Peter's hand, her blue eyes sparkling. "We're in no rush."

"Hey, where's Martha?" I asked. "Didn't she want to stay for dinner?"

Sarah grinned. "She's totally exhausted. She shopped until she dropped. Her credit card was howling by the time we were done." She showed me the clothes that Martha had insisted on buying for her. "They're for my trousseau, whatever that is."

I shook my head in wonder. Martha was one of the most generous people I'd ever met, and she treated Sarah like she was her own child.

"How about a toast?" Joe said, holding up a bottle of cabernet he'd retrieved from our wine cellar.

"Daddy, we've done so many toasts recently, I think I might have to go to rehab when I get back to New York!"

"Ah, how often is it that your only daughter gets married? And to such a great son-in-law. Your mother and I couldn't be happier."

Peter smiled, and I found myself in the circle of Joe's arms, where everything was okay again. I pushed the matter of the troublesome note out of my mind for now.

A little black cat wound his way around my legs. "Hey, His Nibs is back!"

"He's the oddest cat I ever met," Peter said. "I've never seen a cat cozy up to a dog that way."

"Ah, but who doesn't love Jasper?" I poured some kibble into a dish and set it next to the dog bowl, and we all laughed at the contrast between the delicate crunching from the cat and Jasper's loud and enthusiastic gobbling as he banged his metal bowl around, scarfing up his food as fast as he could go.

Over dinner, I waited for a lull in the conversation, and then I said, "Sarah and Peter, I want you two to promise me something."

"Yes, Mom?"

"Promise you'll always be honest with each other—" At Sarah's impatient indrawn breath, I held up a hand. "Not only that, but always make time for each other and remember that the relationship is the most important thing in your world. Nothing else matters."

Sarah smiled. "We'll be fine. Don't worry about us."

I thought about the note again, and prayed she was right.

In our bed that night, wrapped in Joe's arms, I thought again about how very lucky I was, but how ephemeral happiness could be.

"Whatcha thinking about, Daisy?"

I sighed and snuggled closer. "I've been thinking about all the broken relationships surrounding us. And now here's our Sarah and Peter starting out fresh. What innocents they are. They have no idea of how much they'll have to face in married life."

"They'll work it out for themselves, Daisy." Joe kissed me as if to break the spiral of my dismal thoughts. "We were much younger than they are now when we got married. Peter has a good head on his shoulders. He'll keep our daughter in line, or die trying."

"Poor boy," I said. "He's got his work cut out for him."

We chuckled, and Joe drew the sheets over our heads. I sank gratefully into his embrace, warming my skin against this body that I knew as well as my own, determined to cherish every single moment.

Late the next morning, the streets were clear enough that Peter and Sarah could leave to go back to New York. We said a tearful good-bye and reassured ourselves that Christmas was not that long to wait before we'd be together again.

As I headed down to the store, I thought about Nancy Fowler's mysterious blank past. I remembered the last time I'd seen the Fowlers at church, and how they were driving Nancy's Porsche in the snow rather than Frank's practical SUV. Why? Because it had some serious front-end damage from a hit-and-run?

I still had about twenty minutes before the store was

due to open, so I decided to drive over to their house to see if I could get a peek at Frank's vehicle.

The Fowlers lived south of Millbury, in a wealthy neighborhood near Ringing Springs Park. When I drove down the street, there was a Dazzle Team cleaning van outside the house. I pulled over to the curb a good distance away from the house, pretending to check messages on my phone.

Suddenly the garage doors opened and the Porsche backed out at high speed, with Nancy driving and Frank in the passenger seat.

I quickly slid down in my seat, but they zoomed off in the opposite direction. I popped up in time to see the doors closing on an empty garage.

Chapter Sixteen

I grabbed my phone, ready to call Serrano, but I was still smarting from his recent curt dismissal of my discoveries. I knew he'd insist on some cold hard facts, so I called Dottie Brown instead. I didn't need much of an excuse to call her. Dottie loved to talk.

"Hey, Dottie, I happened to be driving by the Fowlers' house this morning and saw one of Kathleen's vans. I didn't know that she cleaned for the Fowlers, too."

"Oh, yes, she's got quite the business going, my girl does." Even over the phone, I could hear the pride in her voice.

"That's wonderful. Good for her. She's a real go-getter, just like her mom."

Dottie laughed.

"You know what's funny, though?" I said. "The Fowlers were driving Nancy's Porsche. I'm so glad I have my all-wheel-drive Subaru in this kind of weather. I don't know why they didn't just take his SUV."

"Oh, that's because Frank's car is in the shop," Dottie said. "He's getting the headlight replaced. I think he drove into a pole in a parking garage or something."

"Ah, I see. Well, good talking to you, Dottie. See you soon."

Did Fowler really damage his car banging into a pole, or from running down an elderly woman and leaving the scene of the crime? But why, for the love of God? What on earth could Althea have done to him?

I drove back to Sometimes a Great Notion, still puzzled. I didn't have much time to think about it for the next few hours, though, as droves of customers came in, each searching for the perfect present.

"Oh, I'm already tired of making lists and checking them twice," said one woman, sighing. "And it's not even December yet."

I laughed and helped her find gifts for several of the family members on her list. "Here, try this." I gave her a pot of hand cream from the lavender farm. "It's very relaxing."

She bought a German tape measure with a spring action from the 1920s adorned with a celluloid basket of flowers, and several vintage needle cases and pincushions.

A male customer wandered in next, appearing lost and uncertain, as men often did in my sewing notions store. "I'm looking for a special gift for my wife," he said. "I know she's into sewing, but that's the extent of what I know. I usually buy her jewelry for Christmas, but I'd like to find something different this time."

He seemed drawn to one of the most expensive items in the store, which was a gorgeous nineteenth-century sewing box and writing desk of black ebony wood with a bone inlay. I opened the carved wood lids to show him the many small compartments for writing and sewing notions. It was lined with the original blue silk, and there was an oval mirror inside the top lid. It even had the original key.

"This one might be a little expensive," I murmured.

He took a look at the price tag and shrugged. "Cheaper than diamonds. Wrap it up. I'll take it."

"It's truly a magnificent piece. I'm sure she's going to love it." I took my time wrapping it so it was ready to gift, finishing the package with my signature peacock-blue grosgrain ribbon. He seemed as happy with the fact that he didn't have to wrap it as he was with the purchase itself.

At this rate, I'd need to hit some estate sales and auctions soon. My usual wealth of stock upstairs was almost depleted. I could see that the other shops in town were doing a good business, too, judging by the bags I saw customers carrying from the chocolatier and gourmet pantry.

Serrano strode in about half an hour before closing time. "Here, I brought you an early Christmas present."

He slapped an envelope on the counter. I eagerly opened it and pulled out a stack of glossy black-and-white photos that were obviously from Cyril's modeling shoot.

I'd been right that the rustic setting would be a great fit. Cyril was standing behind a stack of painted shutters, wiry arms crossed, his long gray hair contrasting with the dark shadows and shafts of sunlight coming through a gap in the side of the barn. Alex Roos had used the vintage camera to perfection, doing justice to Cyril's tough personality and the rugged face that had weathered a hard life, yet was still striking and sexy in its own way.

Tears pricked my eyes as I looked into my old friend's face, seeing the familiar belligerent expression. I pretended to study the photos some more, willing the tears to recede before I looked up at Serrano.

"He looks fantastic," I murmured.

Serrano gestured to the stack. "There's more. Keep going."

I flipped through more photos. It was obvious that rebels Alex and Cyril had broken into the house at some point, because there were shots of the interior. Oddly, there were also photos of the land, the outbuildings, the root cellar, and a close-up of a sampler on the wall. It was a tree of life design, again with a rooster in the tree, just like the one that Althea had in her bedroom.

I peered closer at the photo, moving over to stand under the glow of the lamp on the Welsh dresser. "Hey, wait a minute, this *is* Althea's house. Alex must have climbed her ladder and shot the photo through her window with a long-range lens."

"Strange for a guy to be interested in antique needle-work samplers, ain't it?" Serrano's comment echoed the thought in my head. "I've saved the best for last."

I moved the photo of the sampler to the back of the pile and gasped as I saw the last few shots.

Even though their faces weren't clear, I was sure that the couple locked in a passionate embrace inside a home under construction was Sally McIntire and Beau Cassell. The next photo was even more graphic, with Sally's face clearly shown as she threw her head back in ecstasy, Cassell standing between her legs. The last one was Beau Cassell looking directly at the camera, his face dark with anger.

"Holy smokes," I whispered. He looked like he wanted to kill whoever was on the other side of the lens.

Serrano pointed a finger at me like he was cocking a gun.

Then reality hit me. "Ew. A new construction site is not a very comfortable place to carry on like that. All that sawdust and nails. All those splinters! *Jeez.*"

"Daisy, focus, please. Haven't I been saying all along that this guy is my numero uno? By the way, forensics showed that Roos's body was in the tool chest of Cassell's truck at some point."

"I knew it!"

"And after the hit-and-run, I brought Cassell in for questioning again. One of his construction trucks had some front end damage. He blew a gasket, claiming he was being victimized and that his vehicles were parked inside the enclosure that night. But then he admitted that the guys are sometimes careless and leave keys in the trucks."

Serrano's lip curled as he looked at the photos of the tryst with Sally McIntire.

"Then he went off on a rant about how his useless little foreman has a lot to answer for. Neighborhood kids often climb over the fence and mess with the equipment and steal his materials. Maybe one of them took a truck out joyriding."

"Are there any witnesses to the accident?"

He shook his head. "No, and Althea Gunn is still in a coma and can't help."

I told him about the Fowlers driving the Porsche in the snow and Frank's story about hitting something in a parking garage. To my surprise, Serrano didn't scoff like he usually did, but said he would check out the local body shops.

After he left, I closed up Sometimes a Great Notion. The note that I'd found in Stanley's jacket was stuffed in my pocketbook. I'd wrestled with how to handle this all day, but I'd finally decided that it might make Ruth feel better if she knew she wasn't the only one who had cheated. It might relieve some of the guilt that was weighing on her and give her some peace.

I called Joe to say I had a quick stop to make and drove over to Ruth's house. Even before I got to the front door, I sensed something different about the place. Like the vacant property at Cassell's development, this one gave off a gloomy vibe now, with the darkened carriage house, newspapers piling up on the driveway, and the steps that hadn't been swept free of snow since Kathleen wasn't coming to clean anymore.

I hadn't called Ruth to tell her I was coming, not knowing how to approach the delicate matter over the phone. I had to ring the bell a few times before she finally appeared.

She actually looked a bit more like her old self, with her makeup done and dressed in her elegant clothes.

"Daisy! What are you doing here?"

"Oh, I—er—just came to see how you're doing. And there's something I wanted to show you."

She opened the front door a crack to let me in. Even standing in the foyer, the house looked bare. Many of the paintings were gone from the walls, and the living room was completely cleaned out from what I could see. She must have shipped the rest of the furniture off to Backstead's for an auction. Apparently once Ruth had made up her mind to leave, she wasn't wasting a minute.

"I'll be glad to get out of here, Daisy. The place is already listed with the Realtor. There's nothing but sad memories in it for me now. I'm looking forward to starting fresh in the city. Who knows, maybe I'll meet someone new."

We were still in the foyer, and she made no move to invite me further into the house.

"Yes, maybe." I shifted uncomfortably and swallowed. "Look, Ruth, I really don't know how to tell you this, so I'll just jump right in. Last night, when I put on the rain jacket that I bought at the estate sale, the one that belonged to Stanley, I found this in the pocket." I fished the note out of my bag and handed it to her.

She scanned it quickly, her mouth thinning as she read.

"Why did you show me this, Daisy?" Her voice was very quiet. "Are you deliberately trying to hurt me?"

"No!" I gasped. "Of course not. I just thought it might make you feel better to know that you're not the only one who—um—cheated." My voice trailed off as I realized I'd made a terrible mistake.

"Well, I wish you'd never said anything." Her beautifully made-up face twisted into an ugly snarl. "You know, I used to hate myself for being so weak with my feelings for Edward. I would lie in bed at night, wishing Stanley would have died in a car accident or something, anything, rather than being stuck with this shell of who he was. He wasn't the man I married, but I still had to care for him, whether I wanted to or not."

I sucked in a breath and backed toward the door.

Ruth ripped the note into tiny bits and threw them at me. "How *dare* you? Why the hell do you have to be such a busybody all the time?" Her eyes were full of angry tears. "In spite of my own faults, I still wanted to believe that Stanley was a good and honorable man. *Thank you*, Daisy Buchanan, for shattering the last decent memory I had of him. Now get out. I never want to see you again."

As I stumbled out of the house, tears filling my own eyes, I damned myself over and over. Ruth was right. What on earth gave me the right to be such a self-righteous ass? I got back in my car and drove down the driveway too fast, desperate to get away, sucking in a breath as I fishtailed a bit out onto the main road.

The snowflakes were getting bigger now and splattering against the windshield in clumps instead of the pinpricks they were before. I wiped the tears off my cheeks as I drove, a sick ache in my heart.

Now I wondered if I should have told Martha that Cyril was still alive. Did I really have the right to keep this from her? Who the hell did I think I was? I had another awful thought as I realized how pissed off Martha would be at me when she finally found out, but then I remembered the most important part, about keeping her safe.

Still, it was as if I was damned if I said something and damned if I didn't.

I had just reached Millbury, turning onto Main Street, when I blinked at an approaching apparition. I pulled the Subaru over to the side and stopped, watching in wonder as two white horses pulling an antique sleigh walked slowly up the deserted, snow-covered street.

Even with the car windows rolled up, I could still hear the dulcet tones of Tony Zappata as he serenaded Eleanor in his beautiful tenor. Not with one of his usual operatic arias, though. If I wasn't mistaken, it was the Partridge Family's "I Think I Love You."

As the sleigh passed me by, resplendent in its dark green paint with gold pinstriping and crushed red velvet interior, Eleanor raised her champagne glass to me and winked. I glimpsed a cannoli in Tony's hand as he blasted his love to the sky.

I chuckled. Maybe my meddling wasn't *all* bad.

On Sunday, Patsy called. "Yo, Daisy, I found another house that I think is great, and I put in an offer. Claire really likes it, too. Even Angus approves, and you know what a pain he's been about this whole thing."

"That's wonderful. I'm so happy for you."

"I wanted you to see it, Daisy, but it was such a rush job, because other people were bidding on it."

"Oh, I understand, and I'm sorry I haven't helped you more on the house hunt. The store has been crazy lately with the Christmas rush."

"No prob. But I was calling to see if you might have time on Monday morning before the store opens? We're doing the home inspection at 9 a.m."

"Absolutely. I'd love to see it."

"Claire's school is closed that day for the Thanksgiving break, and I was going to have her stay with my sister, but she tortured me until I agreed to let her come. So I'd love your eagle eyes on the place, but perhaps you could keep an eye on Claire, too? Daisy, this is the biggest purchase I'll probably ever make in my life. I want to make sure I do it right."

"I know what you mean, and don't worry, I'll keep her

occupied while you talk to the home inspector. Text me the address and I'll meet you there."

As requested, on Monday morning, I drove to the address Patsy had provided. It wasn't the grand country mansion of Claire's painting, but it was a pretty Victorian duplex on a side street just off Hemlock Lane, not far from where Martha lived. It was set a good distance back from the road, and I glimpsed a nice backyard with a tire swing hanging off a majestic oak tree.

Angus pulled up right after me. "This one's got good bones, don't it, Daisy?" he yelled as he got out of the truck.

"Well, I'm interested to see the interior, but yes, it looks like it has a lot of possibilities."

He nodded. "A house is like a woman. You can tell right off the bat whether you want to put up with her crap or not. As long as she looks good underneath all the froufrou when she wakes up in the morning, you've got yourself a winner."

I shook my head at him. "You're such a guy."

Patsy and Claire arrived next, followed by the home inspector and the real estate agent.

Claire rushed up to me and gave me her usual enthusiastic hug, which I returned and savored for as long as I could.

"Is this a duplex, Pats?" I asked.

"Yeah, that's why it's such a great investment. The price is a bit of a stretch, but there's already a tenant whose rent will pay more than half the mortgage."

"What a great idea. Let's go take a look."

As we walked up to the house with the agent, I heard Patsy murmur to her, "If someone died here, for God's sake, don't tell Claire."

"No, it's okay, I think they went to a senior community because they needed a one-level home."

While everyone else started in the basement, Claire dragged me upstairs to a bedroom that was painted a pale

lilac. Her favorite color. Even though it wasn't the grand
place of her dreams, I could see she was already sold.

"Look at this!" I said. "It doesn't even need painting,
does it?"

She grinned at me. "I know, Daisy, isn't it so cool? But I
told Mommy I would help her paint the other rooms."

The bedroom was a good size, set at the back of the
house with two huge windows, one with a window seat that
looked out over the yard and the oak tree with the tire swing.

"I think I'm going to put my dollhouse in this corner."
Claire made a circle with her arms in the corner next to the
window seat.

"Perfect." I stared at it and remembered all the work
Cyril and I had done on the Victorian dollhouse only a
month ago. Actually, he'd done most of it, painstakingly
gluing on the tiny wooden shingles, one by one, restoring
the floors, and attaching new balustrades and gingerbread
trim. My heart ached all over again.

"Mommy said you and Uncle Cyril spoiled me with the
dollhouse," she said, slipping a hand into mine.

"Ah, how could anyone ever spoil you enough?"

"Do you think he's ever going to come home?"

I sucked in a breath and held her hand tighter. I didn't
have it in me to lie to a child, but I didn't want to upset her
either. "I truly hope so, Claire. I know that he loves all of us
very much, and if there's a way, I'm sure he'll figure it out."

She sat on the floor and pulled a little book out of her
pocket. "I'm keeping a diary of our house hunting adventure."

I smiled at her. "I have a good feeling that this story is
going to have a happy ending."

"Can you keep a secret, Daisy?"

I laid a hand on my heart. "My dear Claire, I am the
soul of discretion."

She giggled. "Well, I was watching this show on TV
about money management and how you need to make goals

for yourself. You need to plan ahead. So I made a five-year plan for me and my mom. Some of it has already come true."

She showed me the diary. One of the goals was for her mom to quit the diner. There was a big red check mark next to that item.

Next up was to find a house and to have a housewarming party.

"Guess you might be able to check those two off the list soon, as long as everything goes well with the inspection today. I'll have a chat with Martha about the party. Shouldn't be a problem. What's next?"

Claire flipped the page, and there were already two items planned for next year. First was to get a dog, and then to find a husband for her mom. I chuckled at the requirements that any suitor would have to fill. *Must like cheese pizza, but not with any toppings. Must like to read. Must love animals. Must have a nice car.*

It went on and on, but then there was a list of possible matches. Given that Claire and her mother lived in a sleepy little village like Millbury, it was not that long. Two of the candidates caught my eye: Serrano and Chris Paxson, who owned the bicycle store.

"How come Detective Serrano has a question mark after his name?"

Claire pondered it thoughtfully for a minute and then shook her head. "He's very nice, but I don't think it would work out."

"Can I ask why you think that?" I held my breath. Could a nine-year-old really give me an insight into the dark, complex creature that none of the women in our village had been able to figure out thus far?

"He's very bossy, and so is my mom. I think they'd fight all the time."

I laughed out loud.

"Plus I just don't see why he can't go to the grocery store himself."

"Whatever do you mean?"

Claire sighed and closed her diary. "He stops over *all* the time because he's forgotten to buy tea bags, or he needs a roll of paper towels, or jeez, one time he even asked her for shampoo!"

Patsy and Claire lived at Quarry Ridge, which was the same development as Serrano. And from my experience with the anal detective, he never forgot a thing.

Interesting.

Although I didn't think he was Patsy's type. She'd certainly never oohed and aahed over him like the rest of the village's female population.

I bit my lip to stop from smiling. "What's so wrong about asking for shampoo?"

"Oh, Daisy," she said, as if explaining to a four-year-old, "girls and boys use *totally* different kinds. Besides, the boys I know wouldn't even care about shampoo."

I had to admit she was right. If there was none available in our shower, Joe would just lather up with the bar of soap.

"Plus, I think that Chris Paxson might want to impress his new girlfriend, so he'd give her *adorable* daughter a really nice bike." She gave me an impish grin.

Even as I shook my head, I felt a pang at how quickly she would pass this sweet stage of innocence. Too soon would come the disappointments, the hurts, the heartache. I wished I could keep her this way always, full of fun and hope for the future.

"You little wheeler and dealer!" I arched an eyebrow at her, and she giggled. "Come on, why don't you show me the rest of the house?"

As we walked around the second floor, I could see what Angus meant about good bones. Some of the house was a bit dated, true, and there was certainly plenty of wallpaper to strip away, but it was obvious it had been well-maintained. The changes Patsy would have to make were mostly cosmetic. I sighed in satisfaction.

We met up with the rest of the gang in the kitchen.

"I'm not a fan of these cabinets," Patsy said. "Daisy, what do you think?"

They were oak, and not in a contemporary style, but plentiful and still in good condition. I opened up one. "The important thing is that they're well-made. Solid wood inside instead of that pressed board stuff. You can always reface them, or just paint the doors, which is a relatively cheap fix."

"You can help me with things like that, right?" she said to me and Angus. "And with moving?"

I nudged Angus. "Hey, Angus, isn't there some kind of rule that you don't have to help people move house once you turn fifty?"

Patsy snorted with laughter. "Don't be spoilsports, youse guys! Besides, there won't be much. All we have is our clothes, our beds, and a couple of dressers. We probably don't even need a moving van. It can all fit in the back of your pickup, Angus."

"Don't forget my art easel, and my desk, and my toys," Claire piped up. "And my dollhouse."

Angus ruffled her hair. "Sounds like we're gonna need another truck, missy."

Chapter Seventeen

There was another zoning meeting scheduled for Thursday night, but when I woke up that morning, a freezing rain had formed a crisp, hard crust over the snow. Angus's words echoed in my brain about contentious motions being pushed through on inclement days with poor attendance, and I resolved to spend as much time as I could between customers at the store to make some calls and try to ensure a good turnout.

Jasper and I walked down slippery Main Street, where it didn't take long before I was chilled to the bone in the rain that was still coming down.

"Stop pulling, Jasper," I said sharply, as he tugged me toward the next tree and I skidded on the glassy surface of the sidewalk.

My wet gloves were proving worse than useless in keeping my hands warm. I slipped the leash around my wrist, peeled off the sodden wool and blew on my close-to-frostbitten fingers. I wasn't really paying attention when Jasper made another lunge.

I landed on my behind with an excruciating thump. "Aargh! You silly dog!" I yelled. I lay there for a minute, gasping in agony while he stood over me, his tongue hanging out, panting. The scene outside the church when Grace Vreeland had broken her ankle on the ice flashed into my mind. I couldn't afford to be out of commission at this time of the year. I had way too much to do.

As the frigid wet seeped into my jeans, I realized I'd better try to get up. I rolled painfully to my knees and eventually to my feet. Jasper looked up at me with an anxious look on his face as I huffed and puffed and limped home, but he walked obediently now at my side.

Joe had already left the house early, off to sell another consignment of his handmade rocking chairs to Jeanne's Dollhouses and Miniatures in Sheepville.

I got showered and dressed with difficulty, wishing he was still home, but when I got to Sometimes a Great Notion, I saw that he'd already cleaned the slush off the sidewalk and put down some pet-safe ice melt. *Thank you, my darling.* I thanked the heavens again for blessing me with such a man. I swiped my boots on the heavy-duty mat inside the entrance to the store, hobbled over to the counter, and started the coffee brewing.

Thinking about Grace had reminded me of Althea. I wondered if she was still in a coma. I'd heard that Grace was recuperating with her daughter in Florida, and I doubted if anyone from the church had visited our head bell ringer and secretary. I wouldn't bet any money on it.

Even though I was sure Althea was the killer, I resolved to pay her a visit after work and before the zoning meeting. Innocent until proven guilty, as Serrano would say. Perhaps she might feel my presence and it would give her some comfort. It wasn't good enough to show up in church

and pat yourself on the back. It was a person's actions that
spoke louder than words.

*Plus you hope that you can pry some information out of
the poor, defenseless soul if she's awake.*

I glared at my mannequin.

"You know, that kind of snarky comment is quite unbe-
coming, Alice." I turned my back to her and did my best to
drag a box from behind the counter and pull out some
fresh items to display. I was still moaning when Martha
and Eleanor came in, although I did cheer up at the sight of
a foil-covered platter in Martha's hands.

Eleanor shivered. "Mother Nature needs a boot up her
behind. Just think, we have months left of this crap before
spring."

"What's the matter with you?" Martha asked. "You look
pale."

"My back is killing me. Jasper pulled me down on the
ice this morning," I murmured. "But I yelled at him, and
now I feel so bad. I never yell at him."

"It's okay," Eleanor said. "He won't hold a grudge.
That's why I like dogs better than most people."

"Have one of my millionaire shortbreads, Daisy." Martha peeled back the foil to reveal one of her best creations.
"These treats will cure what ails you."

"Oh, wow, these are my favorite! Thank you, Martha." I
reached for one of the bars of rich shortbread laden with a
layer of caramel and topped with chocolate, but I winced
as the motion pulled at my sore muscles.

"Here, sit down. At least until a customer comes in."
She fussed around, settling me into a chair with a cushion
against my back and bringing me a mug of coffee.

"But I have merchandise to display."

"Eleanor and I can do it. Just tell us where to put everything."

I breathed a sigh of relief as my friends brought down the

last of my stock from upstairs. Eleanor filled a Soap Box
Derby car with some children's alphabet books from the
1940s, a couple of Victorian lace petticoats, and a Rag-
gedy Ann doll. Martha arranged a small primitive armoire,
painted in a sugar-pink wash and filled with dolls' clothes,
next to an old Pepsi cooler. She placed a vintage red
painted coffee grinder and a Dazey butter churn on top of
the cooler.

Together they hung a Rising Sun patchwork quilt from
Lancaster County in the bare space on the wall where
another had just sold. I sat in my chair and folded some
linen tea towels and a pair of hand-embroidered floral silk
curtain panels.

"Everything looks great, guys. Thanks so much." Now
that I'd sucked down some caffeine and gobbled one of the
bars, I did feel a bit more like myself. "So, how was your
date the other night, Eleanor?"

"What's this?" Martha planted her hands on her hips.
"A date? With whom, may I ask?"

I grinned. "Tony Z and Eleanor, sitting in a tree. Actually,
it wasn't a tree, but a very romantic horse-drawn sleigh."

"Really?"

Eleanor shrugged as if it was no big deal, although her
mouth curved in a self-satisfied smile. "As you said, at our
age, what are we waiting for?"

"Did he kiss you good night?" Martha demanded.

"Yes, he did. It was a very good one, as a matter of fact."

I was about to press for more details, but the doorbell
jangled, and I set my coffee down with a sigh, ready to wait
on a customer.

Serrano strode into the store, looking especially dashing
in his weathered black leather jacket and jeans. His eyes lit
up at the sight of the shortbread bars, and if I thought Martha had fussed over me, it was nothing compared to the way
she hovered over the detective.

At this rate, there wouldn't be many treats left for any customers, but I didn't mind. I was more concerned about how I could stash some away for myself.

"Ladies, I missed you," he said.

"The feeling is mutual, Detective," Eleanor murmured.

"So, what's up?" he asked.

Martha heaved a sigh. "Well, there's still no sign of my dear Cyril. Although it's funny; when I was working at the soup kitchen the other day, I could have *sworn* I saw someone who looked exactly like him."

Eleanor and I exchanged glances.

"But it was probably just a hallucination, brought on by so much stress. I must admit I do enjoy helping those poor people, but it will be a blue, blue Christmas this year. Oh, and the gala. I don't suppose I'll be able to attend now. I'm so sorry about all the work you put into fixing the gown for me, Eleanor."

Eleanor licked the caramel out of the side of her shortbread bar. "I could go with you. I could be your date. I have a nice dinner jacket."

"Don't be ridiculous. You're too short. Never mind the wrong sex."

"Ah, yes, but sometimes when sex is wrong, it can be so right." Eleanor winked at Serrano, who cleared his throat.

"I would be honored to take you to the ball, Martha," he offered.

She beamed at him. "Now *that's* more like it. But I wouldn't feel right going with anyone other than my dear Cyril. Thank you for offering, though, Detective. It was very gallant of you. "

I narrowed my eyes as I observed Serrano in action. I thought I was starting to figure him out. He went for the unattainable, like Patsy, who wasn't interested in him, or the safe option, like Eleanor or Martha, knowing that nothing romantic would ever happen.

"Patsy found a house," I said, watching carefully for his reaction.

"Yeah, uh, I heard. I'm going to help with the move."

Martha gasped. "We must plan a celebration for her. Sort of a combo Christmas and housewarming party. I'll take care of everything. I need to surround myself with friends at this sad time in my life."

My phone beeped with a text, and I struggled out of the chair to grab my cell phone off the counter. It was a photo from PJ. I enlarged it to see a scene outside a mine shaft. I recognized the imposing figure standing in the foreground, captioned here as *Randall Willensky, foreman of the Bonny Castle Mine*.

Three seconds later, the phone rang.

"You're never going to believe this." PJ sounded like she'd been living on nothing but coffee and cigarettes for days. "See that photo? It wasn't in the newspapers, or on the Internet. Found a journalist here who had the image in his computer files. There was a bad accident at the local mine, and the foreman was blamed for negligence and run out of town. Did ya recognize the dude?"

"Yes, it's Randy, Beau Cassell's new foreman." I clicked the phone on speaker so everyone could hear. "I read about that mine accident, but I never knew Randy's last name and there were no pictures of him, so I didn't put two and two together."

I quickly told PJ and the trio in my store about my encounters with Randy Willensky outside the zoning meeting and again at the town hall, but as I did, I realized that Beau Cassell had always referred to his foreman as "little." The old man from the development had called him a pip-squeak, too.

"But I've seen Randy up close, and no one would describe him as small. He's not Beau Cassell's foreman after all, is he? But why would Frank Fowler lie about who he is? What the heck is going on?"

Serrano didn't comment, but I could tell he was taking it all in.

"I might have the answer to that," came PJ's rasp. "According to local gossip, the owner of the mine had a real wild child daughter called Mandy who disappeared right after she turned sixteen. I've seen an old photo, and I'd be willing to bet any money it's Nancy Fowler, even though she's changed her name and her hair color. Her criminal record was expunged because she was under eighteen, but it wouldn't contain the kind of details she'd want made public, especially when running for higher office. I'm not just talking *pots* and pans here, if you catch my drift, but some serious shit."

Martha raised her hands in puzzlement. "Pots and pans?"

"You know, grass, weed, reefer, herb," Eleanor explained, although Martha still looked a little confused.

PJ chuckled. "*And* a DUI, shoplifting, you name it, this chick did it all before she was even out of her teens. In a small town like this, people have long memories. Buy 'em a shot and a beer and they remember a lot."

I chewed on my bottom lip. "So Willensky has tracked Nancy down, perhaps to blackmail her about keeping the story quiet? It certainly wouldn't look good for the future governor to be exposed as a former drugged-up alcoholic criminal."

I remembered how protective Frank was of Nancy. *What a magnificent woman she is. I'd do anything to protect her, you know.*

Outside the town hall after the zoning meeting, Randy had been saying to Fowler that he owed him. I'd assumed it was something to do with Cassell and the land, but perhaps it was for extortion payments.

"Oh my God, did Frank try to get rid of his blackmailer, only to run down the wrong person?" I exclaimed. "Althea's very tall for a woman, and she wore a man's hat most of the time. Both Randy and she wore long black down coats. They may have looked the same from the back."

"She was probably a dead ringer for him," Eleanor said.
PJ snickered on the other end of the line.

I tried to keep a straight face as I scolded Eleanor. "That's
very inappropriate. And PJ? Good work. Now come on home.
But drive carefully."

After I hung up, Serrano said he was going to bring Fowler
in for questioning, Eleanor mumbled something about opening her store, and Martha wrapped her coat around herself
and said she had a slew of errands to run. I reminded them
about the meeting that night, and urged them to try to drum
up as much support as possible.

I made as many phone calls as I could between customers, although I reached a lot of answering machines and
voice mail systems.

A couple of hours later, Serrano called. "Yeah, so I
brought Frank Fowler in. It didn't take long to crack him.
He's confessed that he was the one who ran Althea down,
mistaking her for the guy who was blackmailing him and
his wife."

"Ah! So I was right!"

"Daisy, you know, a broken watch is right at least once
a day."

"Jeez, Serrano, give me a little credit. What's going to
happen to Fowler?"

"He's under arrest. Felony hit-and-run, plus attempted
murder, even though he hit the wrong person, the gavoon.
He'd better be praying that Althea Gunn doesn't snuff it. It
doesn't look like the old bird is ever going to wake up, though,
and chances are she'll be brain damaged if she ever does."

"Poor Althea. What about her cat?"

"I stopped by his foster home to see him the other day.
He's as fat and happy as ever."

Seeing as Serrano was on the phone and not standing in
front of me, I didn't have to hide my smile. I'd always known
there was a soft heart under that tough-guy bravado.

"So that solves the question of the hit-and-run, but who killed Roos? Did Frank think Roos had uncovered Nancy's past and was going to blackmail him, too?"

"Who the hell knows, but the Fowlers were at a political event that night after the funeral. They didn't leave until well after midnight, and then a driver took them home, so they're in the clear for that one. Sounds like Fowler's shelled out a fortune to Willensky already. I'd like to bring that son of a bitch in, too, but he's nowhere to be found."

"Was Frank doing favors for Beau Cassell to come up with the money to pay off Willensky? There's another zoning meeting tonight, and I have a suspicion that Fowler is working behind the scenes to help our sleazy builder."

Serrano sighed. A deep sigh. "I was so sure that Cassell was our guy, but he has an alibi. After I saw those pictures, I had a chat with Sally McIntire. Forensics think that the photographer was killed somewhere between 10 p.m. and midnight, at which point Cassell was apparently banging Sally. His prints are all over the tool chest and the truck, but then again, it's his truck.

"And Daisy, there's something else. We managed to get a couple of prints off the rope in the tool chest. They're a match for Althea Gunn. And there was a green woman's sweater in the cab. I still can't figure out how she could have hauled a full-grown man into an attic, though."

"Don't lose hope, Detective. You'll figure it out."

Serrano gave a glum chuckle. "Yeah, just like you, Ms. Buchanan, I never give up."

After work, I closed up the shop and headed over to Doylestown Hospital. I would be cutting it close to get to the zoning meeting in time, but I couldn't wait.

Althea had been moved out of intensive care and was in a private room. As nice as it was, there was still that weird smell that hospitals have, of disinfectant, of food left sitting out on trays, of desperation, sickness, and fear.

I stared down at the patient, who had been a tall, thin woman before, but was now incredibly gaunt, with a gray cast to her skin. She was hooked up to a mass of monitors, and her heartbeat was steady, but I wondered what was going on in that brain, if anything.

I set the vase of flowers I'd brought on the table next to her. There were no other cards or flowers, or any sign that anyone else had been to visit. I sat down at her bedside, and for the next half hour, I talked. I told her that her cat was fine and well–cared for and not to worry about him. I told her about finding the sampler at her house, and that I knew her secret, and it was okay.

Suddenly her eyelids flickered. An expression of abject horror spread across her face.

"Gah! No, tell me it isn't so." She squinted at me, as if trying to block out a horrible vision. "Save me, oh my Lord, save me from the depths of hell!"

"Jeez, Althea, it's me. Daisy Buchanan."

She moaned.

"You're not in the Devil's Kingdom. You're actually in Doylestown Hospital, in rather a nice room."

I rang for the nurse, who rushed in and checked her vital signs. When she was satisfied that Althea was stable, she hurried out again, saying she was going to page the doctor.

"Althea, did you hear any of what I said just now?"

She looked confused, so I decided to take it slowly from the beginning. I had no idea how much time I had before the doctor showed up and asked me to leave, and I knew I was pushing it with a woman who had just awakened from a coma, but this was important.

"I have to ask you some questions. Please think carefully." *Or as much as you can.* "Did you take Beau Cassell's truck the night that Alex Roos was murdered?"

She nodded slowly. "We had to move a piano for the church. Beau let me borrow his truck, but I returned it to the site that night." Her voice was dry and cracked, and I poured her a glass of water, helping her to drink a little.

"Did you pick up Alex Roos on the road outside the pub?"

"Yes, I—ah—I needed to talk to him about something."

"The sampler?" I asked gently.

She looked at me again with fear in her eyes.

"It's all right, Althea. I know your family history. It's okay. You can talk to me."

She sighed. "Roos came here to write a book. The biggest story of his life. One that would have destroyed mine."

She fell silent, and while patience wasn't my strong suit, I waited for her to talk.

"Can I tell you how many nights I've woken up in a cold sweat? All those poor, wretched people that Otto Gunther chased down and brought back to a life of misery? They call to me in the dark, Daisy, begging me to save them, but I *can't.*"

I stared at her. She had always seemed like such a formidable woman. Here, in this hospital bed, I saw the real, vulnerable Althea, who cared deeply about others and had suffered for the sins of her forefathers.

"Roos's ancestor was a slave," she said in a tortured whisper. "He escaped to this area, but was captured and killed. I'm not sure, but it may have been my ancestor who tracked him down. Otto Gunther performed some unspeakable acts, and if he was the one who got to him, I expect he was the one who did the killing. I can't bear to think about it. I'm so ashamed to be related to that monster."

"But Alex Roos didn't look black." Even as I said it, I realized how stupid I sounded. What I'd thought was a permanent tan was probably his natural skin tone.

"This was generations ago, Daisy." Her voice was getting weary, and I glanced at the doorway. No one was coming yet, but I knew I was running out of time.

"So then you had to kill him to stop him from writing the book?"

"No!" She tried to sit up in bed, but fell back against the pillows. "I tried to reason with Alex when I dropped him off at the carriage house, but he was set on telling the story of his family. So I stopped in at the shivah for a few minutes. Then I took the truck back to the construction site, and Grace met me there and gave me a ride home. But I didn't kill him, I swear. You have to believe me!"

"What time did Grace pick you up?"

"I think around 8 p.m."

If Roos was killed at midnight, then she wasn't the culprit. But who was? I'd run out of suspects without alibis. "Why on earth didn't you say something earlier about giving Roos a ride?"

"I didn't want to draw attention to myself and the reason I wanted to talk to him. Also, I'd forgotten the rope that we used to secure the piano. I'd left it in the tool chest, and I was worried that it might incriminate me. That detective is too smart, and you're not too bad yourself." A tear ran down her thin face and slipped onto the pillow. "Oh, Daisy, I've been so ashamed."

"Althea." I gently took her hand. "*You* didn't do anything wrong. You have nothing to be ashamed of. We can't help our histories. All we can do is live in the present and try to make that the best it can be. And you've been wonderful, with your work for the church and your generosity to so many charities. I think it might be time to forgive. Yourself, especially."

I had an inkling that there was another reason she hadn't said anything before. "Were you also worried that Beau had something to do with it?"

She nodded, murmured something about cigar smoke, and then she closed her eyes and apparently fell asleep.

A tapping noise sounded down the corridor, and I turned

to see Grace Vreeland hobbling into the room, a cast on her foot. "Daisy! What are you doing here? I just got back from Florida, and the nurse told me Althea woke up?"

She stared down at her cousin, who was out cold. I stood up so that Grace could take my chair.

"Yes, and she was talking normally. I'm no doctor, but I'd say she's going to be fine."

"Oh, praise the Lord!"

"Grace, I have to ask you something very important. Can you confirm that Althea borrowed Cassell's truck *with* his permission? And that at eight o'clock you gave her a ride home from the construction site after she dropped it off?"

"Yes. I told her I'd give her a ride, but that I'd need to be home in time to watch *Law & Order*. What's this all about?"

"Just wondering if Althea has been protecting Beau Cassell in some way."

"It wouldn't surprise me. She thought the sun shone out of that man. She worked her butt off for him, but he never appreciated it and paid her peanuts. She'd be cooped up in that little trailer, bundled up in that old green sweater every day, freezing to death. I always told her to get another job, but she said she loved her 'career.' Humph. Some career."

Seeing as Grace was Althea's cousin, the story of Gunther the slave catcher was part of her family history, too. I'd hazard a guess that she didn't know about it, but I could save the telling of the tale for another day.

I said good-bye to Grace and hurried down the shiny tile hallway back out to the parking lot. Althea wasn't the killer, I was sure of it now. I called Serrano again as I got into my car.

"I got it all wrong, and you were right." I quickly explained about her having permission to borrow the truck. "I bet it's Beau who killed Roos. I know he has an alibi, but I'm certain it's him."

"So we arrest him on the strength of your gut feeling, do we, Ms. Daisy?"

"If Althea *had* been the killer, she wouldn't have trashed the studio. She wouldn't have wanted to damage property like that, and she's so thrifty, she would have kept the camera equipment, too. There's something missing here."

Serrano cleared his throat. "I gotta go."

I blew out a breath. *Okay, class. One, two, three, eyes on me.* "Did the woman's sweater that you found in the cab of the truck smell of mothballs?"

"Excuse me?"

"The sweater. If it *had* come directly from Althea's house, it would have smelled of mothballs, like the rest of her clothes. I bet she left it in the construction trailer when she retired, in which case, it's had a few years to air out. I think Beau planted it in the truck."

"Daisy—"

"Look, no one expected Althea to wake up," I said, desperately trying to hold his attention. "It's easy to pin everything on someone who can't defend herself. Beau never mentioned about her borrowing the truck because he wanted us to think she stole it, and he also didn't want to draw attention to the time line of when Roos was killed. I bet if you check Althea's house you'll find where he planted the cameras, too."

Serrano laughed. "You need to sign up for the Olympics. There's at least a triple jump in your logic."

I snapped out a good-bye and hung up on him first.

Chapter Eighteen

Outside it had started snowing again. I'd planned to pick up Joe before the meeting, but there wasn't enough time now. I'd be lucky if I made it in time as it was. I called the house, but got the answering machine and had to leave a message.

As I drove out of the hospital parking lot, the tires locked up on the ice, and I shuddered to a stop. I started off again, more carefully this time on the untreated roads.

My knuckles were white as I drove up Sheepville Pike, the windshield wipers making ridges of icy snow at the edges of my field of vision. A salt truck pulled out in front of me, and I followed it the rest of the way into town, hugging its gritty path.

"Thank you," I whispered to the charcoal sky.

When I finally made it to the town hall, I leaned back in my seat and closed my eyes. In spite of the fact that I was already late, I sat there for a minute, waiting for my heart rate to calm down and the shaking in my arms to subside.

Martha and Eleanor hurried up to me as I walked into the meeting.

"Daisy, I was worried about you." Martha enfolded me in her arms.

"I was worried about me, too. It's no fun driving out there tonight."

"Tell me about it," Eleanor said. "I drove with this maniac in the Death Mobile. I'm about ready for a stiff martini, or three."

I looked around the empty room in dismay. "Doesn't look like many people made it, does it?"

Eleanor shook her head, her expression glum.Beau Cassell was already seated at the front, laughing and chatting, and I gritted my teeth at his cocky attitude.

The meeting got underway, minus Frank Fowler. As they went through the usual routine of the agenda, reading the minutes from the last meeting, I whispered to my compadres about my visit with Althea and how now I was sure Cassell was the guilty party, but we still had no real evidence.

"Hey! Isn't that the creepy foreman guy?" Eleanor nudged me and pointed to where a figure in a long black coat was slinking along the back of the room. He surveyed the crowd and then disappeared into the hallway.

"My God, yes! Hold on, I'll be right back." I walked as quickly as I could without drawing too much attention to myself toward the doorway where he'd slipped out. The long hallway was empty. I ran to the end of it and down the next one, but there was no sign of him.

I called Serrano. "Willensky must have shown up tonight to try to collect more money from Fowler, not realizing that Fowler's in prison."

"Daisy, *do not* try to approach this guy. I've got men on the way. I'll be there in seven minutes."

"Hurry up!"

Eleanor appeared at my side. "Where'd he go?" She brushed snowflakes off her hair.

I shook my head. "Disappeared like a rat up a drainpipe. Serrano's on his way, but I don't think he'll get here in time. Willensky will be long gone by then."

"That weasel's not going anywhere," Eleanor said. "At least not in a car. I knew who all the vehicles out in that parking lot belonged to, except for one." She held up a distributor cap.

I grinned at her. "Nice going, E."

We walked back into the room to find a triumphant group of Historical Society members.

"The variance was defeated," Martha proclaimed. "Something about the added load on the sewers. I didn't really understand it all, but the end result is a no-go on the development."

Cassell was red in the face and threatening that this wasn't the end of it to anyone who would listen, but considering that the majority of those in attendance besides the board were society members, no one was paying much attention.

Eleanor bit her lip. "Not so fast with the celebrations, gang. Cassell won't give up this easily. He can still appeal. The war's not over yet."

"Well, we won the battle tonight," I said.

As we were walking out to the parking lot, Serrano strode up to us. "We've got the building surrounded, but there's no sign of Willensky."

I told him about Eleanor putting his car out of commission, and Serrano barked out orders to search the area street by street.

"Hey, wait a minute!" Martha looked around in panic. "Where's *my* car?"

The huge old Lincoln Continental was hard to miss, especially in an almost deserted snow-covered parking lot.

"Damn it," Eleanor said. "Willensky must have hot-wired it to escape."

"Don't worry, ladies, we'll get him." Serrano barked some rapid-fire orders into his cell phone and then turned his attention back to us. "Not only is that car easy to spot, but there aren't many ways to get there from here in these parts. We'll grab him at a roadblock."

He was right. Some areas around Millbury and Sheepville were so heavily wooded or bordered by acres of farmland that we usually had to go the long way around.

Serrano gestured to a hunky police officer. "I can have one of my men drive you home."

"Or we could ride with Daisy?" Martha suggested.

"Come *on*." Eleanor grabbed her hand and dragged her toward the cruiser. "Don't be daft."

After they left, Serrano stood in front of me with his hands on his hips, wearing his sternest expression. "Now, Daisy, you must promise me that you will go straight home and stay out of trouble, okay?"

"Yes, sir."

"Oh, and I heard there're some trees down on River Road. You may want to take Grist Mill instead."

Great. Just what I needed on a night like tonight. An even longer trip to Millbury.

"Are you sure you don't want to leave your car here and we could take you home?"

I toyed with the idea of accepting Serrano's offer of a ride, but Joe and I only had the one vehicle, and I didn't like the idea of being stuck at home with no transportation.

I assured him I'd take it slow, and I called my husband again, but he must have been in the basement, working on his miniatures. He never bothered to answer the phone when he was down there, reasoning that by the time he climbed the steps, whoever was calling would have hung up, anyway. I sighed and pulled out onto Sheepville Pike, heading south and bracing for the challenge.

The snow came straight at the windshield, and I blinked to shake my brain loose from the hypnotic kaleidoscope of white dots. My Subaru might be old, but I blessed the car over and over for the way it trundled reliably over the thick layer of snow, carrying me ever closer to safety. When I got home, I was going to pour myself a stiff vodka, à la Eleanor. Never mind the wine tonight.

I comforted myself with thoughts like this as I counted down the miles. Dreams of a hot bubble bath, preferably one that included Joe, helped to push the fear and anxiety down to a level that allowed me to keep going.

When I passed Ringing Springs Park, I thought of one of my favorite poems by Robert Frost. *The woods are lovely, dark and deep, but I have promises to keep, and miles to go before I sleep.*

Not too many more miles, though, thank God. I recited more of my favorite poems to myself until finally I breathed a sigh of relief at the sight of Glory Farm. A left turn up the road onto Main Street and I would have made it. But as I passed the farm, I saw a familiar figure hurrying from the house to the barn.

Cyril!

Forgetting my resolve to drive carefully, I slammed on the brakes and fishtailed into the driveway. I was determined to bring him home. Enough of this subterfuge, already.

I powered over the drifts, standing on the accelerator to keep the car moving until I reached the barn, where the snow was not as deep on the leeward side from the wind.

I jumped out of the car. "Cyril!" I yelled into the storm. "I know you're there. It's okay to come out now."

Snow tangled in my hair, and I peered into the darkness, about to yell for him again, when suddenly he was in front of me, and I grabbed him, clutching him as if he were an apparition that might disappear at any minute.

"Steady on, lass. Don't get yer knickers in a twist."

I laughed and cried and punched him in the arm all at the same time. "Goddamn it, Cyril, you've had us so worried. Martha's been in absolute mourning ever since you disappeared."

A shadow crossed his face. "I feel terrible about that, I do, but I had no choice. I love that woman more than life itself. I'd never forgive meself if anything bad happened to her on account of me."

"Why the hell have you been hiding out like this?"

He drew me into the barn where there was blessed respite from the driving snow.

"When that devil Willensky showed up at the pub, I ran out the back door, praying I hadn't been seen, but I couldn't be sure. After the accident at Bonny Castle, I was the one who led the effort to make sure he would never set foot in a mine again." Cyril ran his thumbs over his closed eyelids. "Those were some real good lads, Daisy. They didn't deserve to die like that."

I touched his arm, and he blew out a breath.

"He deserved a whipping for the way he pushed those workers, ignoring the danger signs and then lying to cover up the truth. The owner were to blame, too, but Willensky took the brunt of it with the authorities, thanks to the lawyer, Fowler, who threw him under the bus. Randy swore that he was going to kill me and anyone close to me for destroying his life. One night I came home to find my house on fire. I rescued me cat and took off."

Cyril ran a hand across his eyes again.

I swallowed against the tears building in my own. "Well, I guess it was better to put Martha through hell to protect her than because you were *really* dead. And yes, I took care of His Nibs for you. You're welcome."

A tired smile spread across his face. "I knew tha would, Daisy. You were the only one I could trust."

"What about Serrano? Couldn't you have gone to the police?"

Cyril sighed. "Serrano's a good bloke, but he can't be everywhere at once. Willensky were the type to hurt her to get to me."

I looked around the barn. "Is this where you've been hiding out all this time?"

But before he could answer, headlights lit up the driveway, and the unmistakable shape of a massive Lincoln Continental swung up toward the house.

Cyril ran joyfully toward the car even as I screamed, "No!"

Shots rang out, and, dodging bullets, Cyril sprinted back across the farmyard. He grabbed my hand and dragged me away from the open doorway of the barn toward the root cellar set into the side of the slope behind the outbuildings. He pushed me inside and slammed the door behind us. A shot pinged against the ancient wood, and I screamed again. I huddled against Cyril's back in the pitch black, praying that the thick door would hold, but knowing it was a feeble hope.

Memories of facing down another gun in my past threatened to overwhelm me, and in my mind I said goodbye to Joe and Sarah and Jasper while I heaved for breath, clutching the folds of Cyril's jacket, which was the last thing I would probably ever touch.

Suddenly sirens wailed in the distance. Then came the unmistakable sound of a padlock snapping shut. A minute later there was the roar of the Lincoln's powerful engine as Willensky sped away.

A long, dark silence ensued.

Finally Cyril's voice, rich with disgust, broke the spell. "Well, that's just brilliant. I've spent all this time staying out of trouble, and now you've gone and landed us right in it."

I couldn't see him, but I knew he was shaking his scraggy gray head. I dropped my hands from the death grip on his jacket.

"Hey, I only stopped by because I was trying to rescue *you*." My voice quavered a little, but the injustice of his attitude was spurring my heart back into action.

"I were doing fine by meself."

I snorted. "Oh, really? And guess what? Willensky wasn't here for you, anyway. He was after Fowler, looking to blackmail him about Nancy's colorful past."

There was another long silence.

"Well, we're buggered now, anyway. Like mice in a trap."

"Look, this attitude is getting us nowhere, Cyril. At least he didn't kill us."

I started yelling for help, but without much hope that anyone would hear us from within this vault set so deep into the ground and far away from the main road.

"Simmer down, lass. Eventually someone will see yer car parked outside."

The complete absence of light was getting to me. I concentrated on my breathing, but the dreaded sweat was already prickling up my back. With my internal temperature zooming in spite of the cold, I didn't know how long I could take being in this small dark space with a cantankerous old man.

Think, Daisy. As it always did when I was in serious trouble, Serrano's cool, sardonic voice seemed to speak inside my head.

I fished around in my pocketbook, searching for the familiar shape of my cell phone. That would give us some light, plus maybe I could get a message to someone. I groaned as I saw the red signal that the battery was about to die. It didn't look as though there were any reception bars either, but I sent Serrano a text with shaking fingers, telling him to look in the root cellar.

I tried to send a text to Joe, too, but then the phone went dead.

"Oh, God. I tried to tell Serrano we were in here, but I'm not sure the text made it through. And would he know what I meant? Jeez. I didn't even say the root cellar at Glory Farm."

I wanted to cry, but what good would it do? I was also getting light-headed, and the burning urge to jump out of my skin threatened to overwhelm me.

"Cyril, I should tell you that I have a real problem with claustrophobia. I've got to get out of here. Now. I'm not kidding."

I jumped as he grasped my hands in the darkness with his cold, work-roughened ones.

"Calm down. Don't go round the twist now. Breathe, Daisy."

I closed my eyes, even though it didn't matter anyway, and clutched his hands as I blew out one breath after another.

The air was musty with the scent of long-ago stored vegetables and the rising damp through the earthen floor, combined with damp wood. And perhaps Cyril had missed showering for a couple of days.

There was a silence, and then he chuckled. "Aye up. This is a fine kettle of fish, ain't it? This place isn't so bad, although I'm right sick o' carrots and raw potatoes. And the ground's hard, and it's perishing cold at night."

"Did you—did you actually *sleep* in here?" My voice sounded faint.

He sighed. "I was a miner, remember? The dark doesn't scare me. And I knew it were safe. That was the most important thing. Here, come sit on one of these boxes. They'll find us eventually."

"When? That storm is getting so bad outside, it'll cover up my car in no time. It could be days before anyone thinks to look in here."

I felt him shove what felt like a wooden crate against the back of my leg. I sank down onto it, and for the next couple of hours, I filled him in on what had been going on in Millbury while he'd been on the run. About my list of suspects, from Jim McIntire, to Beau Cassell, to Althea Gunn. Even Ruth Bornstein.

I frowned for a second as I remembered my last encounter with Ruth. I still wasn't completely convinced that Stanley had died of natural causes, but I guessed I'd never know now.

Talking to Cyril was helping alleviate the panic, so I kept talking as much as I could. I could hear his breathing next to me, but it was getting shallower and he hadn't said anything in a while. Perhaps he was asleep, but I didn't care. I kept going, talking about Roos's history and the sampler at Althea's house. The voices of long-ago slaves called to me.

Freedom, Daisy, freedom.

Images of the tree of life sampler and also the sketched map I'd drawn of the safe houses on the Underground Railroad floated around in my brain, like pictures superimposed on one another, with the safe houses sitting like ripe fruits on the branches of the tree.

Suddenly I realized that Glory Farm would be in exactly the right geographical position to be the branch with the rooster on it.

Hope surged through me, and I jumped to my feet.

"Cyril, I think this place might have been a stop on the Underground Railroad! I've been doing research on the area for the Historical Society. There's not much documented, but there was a brief mention in Rufus Banks's diary where he hinted that this farm could be a stop on the route. And then there's the rooster in the tree!"

"Who's Rufus Banks when he's at 'ome?" Cyril's voice sounded sleepy. "And what bloody rooster?"

"Never mind. Look, I bet that there's an entrance to a tunnel in here somewhere that leads to the outside world. A lot of these old root cellars followed the stream." Thanks to teaching, my mind was a patchwork coverlet of information. "Help me look for some kind of escape door or hatch."

Now that I was calmer and could think clearly, I also remembered I had a tiny flashlight on the end of my key chain. It didn't take long to find my keys, and as I squeezed it, I grinned at Cyril's craggy face in the dim light.

I flickered it over the front wall of the root cellar where the door was. "That side is just rock all the way, but I think it's earth on this other side behind the shelves."

Wooden shelves behind us were laden with dusty canning jars filled with a bounty of tomato sauce and pickles from a long-ago summer. There were also boxes of rotted potatoes and onions, wicker baskets, and garden tools. I pulled experimentally at the side of the structure. "I don't think it's attached to the wall. If we clear off the shelves, we could move it."

"Don't waste the light," Cyril ordered.

"Don't get cocky with me, mister. I own the keys." But I took his caution to heart, and with a quick flash of light to catch our bearings, we felt for armfuls of glass jars in the dark and carried them off the shelves and set them on the other side of the cellar, bumping into each other occasionally in the cramped space.

This must be what it's like to be blind.

Another flash to make sure they were clear, and then Cyril got on one end and I took the other to move the shelves, swinging back and forth, inch by inch, to slowly zigzag them away from the earth wall.

I held up the key light and we stared at the small door built into the wall that was barely four feet tall and had been completely covered by the junk. There was no handle or lock, so we took turns trying to grip the edges to force it open. I was glad of my gloves. My fingernails would have been ripped to shreds by now.

If you don't get out of here, Daisy, who the hell is going to care about your manicure? The undertaker?

Odd that I was usually the least fussy person on the planet about things like that. Odd what pops into your head when you feel that your time is running out.

"Wish I had a screwdriver or a chisel or summat," Cyril muttered. "What else have you got in that bag?"

"I'm a mom. I've got lots of stuff." I felt around some more, my fingers finally closing on promising object. I turned on the precious light to reveal a silver chatelaine containing a pair of sterling silver scissors.

Cyril held out his hand.

"You can't use this. It's an antique!"

With a muttered oath, he grabbed it, and soon the space was filled with the screech of rusty nails prying loose from their hundred-year-or-more-old resting places. I stood next to him, holding the light, and wondering how long the batteries in these things were supposed to last.

Even though I'd been the one pushing to uncover the entrance, the sight of the airless narrow tunnel made me break out in a real sweat this time.

"I don't think I can do this, Cyril." The passageway was only as high as our bodies. "I don't think I can fit through there."

"Of course ye can. Make up your mind, lass. Do you want to come with me, or would you rather stay here while I go get help? I've been thinking what you said about the storm and how long it might take them to find us, and I think yer right. While I'm not so worried about the lack of food, we've got no water. We need to make a move. Now. Or at least I do."

"Don't leave me alone here. I'll go with you."

"Look sharp, then."

"Wait, do you think we should have a code word for panic?" I flashed the penlight for a second, stalling as long as I could.

"Trust me" was all he said before he disappeared into the tunnel.

Chapter Nineteen

It took all the courage I possessed in the world to follow him into that dank hole. I reached out and grabbed the back of Cyril's jacket and held on for dear life. If we were going to die, we'd die together. And if we ever got out of here, if he didn't ask Martha to marry him, I'd ask her for him.

The narrow space was probably only about four feet high and three feet wide. I bumped into the damp sides of the walls enough times to figure it out. I'd never been in such complete darkness before. I opened my eyes as wide as I could, but it didn't make any difference. I fought to calm my raging thoughts and the sense of powerlessness that made my heart pound in my chest.

After a few minutes, it seemed as though all my senses were heightened. The sound of the rasp of Cyril's labored breath, the chill and the smell of the musty earth, the rustle of—What was that? A rat?

"I need the light again, Cyril. Stop for a second."

He sighed. "It's worse if you keep turning it on and off."

I ignored him and flashed the light on the key chain. It barely made a pinpoint in the oppressive black. I stood for a minute, practicing my Lamaze breathing. My back was killing me from crouching over. I couldn't see any rats, but as the sweat dried, I spotted an alcove, hollowed out of the earthen wall. There was some kind of sack stored inside. "What the heck's that?"

My heart was pounding as I ordered Cyril to hold the light. Inside the sack was what looked like a book. "It's a diary!" I gingerly opened it and scanned the pages. "Oh my God, Cyril, if this is what I think it is, it's a record of the slaves who passed through this tunnel on their way to freedom. Do you realize what this means?"

I didn't care about the claustrophobia anymore. I was practically dancing with excitement. "This farm is an historic site! That creep Cassell will never be able to build on here now, no matter what he does."

I gasped. "You know, Althea told me she smelled cigar smoke outside the carriage house. I bet Cassell was listening to their conversation. Roos probably mentioned something about suspecting that this place might have been part of the Underground Railroad. That's why he took all the pictures of this farm."

Cyril nodded. "And when Althea went into the shivah, Cassell beat Roos unconscious, tied him up, and stuffed him in the tool chest. Clever trick, that. To have Althea be the one to drive Roos to his doom."

"My God."

As we stared at each other, the little light at the end of my key chain petered out and we were plunged into pitch black again.

"That's it, then."

Cyril's matter-of-fact voice sounded in the dark. The

reality that we had no more light, and no idea where we were, or if there really was an opening at the end, sank in.

Maybe this was just a holding tunnel and not an escape route. Maybe there were skeletons in front of us from those who never made it.

Cyril began marching again, and I stumbled after him, clutching the sack close to my chest. How had the slaves felt, in the days before battery-powered lights, crawling through this space?

This train is bound for glory, this train. I started humming the old gospel song. I wasn't just looking to save myself now, I was on a mission to save this land and honor the history of all who had gone before.

I segued to one of my favorite Springsteen songs, "Land of Hope and Dreams," and sang out loud about steel wheels ringing and bells of freedom.

"Stone the crows," Cyril cried.

I laughed and sang louder. *Swing low, sweet chariot, coming for to carry me home.*

We kept moving, and after a while, it felt as though we were going uphill slightly. I was sweating and my back was screaming from walking so hunched over.

"Did you hear that? It sounded like a church bell." I strained to hear the bell again. The air seemed fresher, too, and I thought I could dimly see the back of his jacket. I heard other sounds, and now I knew I wasn't imagining the rumble that was almost on top of us, like footsteps.

Suddenly Cyril came to an abrupt stop. "Ow! Me bloody head!" He reached up and pounded hard on what sounded like wood. "Hey, is anyone there? Let us out!"

I joined in with the shouting. Next we heard the screech of objects being dragged across the floor, and after what seemed like an eternity, but was probably only a few minutes, there came the sound of a rusty bolt being pushed back.

We squeezed our eyes at the sudden brightness as a hatch door opened to reveal a very startled Father Morris.

I took the father's hand gratefully as he reached down and pulled me up into the sacristy of the Episcopal church, where items for worship were stored. Cyril climbed out next, and we stood there, shivering from the damp that had chilled us to the bone. A huge heavy cabinet that held vestments and hangings and a rug were pushed to one side.

"I never even knew this door was under here!" Father Morris said. "What on earth are you two doing?"

"It's rather a long story, Father," I said, my teeth chattering, "and I'll tell you in a minute, but right now could you please call the police? There's a dangerous man on the loose, and he very nearly killed us."

"Good heavens! Of course. Come on into the office." While he called 911, I stumbled off to the restroom. I shuddered at my reflection in the mirror and cleaned up as best I could. I'd need a long, hot shower later, but for now, I was at the limit of my energy reserves.

When I came back to the office, I found Cyril sitting wrapped in a blanket and enjoying a cup of tea from the Keurig machine. Our little church was well-equipped in the things that mattered. Father Morris tucked a thick blanket around me, too, and was about to start a coffee brewing when Serrano strode in.

"Daisy, come here." I had barely risen before he swept me up into his arms and held me tight. I held him back, feeling the slight tremor throughout his powerful body. "You scared the hell out of me. When you didn't come home, Joe called. We've been looking for you all night."

"It's okay. I'm right here," I said, rubbing his back briefly.

"Damn it. You promised me you would go right home," he murmured in my ear, so that it was only me who heard the roughness brought on by emotion. And it wasn't anything sexual. It was the fear of loss. Someday we'd talk about the demons in his past. How he had suffered and survived, but couldn't cope with the idea of losing anyone else in his life.

There was a commotion at the door to the office, and a very emotional Martha burst in, followed by Joe, Eleanor, and Tony Z.

Serrano and Joe shook hands, and then I was wrapped in my husband's arms, the arms I had dreamed of during the long torturous crawl through the tunnel. "How did you guys get here without my car or Martha's?" I asked him.

"Tony gave us a ride." Eleanor said, grinning at me. "We looked like a bunch of clowns getting out of his Mini Cooper."

"You are in serious trouble, mister," Martha said to Cyril, tears streaming down her face as she swept him into a passionate embrace, which went on for quite a while.

Father Morris coughed lightly and turned his attention to making cups of coffee for everyone.

"Did you get my text?" I said to Serrano. "About the root cellar?"

"I did, Daisy, but I'm embarrassed to say, I didn't go to the one you meant. I thought you must be talking about Althea's cellar. Especially after how you were going on and on and *on* about Cassell trying to frame her for Roos's murder."

I smiled at him in satisfaction. *Maybe he did pay attention in class after all.*

"And, yes, Ms. Buchanan, the camera equipment was stashed in there, just like you said. We're testing the stuff for his prints as we speak."

"And how about Willensky?" Cyril asked. "Did you find 'im?"

"Yeah, in a manner of speaking. Apparently he drove too fast in Martha's Lincoln in the snow. It did a one-eighty at the corner of Main Street and Grist Mill and crashed into the tree next to the Historical Society. He died instantly."

Father Morris bowed his head, and the rest of us took a moment of silence. More tears poured down Martha's cheeks. She'd really loved that old tank of a car.

Eleanor pressed another cup into the Keurig. "So. Is the Death Mobile totaled?"

"The tree will need to be replaced, but apart from a dent on the bumper, the Lincoln is relatively unscathed."

Martha beamed at Serrano. "They don't make 'em like that anymore. It's indestructible. Hey, I've just remembered where I saw that man before, and not only from the zoning meeting last night. It was the day I was putting up the flyers around Sheepville."

Cyril shifted a little, and I suddenly knew who had taken the notices down. He hadn't gone to the trouble to stay hidden only to have his face plastered all over town. I wondered if he'd ever admit it to her. I'd have a hell of a lot of explaining to do, too, but for now, I was happy to be alive.

"I saw him checking out the car, but a lot of people do that," she said. "Especially the antique car buffs. But then he was staring directly at me. It gave me the willies."

I glanced at Cyril, knowing his blood was running as cold as mine at the thought of how close Martha had come to danger.

Eleanor nodded toward the sack I was clutching. "What's in the bag, Daisy?"

"Oh my God, I forgot about this for a moment. I found it in the tunnel. I think it's a diary that details the farm's history as a stop on the Underground Railroad. Alex Roos wasn't just here to do the calendar shoot. He was here to document the story of his ancestors."

I carefully opened one page after another, finally finding the passage I was looking for. An entry about a runaway slave named Roos who passed through this farm on the way to Canada. He was caught and whipped savagely by a slave catcher named Gunther. He died of his injuries before he could be returned to the South. That must be the reason for the rooster in the tree. The final resting place of Roos the slave.

I read the passage out loud to the quiet room.

"Does this mean that Cassell will never be able to build now?" Martha asked.

Eleanor wrinkled her nose. "Even though the National Register can't *force* the farmer not to sell to him, no matter what he does, the zoning will never be approved."

"Alex had a personal interest in trying to save the land, which is probably why he did the pictures for such a cut rate," I said. "I'm not sure we can prove that Cassell knew about the historical significance, but I bet he did, and he wasn't about to let Roos screw up his development plans."

"I wonder if there are more artifacts buried in that tunnel?" Eleanor mused.

"Probably," I said, "but someone else can go look for them. There's no way I'm going underground again unless I'm toes up in a wooden box."

Serrano's cell chirped and he listened intently, not saying much, his expression grim. He hung up and looked at me. "The cameras were wiped clean. No fingerprints at all. Damn it." He ran a hand across his cropped gray hair. "It's all circumstantial—the sweater, the cameras, the whole bit. We still don't have anything on the son of a bitch."

"At least he won't be able to destroy the village now." I let the blanket fall onto the chair, finally feeling warmed up again.

"No one will," Eleanor said firmly, while Tony Z looked at her with adoration.

"And Cassell will be on my radar forever," Serrano said. "Sooner or later, I'll get him. You mark my words."

Sally McIntire appeared at the doorway. "Oh, there you

are, Father. Saw the lights and figured I'd stop in. I need to talk to you." She was wearing a short red jacket over a black sheath and very high heels with no stockings. I wondered if she'd just come from her latest assignation. She appraised Serrano with a practiced eye and smiled her knowing smile. "Oh, to hell with it, I may as well tell *you* directly. Forget the church."

Father Morris raised an eyebrow, but he didn't interrupt.

"You know that piece of sh—uh, I mean, that no-good Beau Cassell?" she said.

Serrano nodded, his expression neutral.

"And you remember how I told you I was with him when Roos was killed?" she said, as if a statement to the police concerning a murder investigation was just a casual conversational tidbit. "Well, I wasn't. Not all night. Only 'til around 9 p.m. Then I was with someone else."

I didn't dare look at Eleanor. I just dared not.

Sally stamped a spiked heel on the floor, and I hoped it hadn't left a dent in the ancient wood.

"He promised me a tennis bracelet for covering for him, but he kept putting me off. Now tonight he shows up with something that looks like he got it at the charity store! Oh, I can tell it's not real. He's all pissed off about the zoning meeting and doesn't feel like spending the cold hard cash. Well, no one puts one over on Sally McIntire. I'll show him not to mess with me."

Serrano sighed as he escorted Sally out of the office. "Come on, Mrs. McIntire. Let's go take your statement again and see if we can get it right this time."

I finally let myself grin at Eleanor.

She snickered. "Once a night is not enough, eh?"

"Stone the crows," Cyril murmured. "Sounds like the village bike. Everyone's had a ride."

Chapter Twenty

Tonight was the night of Martha's party. As Joe and I walked up the street, her huge old Victorian was lit up like the proverbial Christmas tree. I smiled as I saw the weather vane already installed on the roof. The ebony sky above us was clear and studded with stars, with the North Star the brightest of them all.

Follow the Drinking Gourd, the slaves used to whisper to one another. The old spiritual song was actually a musical map full of escape instructions, and the drinking gourd didn't mean the hollowed-out fruit used as a water dipper, but was a code word for the Big Dipper. Find it in the sky, and just below it would be Polaris, the North Star, always in a fixed position, and their midnight guide to freedom.

I stared at the heavens now, wondering if Alex Roos was looking down from somewhere up above. I made a silent vow to him that I would complete his mission and the story he had set out to tell. The Millbury Historical

Society would also document to the best of our ability our little village's role in the journeys of those who had passed through here, seeking only the most basic of human rights.

"You okay, Daisy?"

I nodded at Joe, but I couldn't speak, so I kissed him instead. He squeezed my hand as we walked up the steps and into the house.

Before us, a wide staircase curved up in an arc. To the right was the grand mahogany-paneled living room where Magic Hat Catering was putting the final touches on tables laden with appetizers. Music and laughter reverberated off the walls of the old home. Martha must have spent a fortune on the mountains of shrimp cocktail, truffled mushroom bruschetta, chicken empanadas, mini beef sliders, and cheesesteak egg rolls. There was also a glorious antipasto platter and an artisanal cheese board. The pièce de résistance was a chocolate fountain with fresh fruit, where Claire was standing in rapt attention. She rushed up to me, a string of silver tinsel around her head.

"Martha let me help decorate her tree because we're not going to be in our house until January. Did you ever see such a big one in your life, Daisy?"

"Can't say I ever did." Like everything Martha set her hand to, this tree was on a grand scale. I would imagine the ceilings in her living room were about fourteen feet high, and the majestic Fraser fir in the corner, laden with ornaments, was almost touching it.

There was already a huge stack of presents around it for Patsy and Claire's housewarming gifts. I walked over with Claire and set my gift bag containing the margarita glasses and blender next to the pile. "It's the most spectacular tree I've ever seen. And I can't wait to see you in your new house."

"I'm determined that they will have everything to set up house properly," Martha said as she swept over to me and Joe and gave us each an enthusiastic hug. She looked like she might cry tears of joy again. Martha had been doing a lot of that lately. "Oh, I have the most wonderful friends."

"Martha, you look fantastic," Joe said. And it was true. The sparkle was back in her eyes, and she wore a black cocktail dress that wrapped lovingly around her voluptuous figure.

Cyril was in his favorite spot at the bar. He poured a glass of chardonnay for me and cracked a beer for Joe.

"How about my special cockle-warming cocktail?" he said to Eleanor, wielding a bottle of whiskey as she came up with Tony Z in tow. I think it was the first time I'd ever seen Eleanor in a dress, and this one was a simple silver sheath that set off her hair to perfection. Tony also looked very smart in a tuxedo with a red rose in his lapel.

"I'm calling it Miner's Gold. Whiskey, ginger beer, honey, and lime."

"Sounds good," Tony said. "I'll have one of those."

"I'll have my usual," Eleanor said. "You know what they say. Absinthe makes the heart grow fonder."

As the guests mingled, and Joe and Cyril started chatting about whether the Eagles might actually have a chance in the playoffs this year, I drew Tony to one side.

"Tony, I don't quite know how to say this, but you know, Eleanor has been through a lot. She's finally taking a chance on love again. Please, don't hurt her."

He smiled at me. Tony Z had the cutest dimples. "I know you mean well, Daisy, but *I'm* not the one you need to give your lecture to. I've been in love with that woman for years. If it doesn't work out with us, I'm not sure my heart can take it."

"I'm sorry," I choked. "Sometimes I really should mind my own business."

Tony clinked his glass against mine. "It's okay. You're a good friend to Eleanor, and I'm enjoying the hell out of my life right now. At my age, this romance is a gift."

I set my glass down and gave him the warmest hug I could. We stood there in companionable silence and watched the preening between Chris Paxson and Serrano as they circled Patsy.

"Looks like there's no shortage of guys volunteering to help Patsy move," Tony said.

I chuckled, but I still couldn't picture Serrano and Patsy together. They were like corner pieces of a jigsaw that would never fit.

Serrano caught my eye at that moment and came over to us. He was wearing a dark elegant suit with a sky-blue tie that matched his eyes.

Tony made a big show of jumping back a step. "Yo, Detective! I can't stand next to you. You look so sharp, I might cut myself." As I laughed, Tony said, "Think it's time for a song, don't you?"

He walked into the middle of the room and promptly launched into an aria, a capella. I was amazed as always at the powerful voice that came from a relatively small guy. Conversation quieted as his beautiful tenor soared up into the high ceilings, the echoes resounding around the room like an angelic chorus. I shivered and rubbed my arms.

Eleanor stood, glass halfway to her lips, her eyes dark gray and unblinking.

"Jesus Christ, I might fall in love with him myself if he keeps this up," Serrano muttered.

"Did you just make a joke, Detective?"

But Serrano was never laid-back for long. Under cover of the applause he said, "You'll be pleased to know that Nancy Fowler has decided to make a considerable donation to the Historical Society. According to her, she was unaware of the blackmail and feels terrible about her husband's actions."

Cyril joined us. "I'll believe her, thousands wouldn't. Guess she came up trumps in the end."

"That's fantastic!" I said. "And Eleanor thinks that we're likely to get a grant from the National Register of Historic Places for Pennsylvania, so it looks like we'll be able to buy the farm after all. Old man Yerkel is tickled that one of his ancestors was a hero. A conductor for the railroad. We'll use the proceeds from the calendar to purchase a different building for the kids' community center."

"And I want to pay to restore the farmhouse." PJ Avery sidled in between me and Cyril.

"PJ! You're back!" I hugged her. "But are you sure? You should think seriously about how you spend your inheritance money."

"Yeah, it's cool. I'm not cut out to be a real estate developer. I'll buy a nice condo for myself and I'm good." She stuck her hands in her wrinkled safari jacket and rocked back on her heels. "Money isn't everything. It's more important how you live your life."

As I beamed at PJ, so proud of her that I could burst into song myself, Martha marched over to us. "Ladies, I have something to show you. Come with me. Excuse us, gentlemen, we'll be right back."

Along with the rest of the Historical Society members and some of the other female party guests, we dutifully followed her in a long, colorful line upstairs. Martha had dabbled in watercolor painting for a while, and one of the rooms on the second story at the end of the hallway was set up as a studio.

When we walked in, the expansive room with its paint-spattered wood floors was bare, save for twelve easels set around the room. Above each one was a spotlight shining down on the photos of our calendar models, all blown up to poster size.

In awe, we wandered around the impromptu gallery, exclaiming at how wonderful our friends and neighbors looked. Some were sexy, yes, some were fun, but they all had such a sweetness and joy shining out at the camera.

Alex was a genius. He had captured the essence, the personality of each man. Regardless of his age or his body, a woman could fall in love with any one of them.

"I hope shoppers will feel the same way we do and scoop up these calendars," Eleanor said as she stood next to me and grinned at Mr. October and his pumpkins.

But it was when we got to the poster with the picture of Serrano that we halted, holding our collective breath. No one spoke for a while, as if we were at some kind of sacred altar.

"Holy Mary, Mother of God." Ronnie the psychic crossed herself.

"Girls, we may not be able to put this one in the calendar," Martha cautioned. "Serrano's boss is balking a bit."

"So it might become a black market item?" Eleanor smiled her cat smile.

"I'd pay a *thousand* dollars for one of these," Ronnie declared. "I'd put it on my bedroom wall, like my poster of David Cassidy in high school."

"Rock on," Eleanor said. "Well, if we can't use Serrano's photo, perhaps we could convince another one of the firefighters to fill in. They all seemed more than ready to take their clothes off." She winked at me. "Gotta love those firefighters."

Martha clapped her hands and announced that we should join the party again, and reluctantly we made our way downstairs.

Dottie Brown was at the bar, enjoying one of Cyril's special cocktails. "Hi, Daisy. Isn't it so great that Patsy found a place? Did you hear that Ruth sold her house, too?"

"Really? So fast?"

"Yes, and she's already closed on it. The buyer was paying cash and didn't need a mortgage. Ruth left tonight for Belize. I have a friend in the travel business, and she just happened to mention her itinerary to me."

"Belize?"

I glanced over at Serrano. *Just when I thought that all the mysteries were solved.*

But I forgot about it as a vision appeared at the top of the stairs. Martha walked slowly down the carved wood steps of her grand Victorian house, dressed in a long russet silk gown, the one she'd planned to wear to the ball, her vibrant red hair pulled back in a chignon.

Serrano raised an eyebrow.

"Wow," Joe said.

"Bella." Tony Z kissed the tips of his fingers.

And as far as Cyril, he was speechless.

"Daisy, you'll never believe it!" Martha exclaimed, as she came up to me, Eleanor following close behind. "This dress actually has to be taken in. *By four inches!* I've been so stressed out that the weight has just fallen off."

Eleanor smiled wryly at us. "I can honestly say I've never been so excited about four inches in my entire life."

I gave Cyril a nudge. "Go on, get on with it," I hissed. "No time like the present."

He cleared his throat and got down on one knee. Out of his pocket he produced an emerald-cut ring that fairly blazed in the light. "Well, lass, we missed the charity ball, but it'd be a real shame to waste that dress. Martha Bristol, will you marry me?"

But Martha was already crying, too choked up to speak.

"She says yes," Eleanor and I said in chorus.

Cyril took Martha into his arms. I think he murmured "Good enough for me," but his voice was muffled by her passionate kiss.

Joe put an arm around my shoulders. "Guess you'll be really busy, Daisy, now that you have *two* weddings to plan."

"Yeah, that should keep you out of trouble for a while," Serrano said.

I grinned at him. "Don't count on it, Detective."

The Millbury Ladies' Home Companion

Joe's Terrific Turkey Chili

Delicious, and good for you, too, with the low-fat turkey and veggies!

- 1 pound ground turkey (or you can use ground beef if you like)
- 1 large onion, chopped
- 1 tablespoon minced garlic (about 3 cloves)
- 1 green pepper
- 1 red pepper
- 1 stalk celery
- 2 cups tomato sauce
- 1 cup corn kernels
- 2 cups cooked beans (such as pinto or red beans)
- 1–2 tablespoons chili powder (start with one, and add to taste)

½ teaspoon hot pepper sauce or Tabasco
½ teaspoon oregano
¼ teaspoon cumin
¼ teaspoon coriander
Sprinkling of allspice
Freshly ground black pepper

Brown the turkey in a large, deep saucepan or soup pot. Drain any excess fat. Add the onion and garlic and sauté for a few minutes until the onion is soft.

Add the remaining ingredients, stir well. Bring to a boil, reduce the heat, cover, and simmer for about half an hour.

Note: The amounts of the ingredients are not set in stone. If you want to add extra beans, a yellow pepper instead of red, or more corn, feel free to experiment! Start with the suggested amount of seasonings, and then as it cooks, decide if you need more heat with more chili powder or hot sauce.

Homemade Ice Pack

A cheap and easy way to make your own

1 cup rubbing alcohol (or vodka, but as Eleanor would say, why waste good vodka?)
3 cups water
2 zip-top gallon-size bags

Mix alcohol and water in one bag and seal tightly, removing as much air as possible.

Insert into a second plastic bag and seal tightly.
Place in the freezer for at least 12 hours.

Note: The mixture will be slushy and the bag will mold easily around sore muscles. It's also good for keeping your lunch cold. To make it more slushy, add more alcohol. Wrap in a towel first before applying to bare skin.

Kitchen Sink Cookies

    3 cups all-purpose flour
    1 tablespoon baking soda
    1 tablespoon baking powder
    1 tablespoon ground cinnamon
    1 teaspoon salt
    ½ pound butter
    ½ cup margarine
    1½ cups sugar
    1½ cups light brown sugar
    3 large eggs
    1 tablespoon dark rum (or whiskey or
        bourbon)
    1 tablespoon vanilla
    3 cups old-fashioned rolled oats
    3 cups semisweet chocolate chips
    2 cups chopped walnuts or pecans
    2 cups sweetened flaked coconut

Preheat oven to 350°F.

Mix flour, baking soda, baking powder, cinnamon, and salt.

In a large bowl, beat butter and margarine until smooth with mixer at medium speed. Gradually beat in both sugars until well blended. Add eggs and rum and beat.

Stir in flour mixture. Stir in oats, chocolate chips, walnuts, and coconut.

For each cookie, drop large spoon of dough onto an ungreased baking sheet, spacing about 3 inches apart. Bake for 12 to 15 minutes, until edges are lightly browned. Transfer cookies to rack to cool. Yield: 3 dozen large cookies.

Note: These are kitchen sink cookies, so have some fun. Last time I made them, I didn't have enough chocolate chips, so I made up the difference with dried cranberries. Also, the dough will be very heavy by the time you've added all the ingredients, so you may have to abandon the mixer and mix by hand. Literally!

How to Care for an Antique Sampler

When in any doubt, the best way to care for an antique sampler is to take it to a professional conservator. Wet-cleaning is usually not a good idea, unless in a museum conservation laboratory. Do not try this at home!

Many old samplers are still in amazingly good condition, perhaps because they were prized by their owners, and were not objects that were designed to be used, but hung on the wall. If yours has some condition issues, there are a few things you can try (but do only what is absolutely necessary).

Carefully vacuum to remove any loose dirt, using low suction a few inches away from the fabric. Examine the piece before you start for any weak spots. If an embroidery thread is loose, strong suction could unravel an entire area.

Moth holes can be carefully repaired by stitching a small square of material onto the wrong side, held in place with a few slip stitches. Do not try to rework any areas of the sampler where stitches have completely disappeared as this will hurt the value. A clever way to cope with holes is simply to leave the sampler as is and mount it on a background of the same color, perhaps a piece of unbleached linen.

If necessary, delicately iron from the wrong side.

Stabilize the sampler by removing it from its backboard and remounting the piece onto acid-free museum board that is slipcased in washed cotton fabric. (Old samplers were often glued or tacked to wood or cardboard, and the acids leaching from those are what caused browning and degradation of the fabric.) If your sampler is badly stained, either leave it as is, or take it to an expert.

Next, install under conservation (UV-protected) glass, using spacers so that the glass does not press on the stitches.

Seal the rear of the frame with an acid-free dust cover, and keep the sampler out of direct sunlight.

Dying Yarn

- ☞ Not only wool yarn, but plant and natural fibers take dye well. If you use a synthetic-natural blend, only the natural fiber will absorb the dye, so you may end up with a mottled effect.

- ☞ Test a small portion to see how it will take the dye. If the ratio of dye to yarn is the same for the full skein, you will see the same effect.

- ☞ You can dye yarn that has been previously dyed as long as it is a light color.

- Before you start, check the care instructions for your yarn. Certain yarns may melt at high temperatures.

- Wash first in mild detergent to remove any finishes.

- Kool-Aid can be used as a great dye with no harsh chemicals. Dissolve the Kool-Aid in a cup of hot water. A pack per ounce of natural fiber, or more for synthetic blends.

- Paint your yarn with the dye, perhaps in a gradient or stripes.

- Set the color by placing the yarn in the top of a double boiler and steam for 30 to 45 minutes. When cool, wash again to remove any excess dye and hang to dry.

Cyril's Cockle-Warming Cocktail

Pour a few drops of maple syrup into a chilled rocks glass and swirl to coat the bottom.
Add the following:

1½ ounces bourbon or rye whiskey
1 ounce brandy
¼ ounce Grand Marnier
2 or 3 dashes of Angostura bitters (or orange bitters)

Fill glass with ice and stir with vigor. Garnish with an orange twist for bourbon, or a lemon twist for rye.
Cheers! Or as Cyril would say, bottoms up!

About the Author

Lie of the Needle is Cate Price's third mystery in a series featuring the proprietor of a small-town vintage notions shop. Cate is hard at work on her next novel. Visit her online at cateprice.com.

WELL-CRAFTED MYSTERIES
FROM BERKLEY PRIME CRIME

- **Earlene Fowler** Don't miss these Agatha Award–winning quilting mysteries featuring Benni Harper.

- **Monica Ferris** These *USA Today* bestselling Needle-craft Mysteries include free knitting patterns.

- **Laura Childs** Her Scrapbooking Mysteries offer tips to satisfy the most die-hard crafters.

- **Maggie Sefton** These popular Knitting Mysteries come with knitting patterns and recipes.

- **Lucy Lawrence** These brilliant Decoupage Mysteries involve cutouts, glue, and varnish.

- **Elizabeth Lynn Casey** The Southern Sewing Circle Mysteries are filled with friends, southern charm—and murder.

penguin.com

31901056003397

M884G1011